THE EYE WITNESS

Eric S. Swindell

ISBN- 13: 978-1508962731

ISBN- 10: 1508962731

Also By Eric S. Swindell:

The Soul of a Young Man

This book is dedicated to my Sister Jalissa, Brother-in-Law
Willie, and Uncle Victor.
For being such a big help.

PROLOGUE

Monday, April 8, 2013

They say New York City is the city that never sleeps. On the ninth floor of the First National Bank of New York, there was an office that never really slept. This office belongs to Jay Jackson, a hard working business man, behind his desk; working way past business hour like he's has been doing for the past two weeks.

There were no other people in the building – other than the custodians. The custodian went through all the offices and bathrooms, cleaning them as they do every morning, noon, and night. Jay spent lots of his morning, noon, and nights in his office behind his computer trying to get every task he was assigned finished. He has held a position of an account executive at the bank for just little over a year and has apparently worked very hard every day. His boss congratulated him a few times on his hard work, dedication and consistency.

He was working on closing a deal, and he was starting his second round of double-checking all the related documents and files. Jay wanted to ensure everything was perfect. Everything appeared to be fine. He pressed a few more keys to finish up and thought he might take a quick bathroom break. He slid from behind his desk and headed to the restroom.

Just only moments after walking out of his office, a male custodian in about his late fifties, parked his cleaning cart right out front of Jay's office. Entering inside, he made his way over to collect the trash from the trash can that was against the wall, behind Jay's desk and does some of his other duties. He bent over and pulled the bag from the trashcan, and sat it on the floor to places in a new one. While changing the bags, he scanned the office and saw nothing out of the ordinary. Once the new bag was placed in the trashcan, the custodian picked up the old one he sat on the floor, stood up straight, and headed back to his cart outside the office.

On his way out, he accidentally knocks some papers off the desk and all over the floor. He bends over to pick them up, places them back on the desk, and then happens to get a glance of Jay's computer screen. The custodian has been working at the bank for a while, and knew something illegal was going on when he saw a pop-up message on Jay's computer monitor that read:

COPYING 109 FILES.....

The custodian then glances down towards the front of the computer tower and found a flash-drive stuck into it. There was something very wrong happening in this office behind this desk, but he wasn't sure of what. He knew that the First National Bank of New York had a very strict data security policy, which prohibited copying bank files to thumb drives. He then looked down to the paper he picked up from the floor. The data on papers gave him more of an inkling of what was going on. He has seen this type of thing before from another bank executive, who was currently in jail.

"What are you doing in here?" Jay said as he entered back in the doorway.

The custodian was scared half to death when he heard Jay's voice. He didn't even hear him come in.

"I... I was just getting the trash," the custodian answered, before pausing for a moment. "I had knocked over some of your paperwork by accident. I hope I didn't mess up any of your work."

There was nothing but silence between them, as Jay stood still, eyeing the custodian, wounding if that was all that had happened.

"Just get out of here," he replied, coming closer inside his office.

Without speaking another word, the custodian made his way past Jay, and out the office, while Jay made his way back behind his desk.

Having a bad feeling about what transpired with the custodian, Jay made his way back to the doorway and looked out into the hall. He found the cleaning cart still parked in the same spot it was in when he returned, however, the custodian was nowhere in sight, and other office's doors nearby were closed. While standing in the doorway, Jay went into deep thoughts when glancing back to his desk. Taking a step closer to the desk, he could tell there were some papers missing. It wasn't long until he remembered seeing some papers in the custodian's hand holding the trash bag as he was leaving out of his office.

"Aww hell no," he said aloud to himself as he rushed over to the elevators. He looked up at the numbers and saw that they were going down. Not waiting for the next elevator to come up, Jay rushed through the door next to them and took the stairs. He ran down them as fast as he could without falling.

Once reaching the bottom, he rushed out the door and into the lobby. Jay quickly moved in front of the elevator doors but found that it had already stopped. He then made his way through the lobby and frantically searched for the custodian that was in his office. After a short look around the lobby, Jay saw no sight of the custodian and took in that he was long gone. While trying his best to keep calm, Jay pulls his cell phone from his inner coat pocket and makes a call.

"What is it?" answered an unfriendly voice.

"We have a problem," Jay replied.

CHAPTER ONE

Two days later

It was like any other Wednesday morning in the home of Thelma Walker. Her daughter, Andrea Harris was an early riser, always up at the crack of dawn. She was indeed a beautiful young lady, sized like a supermodel, with smooth brown skin, and long black hair that met her shoulders. She had just woken up from a happy dream – or more of happy memories from her past. Half awake, she slightly turns her head to the right and eyed the picture that was in a gold frame, sitting on her nightstand table. But it wasn't just any old picture – it was her wedding picture.

She eyed her loving husband she fell in love with years ago, Charles Harris, holding her softly in his strong arms, after being wedded man and wife in the picture. He was a very tall man, with beautiful light brown eyes, shaved head, little facial hair, and thick eyebrows. However, Charles wasn't the first man Andrea had eyes on, he wasn't the first she shared her first kiss with either. But he was the first man Andrea was able to look in the eyes as he said the words 'I love you' and knew that he meant it.

They had a happy life together until the most terrify day in America when two planes were flown into The World Trade Center, causing them to collapse, and kill 2,606 people. Charles was among one of the many workers in the South Tower killed, turning Andrea into a single mother of two boys. She'll never forget the last thing he said to her just before the building collapse and ended their call, *"We will always be together...no matter what."*

Still not fully awake, Andrea pulls the covers from on top her, stands to her feet, and heads straight to the bathroom to take a nice hot shower. Once she finished and stepped out of the shower, she covered her body with a towel and headed back to her bedroom where she sat in front of the mirror attached to her dresser to do her hair. By the time Andrea was nearly finished with her hair, she went and to wake her oldest son, Miles, so he could go to the bathroom and get ready for school. Once he was finished, Miles woke his brother, Ted, to do the same.

It's was now seven-fifteen, a little later then when Andrea would normally leave to take Miles and Ted to school. The schoolhouse was about two and a half miles from where they lived.

"Five more minutes and I'm out the door," Andrea shouted to Miles and Ted, through the closed door of their bedroom. She was standing outside her own room, in the middle of the hall, holding a cup that was less than half-empty of tea.

"We'll be out in a minute," Miles shouted back through the door.

"Okay," she replied, before making her way down the hall to the kitchen.

After losing her husband, Andrea went into a deep depression, and her mother stayed with her to help her out with Miles who was only four years old at the time. Ted wasn't born until a month later. Andrea eventually realized that she had to move out of her apartment in Manhattan, and move back into her mother's apartment in Harlem where she grew up – something she never in a hundred years thought she would have to do. After all the dust had settled with the insurance company, Andrea realized that she couldn't afford the apartment and raise two children without her husband's income.

"Good morning," said Thelma, sitting very comfortable on the living room sofa, in her house robe, drinking a cup of coffee, while watching the morning news.

Thelma was a brown skinned woman in her late sixty. She looked just like her daughter only a little older, with long, black hair, sprinkled with gray that met at the shoulder. Thelma was now retired after working almost forty years at the Harlem Hospital Center. She now spends her time at home getting much-needed rest that she much deserve during the day, but in the afternoon, she spends time with her grandsons, while Andrea is away at work.

"Morning mama," Andrea replied, as she entered the kitchen and finished off the last of her tea. "How are you this morning?"

"I woke up with a little pain in my lower back, but other than that I'm fine."

"You have been waking up with pain in your lower back for the past three days."

"Well, I think it's my mattress. I had it for about ten years now. It's maybe time for a new one."

"We're gonna have to see about getting you a new one." she said, washing out her cup in the sink and then placing it in the dish rack.

"I was looking through the paper this morning," Thelma said, carefully standing up from the sofa with the morning paper and coffee in both hands. She eased her way into the kitchen and held up the newspaper to Andrea to see what she had found. "I was looking at this mattress here. It's on sale and I'm thinking about ordering."

"Don't you wanna go test out a few mattresses to know how it feels before ordering one?" Andrea asked, dying her hands by waving them over the sink, before taking the newspaper out of her mother's hand.

"I would. But you know me. I don't like to go shopping by myself."

"You don't like going anywhere by yourself other than to church."

Thelma couldn't deny her daughter's statement. "Anyway, are you doing anything this weekend?" she asked.

Andrea thought for a moment. "Not that I know of," she answered.

"Good. Then why don't we go to one of those mattress stores this Saturday and maybe I can test out a few."

"Alright, that won't be a problem."

"Good," Thelma said, making her way back to the living room with Andrea following behind, and took a seat back over on the sofa.

Reaching over, Andrea picks up her purse lying on the side of the loveseat and started searching through it for her keys. "Miles and Ted, you got two minutes before I walk out the door." She shouted down the hall as she continued searching for her keys. Then, she spoke aloud to herself, "'Cause I don't know if Alex was gonna open up today or not."

"How are things going at the café?" Thelma asked

Still searching through her purse, Andrea answered, "Some days it's very busy and others are very slow and there's nothing to do but sit around."

"Well, I wish it was like that when I was working at the hospital," Thelma said, taking a sip of her coffee. "Has there been any nice men coming through there?"

Andrea paused. "Mama, please don't start," She replied.

"I'm just asking a question."

"Yeah, and I know where that question is going."

Thelma just eyed her daughter silently for a brief moment. "It's been twelve years." She said. "Don't you think it's time for you to move on with your life?"

"Mama, did you move on after dad died?" Andrea asked as she started back searching through her purse.

"No," Thelma said, standing to her feet again, after placing her cup down on the coffee table, and then slowly stepped to Andrea. "Your father and I were married for forty-six year until he passed on. There was really no reason for me to find anyone else because we were together for a lifetime."

"Well, mama, I don't wanna fall into another man's arm just because the one man I really loved was taking away from me."

In over twelve years, Andrea never got over losing Charles. Thelma would sometimes try encouraging Andrea to moving on with her life, but with the love she had for Charles, she just couldn't. She had no belief whatsoever that there was another man out there that could make her feel the joy and happiness of life the way Charles used too.

"But sweetheart, you're still young and you've got a whole life ahead for you," Thelma told her. "You have more than enough time to build a new life for you and the boys."

"You know, mama, you are so right," Andrea said, finally finding her key from deep down in her purse. "That is why I'm working on building us a new life. That is why since I became the assistant manager at the café and started making more money, I've been able to put a little aside, so I can soon get the boys and me a place of our own."

Between raising Miles and Ted, and helping Thelma pay bills and bring food into the apartment, Andrea's money always seemed to stay low. It wasn't too often when Andrea was able to treat herself to something nice.

Thelma exhale. "Okay, but who will Miles and Ted have to look up to?" she asked.

"They still have me."

"Yes, but they also need a father."

"They had one," Andrea replied, before heading towards the door. "He was working to support his family, and some assholes decide to fly a plane into his job and took him from us, remember?"

They both remembered that day.

"Mama, we're ready," said Miles, coming down the hall with Ted following behind him.

Although Ted was a bit shorter and four years younger, he and Miles could've passed for twins, as they shared their father's light brown eyes, and sported the same fade hair cut.

"Alright, let's go," Andrea replied.

"Bye grandma," both Miles and Ted said as they walked over to give their grandmother a hug.

"Bye sweetheart. Have a good day at school," Thelma said, hugging both of them back. "And I'll see you both when I come get you after school."

Andrea opened the apartment door and allowed Miles and ted leave out first. She followed behind, closing the door behind herself.

Once the apartment door was closed, the door to the next apartment opened, and out walked, Bobbi Carter, a young lady in her early twenties, who became a good friend of Andrea shortly after moving into the building with her fiancé, Jeremy, four years ago.

"Hey Andrea," Bobbi said when she spotted Andrea standing out in the hall. "How are you this morning?"

"I was fine until my mother wanted to start with me," Andrea answered.

They walked side by side to and down the stairs together.

"What she do now?" Bobbi asked.

"I don't even wanna talk about it."

"Okay, I understand," Bobbi replied opening the building door and letting Andrea and the boys go out first. "Hey, I was wondering if you don't mind, but could you loan me a hundred, until the end of the month?"

"Again," Andrea replied, giving Bobbi a confused look. "What for this time?"

Bobbi's eyes wandered around as a nervous smile appeared across her face. "I got another parking ticket," she answered.

"How are you getting all these parking tickets?"

"I don't know, but can you help me out… again?"

"I'll see what I can do."

"Thank you."

They then started walking down the sidewalk together. Miles and Ted had gone ahead and were waiting for their mother at the car.

"You need to start parking in a parking garage like I do," Andrea told Bobbi, as they approached her car. "It doesn't cost that much."

"Well, you're not the first one to give me that idea, so maybe I'll find one to park in."

Andrea was still holding her keys. She placed the car key in the door and unlocked them for Miles and Ted to get in while she continued talking with Bobbi. "Yeah and maybe then you'll stop getting all these tickets,"

"I just might." Bobbi agreed as she continued walking down the street. "Anyway, I'll see you later. Have a good day."

"You do the same," Andrea said, getting in her car and closing the door. She put on her seat belt, placed the key in the ignition and started the car. By the time Andrea had her hand on the gear stick, she double looked over at Miles, who was sitting in the front seat. "I know that is not the same shirt you had on yesterday."

"It's still clean," Miles answered.

"Miles that shirt has a stain on the collar… and look at those pants. They haven't even had an iron to them. I'm not taking you to school in that."

"Come on, mama. It doesn't smell."

"Miles, take yourself back upstairs and change," Andrea said, pointing to the front doors of the apartment building. "I'm not letting my child go to school looking like a bum because that's not what I'm raising."

Obeying his mother, Miles unfasten his seat belt, got out the car, and made his way back up to the apartment to change clothes.

"And don't take all day, because I'm already going to be late for work," Andrea shouted out the window. She then glances back at Ted in the back seat. "How are you looking, Teddy?" She eyed Ted from top to bottom. "Now that's how my babies need to be looking when they step out the house." She said after seeing how nice Ted was dressed.

"Well, grandma told us to get our clothes ready last night," Ted told her. "I did as I was told, but Miles wanted to stay on the phone all night talking with some girl."

Andrea shook her head. "I don't know why, but I can believe that." She replied, looking in her rear view mirror to make sure that her makeup was okay. "You boys are growing up so fast on me I don't know what to say."

"Well, it's not like we're gonna stay kids forever."

She eyed Ted from the rear view mirror and gave him a smile to his response. "I'm glad you know that," she replied, "and I hope you thought about what you're gonna do after you finished high school."

"I'm not even in high school yet."

"I know, but you know it's always good to plan ahead. Do you at least have something in mind on what you think you would like to be?"

Ted started thinking.

After a moment of silence between them, Andrea continued to eye Ted in the rear view mirror. "Teddy…" she said, and then waited for him to make eye contact with her. "Whatever you decide to do in life, don't let it be flipping burgers because I can see you doing better than that. Maybe one day I'll see my baby in the White House."

"Oh mom," Ted replied with a chuckle.

"You'll never know. But as for your brother, I just want to see him able making it on his own, because you know how hard-headed he is."

"He's been telling grandma he wants to be a lawyer," Ted told her with another chuckle.

"I can buy that one," Andrea said, looking towards the front doors of the apartment building. "We have some hard-headed lawyers out there in the world. You tell them to be quiet and they keep on talking, trying to defend their clients."

They both laugh.

The doors to the building finally opened. Miles walks out, looking a whole lot better in Andrea's eyes than he did before.

"There you go. That's what my baby supposes to look like when he walks out the house." Andrea said with a big smile on her face. "You look so much better… and ever more handsome now."

Once Miles got back in the car and closed his door, Andrea placed the car in gear and drove them the two and a half miles to the Harlem Village Academy Charter School.

CHAPTER TWO

After getting Miles and Ted to school on time, Andrea drove as quickly as she could to the Blakemore café in lower Manhattan, where she has worked for almost thirteen years. She started working at the café as a part-time waitress, although, Charles was making more than enough to support the both of them and Miles. However, Andrea wanted to have a little money of her own aside for a raining day. But after Charles's death and the birth of Ted, she switched from a part-time worker to full. Then, after six years of working at the café, being quite qualified and becoming very close with the manager and owner, Ms. Alice Blakemore, Andrea became the assistant manager. And even though she was the assistant manager, she enjoyed being out in the front, mingling with the customers like she did when she was just a waitress. Nowadays, Andrea spends lots of her work time in the back, behind a desk, doing a bunch of paperwork while Ms. Blakemore was away.

Andrea searched for a park after driving in the parking garage she always parks, four blocks away from the café. She would normally try to park on the first or second level, but it looked like all those parking spots were taken. She couldn't find a parking spot until she got up to the third level and parked a few feet away from the stairs and elevator. When opening her door, she reached over to the passenger seat and grabbed her purse as she stepped out of the car and locked the doors.

The café was less than halfway down the sidewalk, next to an alley. When approaching, Andrea could see inside the café through the two big front windows that all the chairs were still stacked on top of the tables, and not a light was on in the front or even shining from down the hall. It was just the way it was when she closed up last night, which only meant, Alex, her co-worker, and best friend, hadn't made it in yet.

She pulled the keys from her purse and unlocked the door. But before Andrea turn the knob and pushed open the tall, white, wooden door, with a larger rectangular window, and enter the dark café, she heard somebody calling her name from a very short distance.

"Andrea…" shouted a very well-known voice.

Slowing turning around, Andrea replied, "Good morning, Shanequa." She continued inside the café while glancing back at her longtime friend, Shanequa Robinson, who followed inside behind her.

"You're getting in kind of little late today, aren't you?" Shanequa asked.

She had noticed that no one had been inside the café, as she entered through the doorway and stepped aside far enough for Andrea to close it back. She was wearing a dark purple nurse's uniform, with dark brown hair that came to her neck while pulled back in a ponytail.

"I know," Andrea replied, closing the door. "I was trying to get here earlier because I wasn't sure if Alex was going to open up for me today or not. But Miles was trying to go to school while lookin' like something thrown away, and you know I wasn't about to let that happen. I sent him right back into the house to change, then I take them to school, and then drive almost like a bat-out-of-hell over here without getting a ticket."

"I can say I know what that's like – but without the kids, of course," Shanequa said as she took a seat at the counter. "As a matter of fact, I thought I was gonna be lucky and have the day off, but I turn around and find that I really do need to go in for my own personal reason – don't ask. So, I thought I make it over here for a cup of coffee before I head in."

Slowly heading toward the hall leading to the back, Andrea eyed her friend, and replied, "Well if you give me a minute, let me go put my purse away, and get ready, I'll put on a pot, on me."

"Okay, take your time. I'm not in a rush."

Without another word, Andrea made her way down the hall to the locker room. She put her purse away in her locker, before putting on her apron and nametag. As she pulled her hair back in a ponytail, Andrea turns to the sink near the door to wash off the oil from her hands that came from hair, before heading into the kitchen.

"Montica, Felicia, and I were going out to lunch this afternoon, and were wondering if you be able to join us?" Shanequa shouted Andrea through the wide kitchen window.

"I don't know," Andrea answered, as she finished gathering the stuff to make coffee. "I mean I should be able to. Where y'all plan on going?"

"There's this place Montica was talking about over on 65th street she wants to go."

"Oh, well, if Montica is picking the place, then I know I can't go."

"Why can't you?"

"Cause…" Andrea replied, looking to Shanequa through the kitchen window. "Montica likes going to those high price places that I can't really afford to go. Remember that restaurant she took us to for her birthday last year? The lowest price on that restaurant menu was thirty-five dollars, and that was for three small Crab Cakes."

"Hey, let's not forget I helped you pay for your dinner," Shanequa playful snapped. "And you can't say the food wasn't worth it."

"It was worth it, but I still didn't wanna be paying that much on one plate," Andrea said as she turned her attention back to making the coffee.

"Well, Montica said she'll treat us out today."

"Why does she wanna do that?"

"Cause she said she hasn't spent any time with her friends in a moment."

"She's the one that work's all day and night at that law firm."

"You know she's been trying to make partner there for the last longest."

Andrea came walking out of the kitchen, carrying two hot cups of coffee in both hands, on two separate saucers, and was also carrying the sugar between her left arm and chest. "I know, but she should still try and make a little time to spend with her friends," she said, placing both cups down on the counter top.

Shanequa grabbed the edge of one saucer and pulled it towards herself. "Felicia and I have both told her that," she said, adding sugar to her coffee. "When I also think about it, she has to make time to spend with her husband and daughter."

"How is Felicia doing?" Andrea asked, not purposely changing the subject about their friend Montica, as taking the sugar from Shanequa. "I haven't heard from her since last Sunday. Felicia would usually call me almost every day and talk for a least a minute or so."

"You of all people should know how busy you can get as an assistant manager."

Holding her cup of coffee close to her lips, Andrea replied, "That's right. She did become assistant manager over at Saks 5th Avenue." She took two sips of her coffee and then continued holding the cup close to her lips.

Shanequa picked up her coffee and took a quick sip. "That's right," she said, placing her cup back down on the saucer. "So, you and Felicia are both assistant managers, Montica a lawyer – tryin' to make partner at her firm, and I'm the head nurse at the hospital. I guess it's like what your mama once told us, you gonna start from the bottom and work your way up, and that's exactly what we did, 'cause we're doing beyond good for ourselves."

"Well, I'm still working up. I have a feeling that I might become full manager here in a couple months."

"Are you serious?"

"Maybe," Andrea said, taking another sip out of her coffee, before finally placing the cup down on its saucer. "Ms. Blakemore has been talking about retiring and there's maybe a chance that she'll give me the position."

"Go head, girl. I mean you already work like you own the place anyway."

"I know, right. And if she was, therefore, to give the position to me, then that would mean more money in my pocket."

"I know that's right," Shanequa said, picking back up her cup of coffee and taking a nice long sip.

"Yeah, and maybe then I won't complain about paying thirty-five dollar for a plate of Crab Cakes."

They then heard the café's back door open and close.

"Is that you, Alex?" Andrea shouted.

"Yeah, it's me," Alex replied, coming to the front. "Sorry, I'm running a late."

He was now standing at the end of the counter, looking down to Andrea and Shanequa as they both looked back at him. Alex was in his late twenties, light tan, with short cut dark blonde hair, and had the most beautiful blue eyes. He was the closest and most trusted friend Andrea had in the café. With Ms. Blakemore approval; during the time when she wasn't at the café, Alex would be the one Andrea puts in charge if she was out sick, on lunch break, running errands for the café, or had personal problems she needed to handle. And also, he would be the one to close and lock up on Wednesday nights.

"You don't gotta apologize, I got here a little late myself," Andrea told him. "I couldn't remember if you said you were gonna open up today or not."

Alex came three steps closer to Andrea. "Oh I was," he said, "but I had a call to come in this morning, and I had to take it."

"Was it about the custody hearing?"

"Yeah and things are looking great."

"That's good," Andrea replied with a big smile. "So when will you be getting little Jordan."

Alex stood still and thought for a moment with his eyes halfway to the back of his head. "Hopeful... by the end of the month," he answered. "I'm not too sure. But I'll keep saying it'll be a whole lot better for him to be with me then with his mother."

"What's wrong with the mother?" Shanequa asked curiously.

"A little over a month ago, I found out she was on drugs," he answered. "I believe all the money I was giving her to take care of my son was all going towards them."

"How long has that been going on?"

"I have no idea," Alex said, leaning against the counter. "I should've known something was going on long ago with the way he was always hungry. I thought my son had a tapeworm and he's only one year old. Anyway, he's in temporary Foster Care right now, until I can prove that I'm able to take care of him."

"And I say you can," said Andrea, picking up her coffee. "If I didn't know you, I would say that you'll be a great person *and* father for Jordan to come live with."

Shanequa started looking a bit confused. "Why would anybody think differently," she asked.

Silence built in the room for a brief moment.

"I did five years, two years ago," Alex answered, breaking the silence.

"Oh," Shanequa replied.

"Yeah, and all I can say about it is that I was young and stupid."

"I think we all were like that one point in life," said Andrea.

Alex then remembered something that he needed to tell Andrea. "Look here," he said, holding up a finger. "I know you normally want me to lock up on Wednesday's night, but there's something I have to do tonight around seven o' clock. So I will have to leave a bit earlier tonight as well."

"Oh Alex, you know Wednesdays are the nights I want to get home early to spend time with my boys."

"I know, but I have something I have to get together if I wanna get Jordan."

"Okay, well, since it has something to do with Jordan...," Andrea said in a playful sad way. "... then I guess I can take the time to close tonight."

"Thank you. Hopeful by next week, everything should be back to the way they were. And to make up for tonight, I'll open up in the morning."

"Alright, I'm gonna hold you to that."

"I know you will," Alex said, taking a step backward. "Well, let me go get ready."

Andrea pulled out her phone from her pocket and looked at the time. "Yeah, everybody else should be coming in at any second." She replied after seeing the time.

"Okay, let me get going, so I can get to work myself," Shanequa said, standing up and started drinking down the rest of her coffee. "Oh, you never answered my question. Are you gonna come to lunch with us or not?"

"If Montica is treating, then I guess I will."

"Good, I'll see you then."

"Do you think you can come pick me up? I don't wanna move my car?"

"Sure, I'll be here around twelve forty-five."

"See you then."

Shanequa left out of the café's front door, as Andrea headed to the kitchen to help Alex start getting ready for the customers.

Sitting in a very classy restaurant with friends, drinking ice tea, and enjoying a delicious lunch was just what Andrea needed, after an unexpected busy morning at the café. About an hour, after Shanequa left out the door and all staff got in, the customers started coming in left and right nonstop.

"So, tell me, what you ladies been doing, besides working?" asked Montica, a bright and educated business woman in her earlier thirties.

"That's mostly it. Working and living our life the best way we can," replied Felicia, who was the same type of person as Montica; bright and educated. Maybe it was because they were cousins, and came and gone the same places when growing up. Also, you would've thought they were sisters with how close they were growing up together and used to wear their hair the same way. However, now Montica kept her hair cut a bit shorter than Felicia.

Montica gave Felicia a side look. "Oh come on, I know you all have something good going on in your lives?" she replied.

"Well other than work, I've just been raising my sons," said Andrea, just before putting a fork full of salad in her mouth.

"How are they doing? I haven't seen them in almost a month."

Andrea finished chewing and the salad in her mouth and swallowed before speaking. "They're growing like crazy," she said. "I just brought Teddy some new clothes two weeks ago and already it looks like I gotta get ready to get him some more."

"I know what that's like," Montica said, picking up her glass of ice tea with lemon. "I gotta get ready to buy Destiny some new clothes as well. My little girl is almost as tall as me, and she is just nine." She then turned to Shanequa. "How are things going with you?" she asked.

"Nothing much, I've just been getting through the day," Shanequa answered.

"I know that's right because it's hard out there in the world."

"Tell me about it."

"Don't have to. You can just turn on a TV and see it for yourself."

"What about you?" Andrea asked. "What have you been up too?"

"Oh me…" Montica said, placing her glass back down on the table. "I've just been working hard. Trying to –"

"… Become a partner at the firm." Everybody at the table said and then laughed.

"Well, you all know I want that more than anything right now," Montica told them.

"We know," said Shanequa. "You've been saying that since you start working at that firm."

Montica picked up her fork that was lying on the side of her plate and started scooping up some rice and beans onto it. "Well, I think I'm getting close to it," she said, just before putting the rice and beans in her mouth. "One of my colleagues is trying to get me on this case that could help me out a lot on making partner at my firm."

"Well, what's the case?" asked Felicia.

"You know I can't talk about any cases I work."

"Why not?" asked Shanequa. "I mean it's not like we're gonna run and tell anybody about them."

"I know you won't, but I still can't talk to you about them," Montica replied, pointing her fork towards Shanequa. "But I will say that this case is a little bigger than what I had before. The police have been trying to put this man away for some time, and now my colleague thinks they now have enough evidence to do so. He was supposed to fax me the information but never did. I've been trying to call him about that, but he's not answering his phone for some reason. I hope everything is alright, because if he does get me in on the case, I hope I don't mess anything up."

"You'll do fine," said Andrea. "You're one of the best lawyers in that law firm."

"Yeah, you're a bulldog…" Shanequa said, bring her glass water up to her lips and took a drink. She placed her glass back down on the table and continued to talking. "Remember that case you handled a few months ago. It was like you own that courtroom."

Montica sucked her teeth. "Everybody knew that woman was innocent," she said. "They just wanted her to be guilty, so they could send somebody to jail, and I wasn't about to let them send an innocent woman, wife, and mother to jail. She was just at the wrong place at the wrong time and just got mix up in what was going on."

"Well, I hope something like that doesn't ever happen to me," Andrea replied, sticking another fork full of salad in her mouth.

"Things just happen sometimes," said Montica, looking across the table to Andrea. "You can't help some of the things that happen in life. I mean you can walk across the street and get hit by a car that you didn't see coming. You can walk outta your apartment and get hit on the top of your head by a flower pot that was unstable three floors above. You never know what's around the corner until you get there. Sometimes you can be at the wrong place at the wrong time or even at the right place at the wrong time. You never know."

Everybody at the table sat quietly as they thought about what Montica spoken words. It had all made sense to them because you'll never know what you could run into… in *this* world.

CHAPTER THREE

Nine o'clock in the evening had come quicker than expected. The kitchen was cleaned, all tables were wiped down, chairs neatly stacked on top, floors were mopped, trash was taken out, and the employees had gone home. The café was closed and locked for the day. However, Andrea was still inside, sitting alone in the manager's office, finishing up on some paperwork before heading home. She had called home earlier to inform her family that she was gonna be a little late getting in and why.

By ten thirty-eight, she finished most of the daily reports, but was starting to get sleepy and was ready to leave. Andrea figured she could finish the reports in the morning and file them away, as she put the papers together neatly, and placed them in the top left-hand drawer. After letting out a big yawn, Andrea grabbed her purse that was resting on the edge of the desk, stood to her feet, came around the desk, and headed towards the door. As she reached for the light switch on the way out, the office's phone began ringing.

"Who the hell would be calling here this time of night?" she said aloud, as she stepped back over to the desk, and answered the phone. "Hello, The Blakemore café."

"Hello Andrea," said a woman on the other end with an English accent.

Andrea smiled when recognizing the voice. "Hey Ms. Blakemore, how are you doing?" she asked.

Ms. Blakemore was out of the country, visiting with her family back in West Bromwich, England like she does every year around this time.

"Oh I'm just getting over a wee sniffle, but other than that, I'm doing just fine." Ms. Blakemore replied. "How are you doing? You surprised me by still being there at the café. I thought I was calling your cell phone, but it looks as if I mixed your number up with the café's."

It was no surprise to Andrea that anyone Ms. Blakemore age could've made that mistake.

"Well, I ended up having to let Alex leave early today – for a good reason," she answered. "So I had to be the one to close and lock up tonight."

"Oh, I see."

"Yeah, but I'm doing great. I'm taking one day at a time."

"That's great to hear. How are things going at that the café?"

"Everything is going well. I just finished most of the paperwork from this month. I'm gonna finish it up in the morning when I get in. And I gotta tell you, we've increased profits since last year."

"That's great to hear, dear because everything needs to be in order for when you fully take over next month."

"Well, I'm sure everything will be…" Andrea paused when Ms. Blakemore words repeated in her head. "I'm sorry, what did you just say?"

There was silence over the phone for a moment.

"I said everything needs to be in order for when you fully take over next month." Ms. Blakemore repeated.

"What do you mean fully take over?" Andrea asked.

"Well, I've been giving this a lot of thought for the past few days, and I think it's time for me to retire. I going to move back here to England to be with my family, because God only knows much longer I have on this earth, and I would like to be with them when it's time for me to leave."

"So are you're making me full manager?"

"I'm making you the manager *and* owner of the café."

"Owner…?"

"That's right, dear."

"Why? You had this café for over thirty years. Why would you just want to give it away?"

"That café is the only thing I have over there. And lately, you've been taking care of it more than I have, so I think it would be best if you have it."

Andrea became lost of words as she sat down in one of the two chairs in front of the desk.

"Are you still there, Andrea?" Ms. Blakemore asked.

"Yeah, I'm still here," Andrea said while still in shock. "Ms. Blakemore, are you sure you wanna leave this café to me. I mean I'm not sure if I could handle this kind of responsibility by myself."

"Why couldn't you? You have been managing that café as good as I did when I was always there. I know you will do fine, and that is why I wanna leave it to you. You should have seen this coming, dear."

Andrea exhaled. "No, Ms. Blakemore, I didn't," She replied. "This is very much unexpected. I don't even know what to say."

"A thank you shall do just fine, dear."

It went silent over the phone again.

"Thank you…" Andrea said, breaking the silent.

"I'll be back in town on the twenty-fifth to finish the transfer papers with you."

"Okay, well, I'll see you then, Ms. Blakemore." she replied, standing back up to her feet.

"See you then."

Just when Andrea was about to hang the phone up, she placed it back to her ear when she heard Ms. Blakemore call her name.

"Yes," she asked.

"Congratulation," said Ms. Blakemore.

Andrea closed her eye and smiled. She had never expected something like this to come her way, but since it has, she wasn't sure on how to handle it.

"Thank you," she said again, as she continued holding the phone to her ear for a moment before hanging up.

She smiled all the way to the front, until she reached the front doors, and released another yawn. Andrea pulled the keys from her purse as she unlocked the doors and stepped out. After closing and relocking the door, she safely made her way down the street to the parking garage. There were barely any cars parked in the garage when Andrea entered and made her way towards the elevator, which, there was already one waiting on the first level. She got on and rode it all the way to the third level.

When the doors of the elevator opened, Andrea didn't have a foot off when she heard the sound of somebody talking somewhere within the garage.

"I had a feeling that you were up to something," said an unfriendly voice. "I hope you don't expect to get away with this."

"I expected to do more than you think, Lieutenant." Another unfriendly voice answered.

Andrea stepped off the elevation and started making her way towards her car, trying not to pay any attention to whatever it was going on in the garage.

"Mr. Jackson, you do realize that you're in very deep water right now," said another calm voice. "You are looking at doing a lot of time behind all of your activities."

"Well, Mr. Williams, I don't think that's going to happen," said the second unfriendly voice. "You see I'm a man who plans ahead. I had everything going just fine, until, Mr. Scott here wanted to stick his nose into things he had no business being in."

"It's a good thing I did find out what you were doing," said someone who sounded like they were in little pain. "I have heard a lot about you, Dean Jackson, and now that I have told Lieutenant Author here about what I saw on your brother's computer, he went and told D.A. Steven

Paige and he's personally going to make sure that your ass is put under the jail for the rest of your natural born life."

Andrea started to get just a little worried with all of what she was hearing and started walking a bit faster to get to her car and get out of there.

"Is that right?" asked the second voice.

"It is, you bastard."

"Well, I don't think so because Mr. Paige is no longer a part of the system anymore." He paused for a slight moment. "As a matter of fact, he's no longer apart of anything legal, because I had a little talk with Mr. Steven Paige earlier yesterday just before you three were picked up. After all the hard work he's done, I kind of thought Mr. Paige needed a rest from all it. He did deserve, wouldn't you say. So, I made sure he got a nice long rest."

"You're sick," said the first voice.

"And so are you, Lieutenant," said the second voice. "Maybe you need a nice long rest like Mr. Paige."

When Andrea was only a few steps away from her car, she looked back – up the ramp leading to the fourth level, and saw a black van, a black GMC Suburban trucks, and a black 2013 BMW 7 Series. Standing in front of those vehicles, side by side, in a curved line, with their backs facing Andrea were seven men, wearing all black suits. However, the man standing in the middle of them wore a full-length black coat that made him stick out from the others six. In front of those men were three others, down on their knees, and what seem to appear to Andrea that their hands were bound behind their backs. Two of the men down on the ground were in formal suits while the third was in a jumpsuit and looked as if he had been worked over.

Andrea's legs felt as if they were glued to the ground, as her eyes were fixed on what was happening. She couldn't believe what she was seeing and hoped that it wasn't real – nothing more than a bad dream she was having.

The man in the full-length coat took a step closer to the men down on the ground. Andrea's heart started beating hundred times faster when the man reached back underneath his full-length coat, pulled what looked like a silver gun, along with a small, dark, round tub, and put the two of them together. Her feet finally released from the spot they were stuck in, and she quickly got to the driver side door of her car. But before Andrea had her hand on the doorknob, the man holding the silver gun shot the man on the ground to the far right. Not even a moment later, shots were fired into the other two men down on the ground. He continued shooting until the gun clip was empty.

Praying that it was nothing more than a bad dream, Andrea opened her eyes and saw that it was not a dream – she had just witness somebody killing three other men for God knows what reason. Her only thought was to get the hell out of there. Without thinking, she nervously looked through the keys in her hands for the one to unlock the car door. Unfortunately, Andrea accidentally made so much noise with the keys that she drew attention to herself. Then, she realized the noise she was making with the keys, trying to find the right one was a big mistake.

"Hey!" shouted one of the seven men.

Andrea jumped and dropped the keys on the ground. She looked in the direction where everything was happening and then wasted no time running back towards the elevators. As she was running, she quickly glanced over her shoulder and noticed that five of the men were now pursuing her. So, she quickly decided to skip trying to get away on the elevator, and run down the stairs, for those men were running fast. By the time Andrea was down on the second level, she heard the sound of those men's footsteps, coming down the staircase after her.

When exiting out of the garage, Andrea was hoping to run into someone that could help her – possible the police. There was only a smattering of people out on the street at this time of night. She bumped into few while yelling for help, however, she was ignored. In the busy city, almost everyone minded their own business. So, Andrea ran beyond the few people out to obscure the line of sight of the men chasing her. She somehow manages to outpace and out-maneuver them. After keeping low and moving fast to prevent being caught, Andrea glanced back and saw no sight of those men. She, however, did not stop running. Suddenly, she heard the sound of a gunshot and saw the window from a car only a few inches near her, shatter. Some of the people hit the ground, while some scattered away.

Andrea then turned off down a dark side alley, hoping she could find somewhere to hide until she felt it was safe enough it come out. She frantically searched for a hiding place in that dark alley but didn't see one. There was hardly anything there – except the dark.

"Hey, bitch!" shouted one of the five men catching after Andrea.

She glanced back once more to see how far behind those men were. With the ally being so dark, Andrea couldn't see much of anything, and also, those men were wearing all black suits. When she turned to see in front of her, Andrea tripped on something, however, was able to catch her balance by pushing herself up when her left hand that hit the ground. She then heard two shots fired, and landed near her. Andrea yelled when she felt flakes of brick explode from the wall and flown against her chest. With the idea of how close those bullets came to hitting her, Andrea kept moving, hoping for the chance that they would lose sight of her. She made a right turn down another alley that let out to the streets. Nevertheless, just like the last street, she was on, there wasn't really anybody on it that would help when she asked. She made her way across traffic to the subway station entrance on the other side.

While trying to keep her balance going down the stairs in her current state of mind, Andrea held onto the railing with both hands, while her purse was hanging half way off her right arm by one strap, but thankfully it was zipped closed. When reaching the bottom of the stairs, she rushed over to the gate, but with no money in hand to put in, Andrea had to jump over and quickly squeeze into the closing doors of a train that were about to take off.

"Got you!" said a very tall and muscular man, as he grabbed a hold to Andrea's arm that was still hanging out of the train.

The train started moving, the man lets go of Andrea's arm and grabbed a hold of her purse, still on Andrea's arms, and hanging halfway out the train. But Andrea wasn't going to let him get it, as she grabbed a hold of the purse, and started pulling to get it in the train. However, the man on the outside wasn't making it easy as he tried pulling it out. Andrea looked the man in his hazel eyes as they played tug-o-war with the purse. With the doors close tight on it, and the both

41

of them pulling, pressured the purse to start ripping. The train started picking up speed, and the man on the outside was running out of running space. He had no choice but to let go of the purse when he saw the wall a few feet ahead of him.

Andrea fell to the floor after pulling her purse inside the train. All of her belonging went all over the floor. For a moment, Andrea sat still, extremely emotional about what just happened. While looking at the content of her purse, she remembers why she was trying to make sure that those men didn't get a hold of it. She got up on her knees and started picking through the spilled content.

"Where is it?" she asked herself. "Oh my God, where is it?" She frantically pondered, until glancing up under the seat by the door, where she found her wallet. She picked it up and opened it and was able to breathe a little easier to know that those men didn't get a hold of her identity.

Meanwhile, back at the train station, all five men stood together as they watched the train disappear down the tunnel.

"Damn," shouted the very tall and muscular man that tried getting a hold of Andrea's purse.

"He's gonna have our heads for this one," replied the one standing beside him. "So, what are we gonna tell him?"

Nobody said anything.

"We gotta tell him the truth…" the tallest of the five answered. "She got away." He turned around, pulled his cell phone from his jacket pocket, and made a call.

"Did you get her?" answered someone with a thunderous voice.

"No… she got away," he replied.

"How could you let her get away?"

"She got away by train. But don't worry, I got a good look at her and I'm sure we're gonna find her before she decides to the police."

"You're damn right, we will. That's why I had Brain run the numbers on her license plate."

"Did he come up with anything?"

"Yes, he did," replied the man on the other end of the phone in a very happily way. "We are tracking a Mrs. Andrea Olivia Harris."

CHAPTER FOUR

The train pulled into the next station and opened its door. Andrea slowing stepped out, holding the ripped purse and contents from out of it together in her arms. After seeing what those men could do, Andrea looked all around the station, making sure that they didn't try meeting her here. Observing the station, she saw nothing, but a couple sitting close together on a pinch, two men about to board the train, and a woman that was on the train two cars down and now leaving the station.

She had no idea what part of New York the train had taken her. All Andrea knew was that she wanted to get home and fast. Therefore, she hurried over and up the stairs to see where she was. When reaching the top, Andrea found that she was much closer to home than she thought. The train had stopped near 125th Street.

With head hung low, Andrea continued to pray and hope that those men paid no attention to where the subway train was heading and was now somewhere nearby. She stood at the edge of the street waved for a cab to pick her up. She first thought about going to the police, but at this moment, all she wanted was to get home and be with her family, after all she came to have faced tonight.

A cab pulled over, and Andrea quickly got in it. She sat as low as she could down in her seat while her head still hung low, so nobody outside of the cab would recognize her.

"Where to?" asked the cab driver.

She couldn't remember her address. It was as if everything about herself had leaped right out of her head, and the only thing that she could remember clearing was what she saw back in that parking garage.

"Miss…" said the cab driver, getting Andrea's attention.

"Just get me to Hamilton Heights in Harlem, please." Andrea finally answered.

Without another word, the driver put the taxi in gear and drove in the direction Andrea asked to be taken. Then, when he entered the area, Andrea told him precise directions to her apartment building. The driver glanced at the meter and read the fair amount back to Andrea. The fare was a bit more than what she wanted to pay, but she paid it anyway without complaining.

After stepping out of the cab, she nervously hurried up the steps and entered the building. She walked over to the staircase, dropped all her belonging on the second step, and had a seat on the third. With her heart still racing, Andrea started to wonder if she was experiencing an anxiety attack, as played over and over again in her head what she witnessed and wished it all be nothing more than a bad dream. Andrea was still in a semi-state of shock and disbelief.

With closed eyes, Andrea took deep breathes while holding her head up, remembering the words that Montica had said earlier in the day, *'Sometimes you can be at the right place at the wrong time.'*

Feeling that she sat long enough, she gathered up all her belongings in her arms again and eased up to the second floor to her apartment. Approaching the apartment door, Andrea remembered that she dropped her keys in the parking garage after those men caught her witnessing their hit. She then suddenly remembered that she kept a spare key in the dirt of the small round planter sitting outside of the apartment. She reached in with her right hand and pulled the key out from the dirt. Then, with one hand, Andrea tried wiping off most of the dirt before placing it in the knob and unlocking the door.

There were neither lights nor TVs on in the apartment, which told Andrea that everybody was asleep. She closed and locked all three locks on the door, laid all her belongings down on the couch, and headed towards the hallway bathroom. After turning on the light, Andrea stared herself in the mirror for a moment, before reaching out with her clean left hand and turned on the sink to wash off the remaining dirt from the other. Once the dirt was off, she cuffs her hands together to allow water to fill in them, and then leaned over to splash the cold water all over her face to wake up from this horrifying nightmare. However, when the cold water touched her face and she opened her eyes, she again realizes that she was not having a bad dream. She was coming to terms with reality, and that her life could be in great danger.

Stepping out of the bathroom, Andrea turns out the lights and slowly walked down the hall, past her bedroom, and into Miles and Ted's. They were sound asleep. She slowly crawled into the bed with Ted with her shoes still on. She wrapped her arms around him softly, while staring crossed the room over at Miles, and wondered if this would be the last time she was ever going to see or hold them.

"Mom..." said Ted with his eyes still closed.

"Yes, Teddy?" she replied.

"Are you alright?"

"I'm fine, baby. Everything is just fine."

"Then why are you in here?" asked Miles, waking up.

Andrea exhaled. "I just wanted to come be with my boy tonight," she answered. "If that is alright since I got off work late and didn't have time to spend with you both earlier today."

"That's fine," answered Ted, sounding more asleep than awake.

"Okay, well, go on back to sleep, alright," Andrea told them, "and I'll see y'all in the morning."

"Alright," said Miles as he rolled deeper into his comforter.

Andrea laid her head against Ted, with her arms wrapped more tightly around him, as she continued eyeing Miles, and wondered what their lives would be like if she wasn't in it. The wear and tear from all the running earlier were catching up with her body. She slowly closed her eyes and fell sound asleep, still terrified, and worried about her life.

* * * * *

The sun started shining through the blinds of Miles and Ted's bedroom window. Andrea was still asleep when she heard the sounds of footsteps entering the room and stopped right in front of Ted's bed. She figured it was her mother coming to wake them up. However, when she opened her eyes, Andrea started feeling as if she a panic attack when she was looking back in the hazel eyes of the man that tried taking her purse from out of the subway.

"I bet you thought we weren't gonna find you," he said.

Andrea couldn't say anything. She just lay there panicking and looking at the terrible man as he reached behind him, and pulled out what looked like the same silver gun that she saw last night without the silencer. The same gun the man in the long black coat used to kill those three men in the parking garage.

"Please don't…" Andrea cried.

Before she could scream, the man had pulled the trigger, scaring her awake. The dream felt so real and scared her so much that she awoke with a yell while sweating bullets.

She looked around the room and realized that she was in Miles and Ted's room, alone. Andrea placed her head down in her hands after it sunk in that her being killed was nothing more than a bad dream.

"Andrea…" shouted Thelma, rushing down the hall, "… Andrea, are you…" She then paused when she stopped in front of Andrea's room. "Andrea, where are you, baby?" she then shouted.

Andrea straightened herself out a little, looked in the direction of the door, and answered, "I'm in here, mama."

Thelma became confused, after she steps in the doorway, and seeing Andrea sitting up in the middle of Ted's bed. "What are you doing in

48

here?" she asked. "And why are you still in your clothes from yesterday? You should be dressed and ready to leave out the door to take the boys to school already."

"I know," Andrea replied, wiping her eyes. "I came in here to be with the boy for a moment since I got home late. But I guess I overstayed my welcome... and overslept a little."

"I'll say. What time did you get in less night?"

"I'm not sure," Andrea said, still trying to wake up.

"Honey, why are you sweating so hard?" Thelma asked, coming towards her daughter. "Are you sick or something?" She places the back of her hand on Andrea's forehead to see if she was running a fever.

"No, I just got a little hot in here last night is all," she answered, and then asked her own question, "What time is it?"

Thelma looked at her watch. "It's almost seven-thirty," she replied in a bit of shock of the time, as this was the first time she looked at the time.

"Oh God, I gotta get the boys to school," Andrea said, sliding to the edge of the bed, and then tried standing up.

"No, they're gonna be a little late, but I'll get them there by the bus," Thelma said, gently pushing Andrea back down on the bed. "You stay here and get yourself together if you're going into work today. Matter of fact, I think it would be better if you take the day off because you have been working very hard lately."

"No, I'm gonna go into work," Andrea told her. "All I need is to take a nice hot shower and get myself together."

"Are you sure?"

Andrea took a deep breath, before she replied, "Yeah… I'm sure. But are you sure that you wanna take the boys to school? I can run them to school myself real quick."

It went quite in the room for a moment as Thelma gave Andrea that special look.

"You think I don't know how to get my grandsons to school?" she asked. "I may be old, but I can still move faster than what you may think your old mama can. Besides, I need to make a stop at the drug store on my way back." She then headed towards the door, but before stepping out into the hall, she turned back around and faced Andrea again. "Oh, by the way, I was looking out the window this morning and noticed that your car wasn't parked out there."

Andrea had a problem, as she quickly remembered that she left her car in the garage in a hurry last night. She wasn't sure to what she could tell her mother about the whereabouts of her car or to anything that happened last night. Therefore, Andrea pondered on what lie she could give.

"It wouldn't start last night," she lied

"What was wrong with it?" Thelma asked.

"I'm not sure. I had one of my co-workers look at it, but he wasn't sure about what was going on with it, either. So I left it down in Manhattan and he gave me a ride home. But he's gonna have someone else look at it today for me and see if they can get it running."

A strange look came across Thelma's face as she felt that Andrea's story wasn't the truth.

"What is it, mama?" Andrea asked.

"Oh, nothing – I was just thinking," Thelma answered. "I saw on the News this morning that there was a murder that happened last night in the same parking garage you always park in during the week, and I was just hoping that you didn't have to leave it in there."

Andrea stare blankly at her mother as her heart begins beating a hundred times faster like it did several times last night, after hearing Thelma mentioned the most horrible crime that she witnessed.

"Sweetheart, are you okay?" Thelma asked, bringing Andrea back to earth.

"Yes," Andrea answered. "I'm fine. You said that there was an m-m-murder."

"Yeah, in the parking garage you always park in down the street from the café." Thelma filled in the rest of the story. "It's all over the news."

"Who was murdered?"

"I'm not too sure. You yelled and I came running to see if everything was alright with you by the time they were about to go into more detail."

"Oh," Andrea said as she closed her ears.

"Yeah, well, what can we say? This whole world is going to hell… and one day we all are gonna go down with it." Thelma was about to walk out the room again, but then something else had come to mind to ask. "Oh, and what happen to your purse?"

Andrea had quickly come up with another lie. "I slammed it in Alex's car door and he pulled off before I could get it out. I have another one though that I can use to put all my junk in."

"Oh… okay." Thelma knew something wasn't sounding right with her daughter but wasn't gonna take the time to try and get to the bottom of it all.

They silently stared at each other for a brief moment without saying a word.

"Let me get these boys to school and I'll see you when you get home tonight," Thelma said, breaking the silence. Then, without another word, she left out the boy's room, headed back to the living room, and sent Miles and Ted to give their mother a hug before leaving out the apartment.

Andrea told them to have a nice day and that she would see them tonight, but just when she wrapped her arms around Miles and Ted and held them, she didn't want to let them go. She didn't even want to let them out of her sight. She was scared. But finally, she did let go, and walked with them to the front door, and gave them to the care of their grandmother.

Once the apartment door was closed, she turned and picked up her cell phone, lying on the kitchen table with the rest of her belongings, after being moved from the couch by Thelma. After searching for the number, Andrea hit Alex's name and called his cell.

"Hey, I just got in the door," he answered.

"You're there kind of early," Andrea replied.

"Yeah, I know. For no reason at all, I thought I just come in earlier and get a head start on some things."

"Oh okay," she said while exhaling.

"Is everything alright?"

"Yeah, everything is fine. I was just calling to let you know that I was gonna be late coming in today."

"How late do you think you're gonna be?"

Andrea didn't even think of the question.

"I don't know…" she answered. "But, there is a possibility that I may not make it in today. And if so, will you be able to hold everything down by yourself."

There was a quick moment of silence over the phone.

"Andrea," he said slowly, "this wouldn't be my first time running the café without you or Ms. Blakemore here."

"Yeah… right."

"You sure you're okay? You're sounding a little funny."

"I just got a lot on my mind right now, with Ms. Blakemore is turning the café over to me."

"Is she really?" Alex replied, sounding more them happy for Andrea on the other end.

"Yeah… But I'm not gonna talk about it now. I tell you more about it when if I get there."

"You better. I know you're happy because you've wanted an opportunity like this for the longest time."

"Yes I have and I got to go because I need to get dressed."

"Alright, see you when you get here."

They hung up, and Andrea headed to the bathroom.

The whole time while in the shower, Andrea tried freeing her mind from the previous night's event. However, it wasn't easy. After witnessing three people being killed, being chased, and having bullets flying through the air at her – was all part of something that you would never forget.

As she stepped out the shower, Andrea grabbed a towel and wrapped it around herself as she crossed the hall over to her room. After drying off with another towel, she looked through her closet for something to wear. Once dressed, she sat in front of the mirror and did her hair while thinking about what she needed to do.

"You need to go to the police." She told her reflection in the mirror, as she brushed her hair. "You know that it's the right thing to do… and who knows, you may help the police out a lot by going to them. So that's what you gonna do." She paused. "The sooner you do that, the sooner you will feel better about yourself and go on with your life. So you got to go." She sat the brush down on the dresser and stood to her feet. "Everything will be fine."

She reached up onto the closet shelf and pulled down a shopping bag from Macy's, which had inside a black and white design purse that she bought a few weeks ago as a little treat for herself – and because it was on sale. With the other purse being ruined, Andrea had no choice but to now use this one. She opened it as she headed back down to the living room, sat it down on the edge of the kitchen table, and begin placing all her belongings from the old purse into the new. Then, briefly closing her eyes, Andrea took a deep breath, before walking toward the door and opened it.

When halfway outside the apartment, Andrea was surprised by a hand that came from out of nowhere, grabbing her by the neck and dragged her back inside the apartment. The door was slammed shut, and Andrea was pushed up against the closest wall.

"I bet you thought we weren't gonna find you," said the same man from the subway and Andrea's nightmare.

He was holding Andrea so tight that she couldn't even try screaming for help.

"Please... don't hurt me... please." Andrea managed to say as she once again looked up into the hazel eyes of her capture.

The man was almost as tall as the apartment's front door they had entered, with braided hair, nicely trimmed facial hair, and a very muscular body. He was wearing a black suit and shirt with the first button undone.

"Don't worry Miss," he replied. "I'm not gonna do to you what he did to those three last night."

Tears began rolling down Andrea's eyes.

"I won't tell anybody, I promise," she cried.

"Oh, we know you won't," the man said, looking deep into Andrea's brown eyes. "... 'Cause if you do tell anyone what you saw, you will share the same fate as those men. I would hate to have to see him do that to you, Andrea. He's gonna try giving you a chance to just walk away from all this and be happy with your family. And yes, we know all about your two sons Miles and Ted Harris, along with your mother Thelma Walker. I'm sure you don't want anything to happen."

Andrea just started praying in her heart.

"Now, you're gonna walk out of this house, go to work at the Blakemore café, and then you're gonna bring your ass home. Do you understand?"

"Yes... I understand," she cried. "Just don't hurt me, please."

"Just keep your mouth shut! That's all you have to do to keep your life. But if you talk… there's a bullet in this chamber with your name all over it." The unknown man said as he held a Glock forty-five up to Andrea's face.

Andrea's heart felt like it was about to beat right out of her chest when seeing the sight of that gun pointed at her.

Then, with nothing more to be said, the unknown man moved the gun from Andrea's face, released her neck, swung open the door and stormed out the apartment, leaving Andrea standing there against the wall, crying her eyes out.

CHAPTER FIVE

Scared half to death, Andrea did as she was ordered. With no other transportation, she caught the subway and rode it all the way to lower Manhattan. With the possibility of the three victims' blood running underneath her car, while behind yellow crime tape in that garage. It was no longer in Andrea's thoughts to go to the police, now that she was fully aware the killers knew who she was, along with her family.

Coming from a different direction, she arrived at the café a little more than an hour and a half late. Andrea glanced up the street towards the parking garage and was able to see only little from where she stood. When entering, Andrea paid no attention to anything or anybody in there. All she wanted was to put her purse away in her locker and get to work.

"Are you okay?" asked Alex, coming out of nowhere and startling Andrea.

"I'm fine," Andrea replied, trying to keep her breathing under control. "Why you ask?"

For a second, Alex looked at Andrea's body language before pointed up towards the TV hanging from the wall, slightly over the cash register at the end of the counter. "Because of that," he said. "Isn't that the same garage you park in?"

Andrea looked up at the TV for only a moment before heading towards the back to put away her purse. Alex followed behind.

"Isn't that the same garage, Andrea?" he asked again.

"Yes it is," she finally answered. "But I was long gone before any of that happened," she lied, opening her locker door and hung her purse on the hook, and then grabbed her apron off the other.

"That's good to hear because I was a little worry."

"Worried about what?" she said, pulling her hair back in a ponytail.

"Worried that you could have been somewhere near all of that mess."

Andrea closed her locker and walked over to the sink to wash her hands. "What would make you think that?" she asked.

"'Cause I told you that I couldn't close last night and let you do it. And on the fact that I know when you close any other nights, you'll stay a little late to do some paperwork. According to the news people that shooting had to happen around the time I know you to leave here. So that's why I got a little worry about you."

"Well," Andrea replied, putting on a fake smile as she pulled two sheets of paper towels to dry her hands. "I did stay to finish a little work, but I left a bit early so I could get home to my boys. So you don't have to worry about me because I was probably walking through the front door of my mama's apartment by the time those men were killed."

"You have no idea how much better that makes me feel to hear that."

"You don't know how good it feels to not be involved in all that," Andrea replied, throwing the paper towel in the trash can by the sink.

"So where did you park this morning? 'Cause I know you couldn't park in that garage."

She thought about the lie she gave her mother this morning, and tried turning the story around and added a little truth.

"Actually… my car wouldn't start this morning. So, I had to take the subway," she said.

"Are you serious?"

"Yeah, can you believe that?"

"Do you have an idea what's wrong with it?"

"Not really. You know I don't know that much about cars. But I one of my neighbors was more than happy to take a look at it for me and see if he could find the problem."

Alex then remembered his conversation with Andrea over the phone this morning. "Is that why you called saying you were gonna be coming in late today."

"… Yeah, that was the reason why I called," Andrea answered. Then, turned and headed out the locker room to the manager's office. She had just remembered she needed to finish the paperwork from last night.

Alex followed behind her again and changes the subject. "So, can you now tell me more about you taking over this café?" he asked.

Having a seat behind the manager's desk, Andrea opened the top left-hand drawer, pulled out the paperwork, and placed them on top of the desk. She grabbed a pen from the cup holder and continued working from where she left off. "Well," she started. "Just when I was leaving last night, Ms. Blakemore called to see how everything was going… then she just came out and said she wanted to give the whole café to me next month."

"Just like that," said Alex, "You're gonna be the owner of this place next month."

"That's right. She wants to move back to England to be with her family."

"I can understand that, but also, things won't be the same without her around here."

"I know, but she's old and she wants to be with her family before her last hour comes."

Alex chuckled. "You know for a moment there you sounded like Ms. Blakemore and your mother."

They stared at each for a moment in silence, before Andrea burst out laughing.

"Anyway," she said, "she'll be back in town on the twenty-fifth so we can finalize the paperwork. So we need to make sure that everything around here is in order."

"Will do, boss lady."

"Okay, now if you'll give me a moment, I need to finish up this paperwork from last night and file it. And then I'll be out there in a few minutes."

"Okay," Alex replied, taking a step back. "But don't take too long, because it started off a little crazy out here this morning. So there's no telling what it's gonna be like this afternoon."

"Yeah, there's no telling," she agreed.

When Alex was nearly out the office's door, Andrea called for his attention again, after a brilliant thought came to mind.

"What's up?" Alex replied, turning around in the doorway.

"When I take over next month… there's gonna be an opening for an assistant manager, and I was wondering if you would be interested in the job?"

"Andrea, don't play with me," he said with a big smile on his face.

"I'm not playing. Are you interested in the job?"

"Very."

"Okay, the moment I become manager and owner, you'll become the assistant manager, and I'm gonna need for you to be on top of things. Well, that's after you apply for the job, of course."

With opened arms, Alex rushed around the desk and hugged Andrea as tight as he could without suffocating, while Andrea was still sitting down. "You got it." He told her. "Thank you so much."

"Well, I believe you earned it," Andrea replied, holding Alex's arms. "And you're gonna need the extra money to take care of Jordan when you get him."

"Yeah, you're right about that." He agreed, letting Andrea go and took a step aside.

Then, a brown skinned-man, with close cut hair, and thin but still a strong man, by named Hakeem, stuck his head inside the office. "Can we get some help out here, please," he asked with the little attitude that he always has.

"We'll be out there in just a minute," Andrea answered.

"Thank you," Hakeem said, slowly pulling his head back out of the office.

When Hakeem was out of sight, Alex glanced down at Andrea, and asked in almost a whisper, "The moment you take over can we fire Hakeem, please?"

Hakeem was one of those employees that came in and did his work, but at the same time, had this attitude of feeling in control towards a few of his co-worker, leaving the few to dislike him.

"It has been a thought..." Andrea replied, and then paused for a second. Then, when continuing, she chuckled a little, "... but I'm not trying to get into a lawsuit after I take over."

No more than about twenty minutes did it take for Andrea to finish the paperwork, then another three minutes to file them away, neatly. After, she headed to the front to serve any customers that hadn't been served yet. Andrea was still a bit jumpy. Her nerves became a bit shaking after someone would enter the café.

For a moment, Andrea gazed around the room, wondered who all was there in the cafe. It felt as if there were eyes watching her from every corner – which there wasn't. She tried ignoring the tricks that her mind was playing and headed behind the counter. She went to view the board that hung next to the serving window for the tables that hadn't had services yet.

"Morning Andrea," someone said from the opposite side of the counter.

Andrea tried her best not to jump. She quickly turned around to see who it was and smiled happily when she saw it was one of her everyday customer, Billy Allen. He was Andrea's favorite happy, short and round size customer that always wore a smile on his face when coming into the cafe.

"Oh, hey Billy," she said. "How are you today?"

"Same old, same old, just taking one day at a time." He then held up his cup of coffee to his lips and took a nice long sip.

"Well, that's all you can do, right," Andrea replied, coming closer to the counter. "I've been doing the same thing."

Slowly placing his cup back down on the counter, Billy listened to what was being said on the TV. "There are some sick people in the world," he replied.

"Why do you say that?" Andrea asked.

"That…" Billy said, pointing to the TV.

Like she had no idea on what was being said, Andrea looked up to the TV and listened.

"*In other news,*" said the male news anchor. "*Three men were found shot to death execution style in a parking garage in lower Manhattan. All three have been identified as Martin Scott, Lieutenant James Arthur, and Judge Thomas Williams. We'll take you to Lisa on the scene. Lisa.*"

"Why would anybody kill those men in a parking garage?" Billy asked aloud.

"It's a world gone mad," Andrea replied.

They both turned their attention back to the TV, which now had a female news reporter on it at the crime scene.

"*Thank you, David,*" she said. "*I'm standing here at the parking garage in lower Manhattan, where late last night, three men were found shot to death. Two of the men have been identified as Lieutenant*

James Arthur and Judge Thomas Williams, who both were reported missing since Tuesday night. As for Martin Scott, there hasn't yet been any information to be released on him."

The view of the TV started zooming out until they were seeing a man, with tan skin, and red hair, wearing a suit standing side by side with Lisa.

"I'm standing here with police Detective Robert Smith." Lisa introduces the Detective. *"What can you tell us about what has happened here?"* she asked, before placing the microphone up to the Detective's mouth to speak.

"I can't tell you much, it's still early in the investigation," said Smith. *"Other, then what happened here was a very traumatic loss for the Judicial System of New York. Judge Thomas Williams was one of the best judges to ever put on the robe. He has helped us get rid of the New York criminal elements. And Lieutenant James Arthur was one of the best officers on the force and to have somebody just take him from us like this makes this case very personal."*

"Now is it true that District Attorney Steven Paige is missing at this very moment?"

"We're not sure at the moment of the where about of District Attorney Steven Paige. It was said that no one has seen him since Tuesday night as well. We are just hoping that he is alive and well."

The name Steven Paige started repeating in Andrea's mind after the news reporter said it on the TV. She remembered hearing the name before but just couldn't remember where. It then came to Andrea that she had heard the name in the garage just moments before witnessing those men being murdered. She also remembered hearing the man that pulled the trigger say something about Steven Paige needing a nice long rest, and he himself made sure that this Steven Paige got a nice long rest, as he did the three victims that are being talked about on the news.

"Do you have any idea on who could've done this?" Lisa asked.

"Not at this moment, but we have some of our best detectives working on this case. So believe me when I say, we will find the people who did this."

"Do you have any witnesses to this event?"

When the news reported asked that question, Andrea started wondering if there were any cameras in that garage. If there were, did they catch her in there during the shooting? She closed her eyes and prayed that there weren't because with the warning she got to stay away from the police, she wouldn't know what to do if the police came looking for her.

"We don't have any witnesses at this moment," Smith answered.

After hearing the police detective saying those words, Andrea reopened her eyes, and exhaled, disappointed in many ways of the detective's answer. However, when Andrea looked back at the TV, it kind of felt like Detective Smith was making eye contact with her. Like he was speaking directly to her, to do exactly what he was about to say.

"If there are any witnesses out there to this event," he said, *"the police of New York would very much appreciate if you would please contact the NYPD and give us any information that you may have."*

"Now why would they think anyone would come forward and testify against something like this?" Billy asked.

"What you say?" Andrea asked, after giving Billy her attention.

"I said why anybody would come forward and testify," he repeated. "I mean, if there was a witness to what happen, they wouldn't be any use to the police, because by the time those bodies were found, the killer or killers would have found the witness and either threaten their life or killed them."

Billy had no idea to how right he was. One of the people involved with the crime had done precisely that. Given the other choice, Andrea was very relieved that she was threatened.

"Andrea..." called Alex from the kitchen window. "Can you see what the man at table four wants, please?"

"Yeah, I got it," Andrea replied.

The customer was at a booth, near the back of the café, with his back against the wall, and a newspaper up to his face.

As Andrea got closer to the table, she reached into the pocket of her apron and pulled her pen and pad. Then, without looking at the customer, she asked, "Can I take your order, sir?"

"What were you talking about with your friend over there?" asked a familiar voice.

"Excuse me?" Andrea asked, giving an ugly look.

The man allowed the newspaper to drop from in front of his face.

Andrea's face went from an ugly look to a terrified one, after seeing who was sitting in the booth. It was the man who held her by her neck less than three hours ago. The same man from Andrea's nightmare and ran alongside the subway train, trying to get her purse from out the train doors and Andrea's hands.

"I asked what you were talking about with your friend over there?" he repeated.

"Wh-wh-what are you doing here?" Andrea asked.

"Well..." he replied, placing the paper down on the table while straightening up in the booth. "I'm trying to have a nice friendly conversation with a pretty waitress at a café. Then, once this pretty waitress takes my order, I'll be enjoying a nice hot cup of coffee."

"Are you following me?"

"Maybe I am... maybe not. That's for me to know and you to find out. Right now what I know is... were you talking about what was on the TV with that man over there? If so, I just hope he's not a cop or anything like that."

"He's a bank teller who comes here every morning to have breakfast."

"Is that right? Damn, he must not have much of a life then."

"Look, I really don't want any trouble."

"And you won't have any as long as you do as I told you."

They stared at one another for a few seconds in silence.

"Now, can I please get my coffee?" The man asked. "I like it black, with a little sugar."

Without another word, Andrea turns her back and heads towards the kitchen to fix his cup of coffee herself. But before entering the kitchen, she noticed that the back door was closing, but had no idea to why it was open in the first place.

What Andrea was unaware of was that someone from last night had exited back out the café's back door, after bugging her cell phone, from right out of her purse, in the locker room. They wanted to hear all of her conversations, as long as the phone was in Andrea's possession.

CHAPTER SIX

"I'm out the door," said Alex, entering the doorway of the manager's office.

"Okay," Andrea replied, sitting at the desk, looking over a couple things up on the computer monitor. "Get home safe."

Barely taking a step back out of the doorway, Alex became concerned when remembering Andrea did not drive work today. As a friend, he didn't want to leave without first knowing if she was going to get home alright. "Are you good with getting home?" he asked. "If you need me to, I'll have no problem with calling you a cab and paying for it myself."

With a smile, Andrea looked away from the monitor towards Alex. "That's nice of you, Alex. But no thanks, that'll be too much coming outta you, and… I have a ride coming." She replied with a truth and a lie. "So you can go ahead and go home."

"Oh okay. Well, would you like me to wait around until your ride gets here?"

"Oh no, you don't have to do that."

"Are you sure? It won't be a problem at all."

"I'm sure, Alex. You go on home, and I'll see you in the morning," Andrea told him as she turned back to what she was looking at on the computer.

"Okay," Alex replied. Then, again, about to take a step back out of the doorway, but then stopped, when noticing how deep Andrea was into the computer. "I thought you said that computer didn't work."

Still looking at the screen, Andrea answered, "It had a few issues, but mostly it's a bit slow – especially on the internet. That's why I rather do all the reports by hand… it's faster. And with the few issues that it does have, I don't want anything to happen, and then I need to quickly access some information." She paused, just before looking Alex's way. "Matter of fact, there was a time when I was trying to access some information on here, and this damn thing wouldn't let me. So that's why I hardly use it."

"Oh. So what are you over there doing?"

"I'm attempting some research."

Alex stepped farther into the office and he asked, "What are you researching?"

Andrea minimized the page she had up – in case Alex got too close. She then glances up at him, and answered his question, "I'm researching some information on something I heard from a customer."

"What like a club?"

"More like a mob," Andre replied under her breath, glancing towards the computer.

"What was that?"

"Oh, it was nothing. Alex, go on home, and I'll see you in the morning."

"Okay, boss lady." He replied, stepping back to the door. "I'll see you first thing in the morning."

"Okay, see you. My ride should be here in a couple of minutes." She lied again.

"Now are you sure you don't want me to wait with you?"

"I'm sure, Alex."

"Okay, if you say so. I really don't wanna leave you along. Not after what happen last night–"

"– Alex… I will be fine. Go home."

Without another word spoken, Andrea watched and then listened as Alex exited out of the café's back door.

Once she heard the doors closed, Andrea pulled back up the page she was on. She wasn't lying when she told Alex that she was doing some research. Andrea was trying to find some kind of information about what she witnessed last night and why.

First, she started by looking up all three victims that were killed. She was hoping to find a clue or two on something they all had in common. Perhaps there was a case they all were working on together. She was performing searches for old internet crime news stories where the officer's names may have appeared. However, she didn't find much. Just a little about Lieutenant James Arthur and Judge Thomas

Williams, but as for Martin Scott, there wasn't one thing about him; he had nothing to do with the law or courts. She then attempted to find some information about District Attorney Steven Paige. Most of what she found on Steven Paige was the same thing she already heard on the news – he's been missing since Tuesday night.

Closing her eyes, Andrea tried to remember some of the things she overheard in the garage. She then remembers hearing one of the men saying a name. The last name was said by the third voice that spoke when she accidentally listened in on the conversation and then remembered hearing the full name by the fourth voice that spoke out. The last name was *Jackson*. She focused a little harder on trying to remember what the first name was. Then, attempting to give up, the name *Dean Jackson* had come out of nowhere, and fallen straight into Andrea's mind.

She keyed in the name and waited to see what came up in the search result. Many things came up, but nothing that had to do with last night. There were nearly over thirty Dean Jackson's listed in the state of New York. It was too bad Andrea wasn't able to see the man's face that pulled the trigger. Maybe then her search would've been a whole lot easier to find out what she was in the middle of.

Picking up her cell phone rest on the edge of the desk, Andrea viewed the time and realized that it was getting late, and needed to be heading home. She started closing out the pages she had opened, until coming across one where she noticed there was a picture of something missing on it.

"Where the hell is my car?" she said aloud, after viewing the crime scene picture of the garage.

There were several pictures taken at different angles and areas of the garage. One picture was taken in an area where Andrea could see the spot where she had parked yesterday morning. But to Andrea's surprise, the exact spot of where she parked yesterday morning was now just an empty space in the picture. Andrea remembered dropping her keys when trying to unlock the door, then with no choice had to run. The question now that ran through her head now was; what happened with it?

After shutting down the computer, Andrea placed her phone in her purse that was resting on the edge of the desk, and slipped it onto her shoulder. She turned out the office light and headed out the front door. Once locking the front door, Andrea got herself prepared to start walking in the direction of the subway station, which was in the same direction as the parking garage.

Andrea wasn't even ten feet away from the café when she heard a familiar voice speak out to her.

"You don't have to take the subway home." said the voice.

Since she had heard the voice twice today face to face, Andrea didn't have to turn around to see who it was.

"That's the only way I'm gonna get home," she replied, slowly turning around.

Across the street from where Andrea was standing, headlights of a GMC Suburban truck turned on, along with the engine. It was the same truck Andrea saw in the garage, not only that, it's been parked there across the street all day. The lights begin coming closer, then stopped feet away from Andrea, and she was able to see inside. Not only was

Andrea looking into that man's hazel eyes once again in the truck's driver seat, but she saw a younger man in the passenger seat.

He resembled the man with the hazel eyes a bit, although, his eyes were brown. He looked even more serious as he sat evenly with his headrest. His hair had very nice waves in it, a light mustache, and was dressed in a black suit and shirt – just like the man he was sitting beside.

"Why take the subway home when you can drive yourself?" he said.

"And how am I to do that, when I don't have my car?" she replied back.

The man let out a chuckle, as the other young man in the passenger's seat stepped out of the truck, and walked around and stood face to face with Andrea.

"Maybe…" he said, pulling a set of keys from his pocket, "if you would look, you'll see that it's right here." With his right hand, he held the keys up to Andrea and pointed behind the truck with his left.

When Andrea glanced in the direction the young man was pointing, she got her answer to where her Atlantic blue, nineteen ninety-nine Ford, Mustang GT went. It was moved from the garage and now in the hands of the two men in front of her.

"What did you do to it?" she managed asked.

The man standing before Andrea, still holding up the keys, answered, "Nothing… saw that you were a little low on gas, so I filled the damn thing up… and you should really think about gettin' an oil change."

Unable to believe a word he said, Andrea stared at the vehicle like something was going to happen at any minute.

"I don't think she believes you," said the man still sitting in the truck. "Maybe you need to show her that there's nothing wrong with it… that it's safe for her to drive home… and back here to work tomorrow."

For a moment, the man standing before Andrea just eyed her, as she continued staring at the car. He then pulling back the keys and headed towards the vehicle. He opened the car door, crawled in, and started the car without even closing the door behind himself. After placing the vehicle in gear, he slowly drove it closer up behind the truck he was previously sitting in.

"Now, do you believe that there's nothing wrong with it," asked the man behind the wheel of the truck.

Andrea didn't respond. She just stared into the man's hazel eyes.

The other young man exited the Mustang and held the door open for Andrea to get in.

"Go on home… and drive safe." the man in the truck commanded Andrea.

Still fearful of what could happen, Andrea slowly walked towards her car. She had no idea what these men were up to, and she was too scared to really think about it. They said all they did was put gas in it, but it appeared that they weren't going to give her no other choice but to get in and see for herself.

As she stood in front of the open door, Andrea slowly looked at the man holding the door open. She then took a deep breath, closed her eyes, and slowly stepped one foot in while holding on to the door. With her heart racing, Andrea slowly shifted the rest of her body into the driver seat, until she was sitting nervously behind the wheel.

"Relax lady," said the man holding the door. "You don't wanna do all that shaking while driving. You might shake and drive into something on your way home." He then closed the car door.

For a very brief moment, Andrea was just sitting still, with both hands firmly on the steering wheel. She was praying harder than she ever had as she reached to shift the car into gear, then gently pressed the gas and handed home. Every second she was driving down the street, she was worried about what might happen to this car and herself.

"You may be right for once," said the young man, climbing back into the truck. "Maybe Dean shouldn't have to worry much... at less not with us watching over her."

"Why you say that?" asked the man with the hazel eyes.

"Did you see how scared she is around us? I bet she wouldn't say a damn thing if someone had offered her ten billion dollars."

"Place yourself in her shoes. If you witnessed what Dean is capable of, and had my little threat placed over your life and your families... would it be worth attempting to tell anyone?"

The younger man thought about the question for a moment before answering, "Maybe." He chuckled. "But at the same time, though... she doesn't know how lucky she is right now. Dean really wants her dead... and he may soon change his mind about keeping her alive."

The man with the hazel eyes shifts the truck into gear, and just before driving off, he replied, "You let me handle Dean. You just keep your mind on the operations."

Andrea soon arrived home. Once she'd parked and turned off the engine, Andrea leaned her head back against the headrest, placed her right hand over her heart, and said out loud to herself, "Andrea... you gotta relax. Everything is gonna to be fine. All you gotta do is keep quiet about the other night. Just hope that the police will soon catch these guys and have them out of your life forever. Hope… that you won't have to stay afraid. This will all pass over very soon."

She was trying to make last night sound as if it wasn't a big deal. For a few seconds, she tried letting every word she said, run through her head until they were settled deep in her mind before stepping out the car and heading inside.

After almost two more minutes had passed, Andrea finally opened the door and stepped out. While heading towards the front door, she repeatedly said out loud, "Everything is going to be fine. It all will be over soon." She then started saying those words in her head after entering the apartment building.

While coming towards her apartment, Bobbi's apartment door, opened.

"Oh hey, Andrea," Bobbi said, once she saw Andrea passing by.

"Hi Bobbi," Andrea replied, holding herself together. "Where're you stepping out to this time of night?"

"Just gonna get a snack from the convenience store down the street. Hopeful I can get there before they close."

Andrea glanced at her watch before replying, "You're heading to the convenience store at this hour?"

"Well, I missed lunch today, and I burned my dinner while talking with Jeremy. My stomach is crying for something to eat."

"Well, why did you wait so long to go get something to eat?"

"Like I said, I was busy talking to Jeremy. We haven't been able to talk the way we use to, and that's making me miss him even more."

Andrea could almost understand how Bobbi felt.

"Would you like for me to see if there's anything in my mama's refrigerator for you to eat?" she asked

"That would be nice. That way I don't have to walk three blocks and make myself hungrier."

"Come on in," Andrea told Bobbi as she placed her own house key into the door knob.

"Hey, were you still gonna loan me that money for my parking ticket?"

"Yeah," Andrea answered, pushing the door open. "I'll give it to you either after I get off work tomorrow or Saturday morning."

"Okay, that will be great."

As they entered the apartment, both Andrea and Bobbi couldn't help but laugh when they heard Thelma on the couch, snoring like a lumberjack.

"What happened?" said Thelma as she woke straight up by Andrea and Bobbi's laugh.

"Nothing mama," Andrea replied. "Why are you sleeping out here on the couch?"

"Well, I guess I just fell asleep while watching television."

"I see you're watching that triple homicide story," said Bobbi.

"Yeah, I've been watching, because that's all that's been on all day long," Thelma said, standing to her feet. And for the first time, she noticed that Bobbi was in the room, although Bobbi was the one to speak to her just only a second ago. "Oh, what are you doing here, Bobbi?"

"Oh, I didn't have anything to eat," Bobbi answered. "So Andrea was gonna see if there was anything here I could have if that was alright. I really don't wanna have to walk down the street in the middle of the night to the convenience store to find something."

"Well, there was a lot leftover from dinner tonight. So you can help yourself to that." Thelma glanced over to Andrea. "I had made you a plate and put it aside for when you got home. It's in the refrigerator."

"Thank, mama, but I had a big lunch at work today," Andrea replied.

"Okay, well, if it's alright, let Bobbi have the plate I had aside for you."

"Thank you, Ms. Thelma," Bobbi said happily.

"You're welcome," Thelma said, heading towards her bedroom, but then stopped and turned back to asked, "Did you get your car working, Andrea?"

"Yes ma'am, I did." Andrea lied. "That's how I got home tonight."

"That's good," Thelma replied releasing a yawn and then turned back around to enter her bedroom. "You girls have a good night." She said just before she closed the door.

"What was wrong with your car?" Bobbi asked Andrea.

They both made their way into the kitchen. Andrea got the plate from the refrigerator and placed it in the microwave for Bobbi.

"Nothing much," she told Bobbi while setting the timer and then started the microwave. "I just couldn't drive it home yesterday night is all."

"Oh okay," Bobbi replied. She glanced towards the TV and watched the news for a moment. "I'm glad you didn't let me walk down the street."

Andrea looked at Bobbi, and saw that she was watching the news, then replies, "Yeah, you will be surprised by what happens out there on the streets."

"This was all they talked about at work today."

"I believe it. There were a few people talking about it at the café today as well."

"It's hard to believe somebody would do something like that to good people."

"You mean… tie up three men and then… shoot them until the gun's empty."

The microwave beeped. Andrea opens the door, pulled out the plate, grabbed a fork from the dish rack, and handed them both to Bobbi who was standing still giving Andrea a puzzled look before taking the plate.

"How did you know they were tied up and shot until the gun was empty?" Bobbi asked, walking over to the table to have a seat with her meal.

When Andrea realized what she had said, she quickly came up with something that could have made it sound as if she wasn't the only person in the world that had an idea to what happened.

"At the café, I heard someone say that they heard it in the news," she said, unsure if that information was even reported on the news or not. "But you know people say lots of things, and God only knows if it was all true or not."

"You're right about that," Bobbi agreed before pausing for a moment to say grace. "But just saying, I would have hated to have seen something like that in person."

"Tell me about it," Andrea replied, trying hard not to think about it. She then quickly changed the subject. "You want something to drink?"

It took Bobbi a moment to answer, due to her mouth being stuffed with the delish roast beef Thelma had made.

"Yes, please," she finally answered. "Your mama still knows how to throw down in the kitchen."

"You know she does," Andrea said, opening the refrigerator door. "What do you want to drink?"

"What do you have?"

"Water, milk, apple juice, and I think we still have a bottle of coke," Andrea said, closing the refrigerator and then looked to the side of it. "And what do you know... we do." She said picking up the half empty bottle of Coke-Cola and held it up in the air.

"I'll take some of the coke," Bobbi answered, just before sticking fork full of yaws in her mouth.

Andrea placed the bottle back down on the countertop and opened the top cabinet above. She pulled down two glasses for the both of them and filled them with ice from the freezer. Then, just when she was about to pour the soda into one of the glasses, Andrea glanced out the window and saw headlights coming up the street and parked on the other side. She knew exactly who it was, and she wished she didn't.

CHAPTER SEVEN

When Andrea woke up the next morning, it was like waking up to her usual everyday routine: up at five fifty, take a shower, and then after getting out the shower, she sat in front of her dresser mirror and did her hair. When nearly done with her hair, Andrea woke up Miles, who would later wake up Ted when done in the bathroom. Everything felt normal. That was until they were all walking out the apartment building, and Andrea was reminded of everything that was happening when she glanced to the truck from the previous night, still parked across the street in the same spot she saw from her apartment window.

For a quick second, Andrea made eye contact with the man with the hazel eyes just before sliding down in the car. After starting the engine, she drove up the road, came to a stop sign and stopped. Andrea then took a looked in her rearview mirror to see the truck pulling out of its spot and coming up behind her. Her head fell back against the headrest as she blew out air, angrily.

"Are you alright, mama?" asked Miles.

"Yeah… I fine." Andrea answered still glancing into the rearview mirror. "I just got a really big monkey on my back right now."

"What do you mean by that?"

"It's nothing," she said, straightening herself up in the seat.

Although he was still young, Miles could tell that there was something going on with his mother.

"Mama, have you been feeling alright?" he asked.

When it was clear to go, Andrea quickly placed her foot on the gas and continued down the street when replying to Miles.

"I'm fine, baby. Why you ask?"

"You've been acting a strange lately."

Andrea let out a chuckle. "What'd you mean I've been acting strange?"

"I don't know. I guess because of the way you were acting Wednesday night when you came in the room with Ted and me."

"I thought it was nice having mama sleep in the room with us," Ted replied from the back seat.

"Shut up, Ted." Miles shouted. "Nobody was talking to you."

"Hey, don't tell your brother to shut up," Andrea told Miles. "And what was so wrong with me sleeping in the room with you two?"

"It was the way you looked."

Andrea thought back to that night. Feeling on edge after what she saw, Andrea knew that she had to be showing it, but she didn't think that Miles was awake watching her as she lay still, pondering about the most horrifying night of her life.

"How was I looking?" she asked.

"Like you had seen a ghost or something," Miles answered. "Mom you didn't look like yourself the other night."

"I just had something hard on my mind that night is all."

"Had something like what?" asked Ted.

Andrea looked to Ted in the rearview mirror. "Something I can't talk to you guys about." She told the both of them. "I wish I could, but I can't."

"Why can't you?" asked Miles.

"I just can't, okay!" Andrea snapped as she lost a little control of herself.

Silence filled the car for a moment.

"I'm sorry," Andrea replied, breaking the silence. "I didn't mean to snap at you like that. I just got a lot on my mind at the moment and I'm trying my best to keep it together."

"What is it, mama?"

"Miles, it's nothing you have to worry about. Trust me. Everything is gonna to be fine."

It was quite the rest of the ride to the schoolhouse.

When Andrea pulled up in front of the school, she turned to face both of her children to have a word with them before they got out the car.

"Everything is gonna to be fine." She repeated to them. "At this time, I really need you two to pray for your mama... okay."

"Mama... you're really scaring me right now." Miles told her.

"Yeah mama," Ted agreed.

"I know and I don't mean too," Andrea said, looking back and forth between the both of them. "Just remember this… in life, unexpected thing sometimes happens, but in the end… things always resolve for the best."

Miles stared his mother in the eyes. "Isn't that what grandma sometimes say?" he replied.

Andrea chuckled. "Yes baby," she answered. "That is something your grandma always says during hard times, and right now I am dealing with some hard times, but it's going to be over very soon. I hope."

"I hope so too," Miles replied as he leaned over to give his mother a kiss on the cheek.

"Same here," said Ted doing the same as his brother.

"Well, I'm happy to know I have all this love around me," she replied. "But look, I don't want y'all to tell your grandma about this conversation, alright. This is to still between the three of us."

"Okay," both Miles and Ted agreed.

Andrea held up both of her pinky fingers. "Pinky promise," she said.

Miles and Ted took a pinky each, "Promise!" they both shouted in a whisper like.

"Okay… now go and learn something."

Miles opened his door and got out with Ted right behind him.

"Have a good day," Andrea shouted just before Miles closed the car door.

Shortly after watching her children enter the school, Andrea put her car back in gear and slowly drove off the school ground. Her new friend had parked across the street from the schoolhouse while Andrea dropped off the Miles and Ted. He pulled out behind Andrea once she was back out on the street.

Almost every stop that Andrea made, she looked in the rearview mirror in hopes that the two men had lost track of her somehow. However, every time Andrea looked back, she found herself disappointed, because the two men were still right on her tail, just like they've been since the moment she pulled out from in front of her apartment building.

When arriving at the café, Andrea found a parking spot near in front. She started looking through her purse for some loose change to put into the parking meter. After finding the correct amount that she needed, Andrea opens her door as she turned off the engine and stepped out. Locking the car door, she turned to insert the coins into the meter, and then made her way inside the café, where she found four customers seated and serviced, and the staff in the back working like they should be.

"Morning boss lady," said Alex from the kitchen window.

"Morning…" Andrea replied as she looked around a little confused on how the café was already up and running before it was time to open. "Am I running late or something?" she asked.

"Andrea it's Friday. We always open and close an hour early on Fridays."

"Yeah, that's right," she muttered.

Alex came from out of the kitchen and stood behind the counter. "I know I've asked you this like a thousand times already," he said, "but I'm gonna ask one more time. Are you alright?"

"I'm fine, Alex."

"Are you sure?"

"Yes, I'm sure. I know I am. Why would you think there something is wrong with me?"

Alex took a moment before answering. "I don't know," he said. "But I've known you long enough to know when something is bothering you. Now, what is it?"

"Nothing, I just got a lot on my mind right now. I've told you that a thousand times and now that was my thousand and one time telling you."

Without another word to say, Andrea headed towards the back to get ready. Alex watched as Andrea disappeared down the hall, then stepped back into the kitchen and got back to work.

Not long after Andrea came back out to the front, the café's front door opened, and in walks Shanequa.

"Shouldn't you be at work?" Andrea asked, coming behind the counter.

"I have an eye appointment today," Shanequa answered.

"Is something wrong with you eyes?"

"I'm not sure, but I might need glass. Things just seem a little blurring to me at times."

"Oh yeah, get that looked at."

"That's why I got this an appointment," she replied. "Anyway, I'm not gonna stay here long, 'cause my appointment is in an hour. I just came in because I was passing by, and wanted to ask you if you wanted to come out with me tonight and have a drink or two."

"You wanna go out tonight?" Andrea said before glancing out the window to the black truck parked right across the street like it always is.

"Yes, tonight."

"I can't. Not tonight," she replied, looking Shanequa in the face.

"Well, why not? You get off early tonight"

"I know, but tonight..." Andrea paused for a split second. "... I wanna get home to my boy and spend time with them because in the morning I have to go out with my mama." It wasn't much of a lie she told.

Shanequa stared at Andrea with a straight face. "Andrea, I'm sure there is not much you have to do with your mama tomorrow, and then you have a whole weekend to spend with Miles and Tito."

"My son name is Ted."

"I'm sorry, my mistake," she replied with a question burning inside her head. "Why did you give him a name like Ted anyway?"

There was silence between them.

"It's a long story, and I really wish not to talk about it."

"Okay," Shanequa replied, ending that conversation, although she really wanted to know the answer to her question. "Andrea, please come out with us tonight. We're going to our favorite spot."

"What do you mean us? I thought it was just you."

"Well... this whole thing was Felicia's idea, and I thought it was a good one."

"Okay, first Montica wants to go out to lunch together, and now Felicia wants to go out to have drinks tonight."

"Yeah, since yesterday Montica has been a little down about something."

"Down about what?"

"I don't know she wanna won't talk about it. But whatever it is, Felicia wants to try taking her out, and see if having a few drinks will get her mind off whatever's bothering her."

Andrea took another glance out the window again. She really wanted to go see what was going on with Montica, but with everything happening in her life, she didn't want to bring her friends into it. She was already struggling and beating herself up a little with her family having to be around.

"As much as I wanna be there for Montica as a friend," she said, "I'm gonna have to pass. I just have a lot going on right now and I just don't have the time."

Shanequa was shocked by Andrea's responds. "What?" she nearly shouted, making eye contact. "I can't believe you outta all people you're gonna turn your back on a friend in a time of need."

Trying to act normal, Andrea kept eye contact with Shanequa and replied, "I'm not turning my back on a friend. I… I… right now I just got something going on that I need to get together."

"Something like what?"

"I can't talk about it right now, but believe me I'm working it out."

"Andrea…" called Alex from the kitchen window. "Can you get table seven, please?"

Andrea turned towards table seven and kept her real reaction hidden when she saw who was sitting there. She didn't even notice them come in.

"I got it," she told Alex, turning her attention back to Shanequa. "Look, tell Montica I hope everything gets better for her... and whatever it is bothering her, stops."

"Will do..." Shanequa replied. "And I say the same back to you."

Then, without another word, Shanequa exit out the café, as Andrea came around the counter and headed over to the table where her two followers were sitting.

"What can I get you two gentlemen?" she asked, pulling her pen and pad.

"You can start by not drawing attention to us," answered the younger man.

Looking down to him, she asked, "What are you talking about?"

"Every time you get nervous you look at our truck," the man with the hazel eyes answered. "I understand that you're a little scared... but Andrea you need to hold yourself together before you end up making things a whole lot worse for yourself than they already are."

"Well, it's hard to hold it together when I have you two on my back watching every move I make," Andrea replied as low as she possibly could for only them to hear.

"Well, you know what," said the younger man, "the boss doesn't have an ounce of trust in you. You're still being alive has him on edge, and us keeping our eyes on you keeps him calm and you... alive."

"I've already told you that I'm not gonna say anything to anybody."

"The boss has different beliefs," said the man with hazel eyes. "And with the way you're acting, you're gonna really make him right about his beliefs. Now, if I were you I would meet your friends at that club or wherever – so nobody will start building suspicions."

"You could hear my conversation from all the way over here?" Andrea asked.

"We can do more than you think," the younger man replied.

The man with the hazel eyes leaned forward in his seat. "Don't worry about what we can do," he said. "Just worry about seeing another day. The only thing we ask you to do is to not say a word to anybody. Now, go out with your friends tonight, have a good time, be there for your friend for whatever it is she's going through, and then take your ass home. Is that clear?"

They looked at else other in silence for a few seconds.

"Yes sir," Andrea answered, sadly.

"Good," he said, leaning back in his seat. "Now we'll take two coffees, the same way I ordered yesterday."

"Will that be all?"

Both men didn't say a word. They just sat there and eyeing Andrea, waiting for her to walk away. Then, only a second later behind their facial expressions, she did.

The younger man then leaned forward in his seat. "I take back what I said," he muttered. "Maybe Dean has a point. Maybe she is too much of a risk to keep alive."

"Dean has a mind of his own."

"She's gonna get us caught."

"Not as long as we keep our eyes and ears on her."

The other young man blew air as he leaned back into his seat.

"Hey," said the man with hazel eyes, "now you remember who the leader was before Dean."

"How can I forget?"

"Now from what I see, everything is going just fine. This will all be over soon and we all will live happy ever after. We all just got to keep doing our parts. You hear me?"

"Yeah, I hear you... loud and clear."

CHAPTER EIGHT

Long after the café was closed and empty, Andrea sat silently in the manager's office. She rested her head in her left hand while thinking back to when her life made sense, which was long before all this madness started. In her right hand, she held a picture of her with Charles from when they first started dating. Andrea kept the picture in her wallet and only pulled it out occasionally to look back on how happy she once was with the man of her dream. She was pondering if Charles was still alive would he have been able to protect her from this madness that she was now facing.

Tears started rolling down from Andrea's eyes as she continued looking down at the picture. She wiped each tear one by one as they came down.

"Here…" said a well-known voice.

The voice startled Andrea that she looked up very quickly, due that she didn't hear anybody enter in the room – not along, entered the café.

"What are you doing here?" she asked, looking into the tall man's hazel eyes as he held out a black handkerchief to her. "How did you even get in here?"

"Through the front door," he answered.

"But the front door was locked. I locked it myself."

"That didn't stop me," he replied still holding out the black handkerchief. "Now dry your eyes."

Andrea gave him a very confused look on how this man was trying to give her a handkerchief to wipe her eyes with.

"What?" he said. "Being a bad guy means I can't have a heart."

Andrea kept her eyes on him as she slowly took the handkerchief out of his hand. For a few seconds, she closed her eyes so she could wipe them, along with the few tears that she had already cried.

"I thought I told you to go meet with your friends," the man said, breaking the little silence that had started building in the room.

"I was…" Andrea answered, balling the handkerchief up in her hand. "I was on my way out the door right now."

"Don't look like that to me."

"Listen, I was doing a little paperwork when–"

"If you were doing a little paperwork, then where the papers that you were so call doing?" the man asked when cutting her out.

There was then silence building between the two of them again, as Andrea sat still in fear.

"You wanna tell another story?" asked the man.

Andrea couldn't find words to respond.

"Is it that hard for you?" he asked.

"What do you think?" Andrea finally answered.

"What so hard about keeping your mouth shut?"

Silence came again in the room.

The tall man exhales as he took a seat in the right chair in front of the desk. "Look, I know what you saw wasn't an easy thing to have witnessed." He told her. "But you got to understand that he's out of control. No one can control him. Not even his older brother who he once looked up to. Now, I did something that wasn't only hard as hell to do, but to me and five others considered to be suicidal. I was able to convince him to leave you alone... and give you this one chance to just walk away. And all you have to do to keep seeing another day is to keep your mouth closed like I've been telling you to do for the past two days – and so far you've been doing well."

"Why would you do something like that for me?" Andrea asked becoming even more confused by this man.

He stared Andrea in the eyes for a moment. "Because the way I see it, you didn't know what you were walking into when you entered that garage," he replied. "You were just in the right place at the very wrong time."

His spoken words got to Andrea. He sounded a bit more like a friend than an enemy.

"Finish shutting this place down and then go meet up with your friends." He said, standing up to his feet and headed towards the door.

"Why?" Andrea asked.

"Because that's what you need to do." He said, turning back around. "From what I hear in your conversation earlier today, you're the kind of

94

person who is there for a friend during hard times. Now, I heard your friend say that another friend of yours is having a hard time. So you need to go see what's going on if that's the kind of person you really are. That's the kind of person your friend made you out to be. So be that person, before you bring the spotlight onto you, and we don't want that."

Without another word, the man walked out the office, leaving Andrea lost and confused with her head resting upwards in her hands.

It was twenty minutes past nine in the evening when Shanequa, Felicia, and Montica were finally seated at an empty booth near the back of their favorite night club they arrived at five minutes ago. Music played throughout the room, as people dance on the dance floor. Waitresses fought through the crowd, carrying drinks from the bar in one hand high in the air, towards the ones who ordered them.

"Why couldn't Andrea come out with us again?" Felicia asked as she slid into the booth first.

"She wanted to spend the evening with her boys, 'cause she had things she had to do with her mama tomorrow," answered Shanequa who was already in the booth.

After Montica removed her coat and took a seat, she replied, "Well, that's what I wanted to do. Go home to be with my daughter and husband."

"No...," said Felicia. "You've been a little down since yesterday for some reason. Now, I don't know what's going on with you, but we needed to get you away from whatever it is."

"I agree. You could be stressed out from all that hard work you've been doing lately with trying to make partner and things."

Montica paused for a moment as she eyed the two of them. "No, I'm not stressed," she replied. "I really just don't wanna talk about what's going on with me, because it's really none of your business."

"Oh really," Shanequa said. "Well, you know talking about your problems sometimes help. You never know unless you talk. Hell, we might be able to help you through whatever is going on, Montica."

"I don't think so."

A waiter approached the table. "Can I get you, ladies, something to drink?" he asked.

"Yes, I'll have a Cranberry Juice, please," said Montica.

"Let me get a Strawberry Margarita," said Felicia.

Shanequa took a second to think about what she wanted. "I'll take a Dirty Martini," she ordered.

"And one Long Island Ice Tea, please," said a voice coming around the waiter.

Everybody was surprised to see Andrea had come and joined them.

"See, I knew you weren't gonna back down on joining us tonight," Shanequa said happily.

"Well, I was," Andrea replied, sliding in next to Shanequa. "But something just kind of changed my mind and got me out here."

"Well, we're glad you came anyway," said Felicia.

"Will that be all ladies?" the waiter asked.

"Yes, that'll be all," answered Montica.

The waiter backed away from the table and headed towards the bar to get their drinks.

"So, what was it that changed your mind again?" asked Shanequa, giving Andrea a funny look.

"Don't worry about it," Andrea said as she faced Montica. "I wanna know what's going on with you and what's got you so down."

"It's nothing, Andrea," she answered.

"Are you sure about that?"

"I'm positive. I just got a few things going on at work, but it's all gonna get straighten out soon. I know it will."

"Is it on that case you're working on?" Felicia asked curiously.

"Yeah, is that case you were telling us about the other day getting to you?" Shanequa asked before Montica had a chance to answer Felicia question.

Montica stared back and forth to both Shanequa and Felicia. "What if it is?" she said. "You two couldn't do anything about it if that was the issue."

"But is it about a case?" Andrea asked. "Did you lose a simple case the other day?"

The waiter returned to the table with their drinks and placed them correctly out in front of them.

"Thank you," everybody told waiter as he left the table again.

"No, it's not about a case," Montica told them while becoming a bit frustrated. "I just don't wanna talk about it, because it's nothing. So please let's find something else to talk about."

"Alright," said Felicia. "But can you please at least smile for us the rest of the time we're out... please."

Montica quickly spread a smile across her face before picking up her drink and took a little sip.

The night felt as if it was going by fast, as they all were having really great time.

Andrea looked at the time on her watch. "Oh gosh," she said, "It's almost midnight. I need to go home."

"Me too," Montica said as she also looked at her watch.

"Man, I miss the good old days, before you all had responsibilities," said Shanequa.

"Yeah," Felicia agreed. "Back when we all use to stay out way past three in the morning and do *God please forgive me* things."

"I remember those days, but don't wish to do them again," said Andrea.

"Same here," Montica said, drinking the last of her second cranberry juice, then slid out of the booth and put on her coat. "I'll talk with you girls later. Right now I gotta get home before my husband sends out a search party."

"You're not the only one," replied Andrea doing the same. "But first, I'm gonna head over to the bar and get a glass of water, and then I'm outta here."

"Okay, well, we'll see you two party poopers later," Shanequa replied.

"Yeah," said Felicia. "And when I see you next time Montica, I want you smiling."

"Yes, please," Andrea agreed.

"Alright," Montica said, backing away from the table. "I'll see you guys later." She then walked from the table and towards the front door.

They all watch as she left the building.

"Something is really bothering her," said Felicia.

"The question is what," replied Andrea. "Is she and Brice having problems?"

"Your guess is as good as mines."

"Well, like I said, the only thing we can do is be there for her" Shanequa told them.

"I told you that," said Felicia.

"Does it really matter who said it, as long as we do it."

"Well, you're right about that."

Andrea looked at them for a moment. "Alright, let me go get some water and then get outta here," she said. "I'll see you guys later." She picked up her purse and headed over to the bar.

Stepping up to the bar, she called for the closest bartender, who walked over to see what she wanted.

"May I get a glass of water, please?" she ordered.

The bartender walked away to get Andrea's water, and Andrea stood patiently for the bartender to return. While she waited, out of the corner of her right eye she noticed a young man in about his late twenties, good looking, brown skin, with a faded haircut and very nice trimmed facial hair, standing right beside her, staring.

She fully turned her head to see who he was. "Can I help you, sir?" she asked.

"I'm sure you can," he replied.

"Okay, listen I'm not that kind of person. I'm a mother of two boys that I'm raising by myself."

"You're not the only woman in the world who's doing that."

"What do you want?"

"Your help, if you don't mind."

"You want my help? And just who the hell are you?"

"I'm sorry," he said, reaching into his jacket pocket and then held up a badge to Andrea's face. "I'm Detective Justin Ronking and I would like to know what you saw in the garage Wednesday night."

Andrea paused as her heart felt like it was about to beat right out of her chest. Her eyes were locked on the badge the Detective was still holding up to her.

"Miss…" he said waiting for her to say something.

"What are you talking about?" Andrea replied, acting as if she didn't know what he was referring to.

"Well, as you may know, three men were murdered in a parking garage… not too far from where you work."

"Yeah, I know. I heard about it on the news," she answered not paying attention to the Detective's last comment.

"I don't believe the news is the way you know about it."

"Well, it is."

"Is it really?"

"Yeah it is."

"Then tell me, why I have several people tell us they saw you running from the garage with a couple of guys running behind you."

Andrea stood silently for a slight second, eyeing the detective. "What do you mean people saw me running from the garage."

Ronking then picked up a folder that was resting on the bar countertop. He opened it and placed a photo of Andrea running out the garage in front of her. "We've shown this to people who said they were around during the time the shooting had to happen. They all said that it was you running out of that garage, Andrea," he told her. "Now I want to know what you saw."

"Where did you get this?" she asked, looking down at the photo.

"It wasn't easy. Someone messed with the garage surveillance system in order not be recorded. This is from a camera they missed."

They looked eye to eye with one another for a moment.

"Now what did you see and why were those men chasing you?" he asked again.

"I really didn't know what you are talking about?" Andrea answered.

The bartender placed a glass of water in front of her and walked away. Andrea forgot all about the water.

"Miss," Ronking said, placing the photo away. "We have men working around the clock on this murder case. Now here we have someone who may have seen something, and would very much appreciate if you would come tell us what you might have seen."

"I have told you, I don't know anything." She said as she tried walking away.

"If you're worried that somebody might come after you talk, then we can place you and your family in a Witness Protection Program."

"That won't be necessary," she said, turning to face him once more, "because I don't have a reason to be put in witness protection. Now if you would excuse me, I have to get home."

"That's right… you have two boys you have to go raise by yourself."

Andrea said nothing more. She just walked until she was out the club and sitting in her car. Then, a few minutes later, Andrea was home where she really wanted to be with her mother and children.

CHAPTER NINE

When the sun was high up in the sky, Andrea opened her eyes and lay still for a moment, before sitting up on the side of the bed. After about three minutes had passed, she stood to her feet, walked out the room, and glanced into the boys' room as they were still asleep. Andrea then headed down the hall to the living room where she found Thelma relaxing on the couch like she does every other morning, in front of the TV, with a cup of tea in hand.

"Morning mama," she said, entering the room.

"Good morning, sweetheart," Thelma replied. "How are you this morning?"

"Tired," Andrea exhaled.

Thelma eyed her daughter in the face. "Did you get enough sleep? You don't look like you did." She said.

"I haven't been able to sleep too well these past few nights," Andrea told her as she turned and headed into the kitchen to make for herself a cup of hot Green Tea.

Thelma watched Andrea in the kitchen from the spot she sat at on the couch. "Well, why not?" she nearly shouted. "Is everything alright?"

"Everything's fine," Andrea answered, pulling down a cup from the top cabinet, and then stepped over to the stove to fill it with the hot water that was already made in the kettle.

While watching Andrea's every move, Thelma asked, "Is there something on your mind that you would like to talk about?"

"No," she answered, pulling a Green Tea bag from the jar next to the stove.

"You sure about," Thelma said, leaning forward and placing her cup down on the couch table, "'Cause the one thing a mother knows is her children, and I have sat here for the past few minutes and I can tell that there's something on your mind. Now, what is it?"

"I can assure you, mama, that there is nothing on my mind to really talk about," Andrea said, entering back into the living room, with her tea in hand, and sat down in the center of the loveseat.

"Are you really sure about?"

"Yes, I'm more than sure," Andrea replied as she took a sip of the tea.

"Okay, well," Thelma said, leaning back on the couch. "I mean you're a grown woman, and I'm sure you have the sense to talk to somebody if you had something going on. But I'm your mother, and I am quite sure I know that there's something is on your mind – and that it's bothering you."

Andrea leaned against the arm of the loveseat. "Mama, I promise you if I had something on my mind bothering me that you would be the first to know about it," she said. "Right now, I'm just a little tired from staying out so late last night."

"Oh yes, I do remember hearing you come in at twelve fifty-six in the morning."

"Montica has been a little out of herself about something, and the girls wanted to take her out to get her mind off whatever it is."

"How she's doing now?"

"About the same," Andrea answered, taking another sip of her green tea. She then changes the subject when remembering what Thelma wanted to do today. "So, did you still wanna go see if we can find you another mattress?" she asked

"Oh no, I'm good."

"You're sure? I thought you said the mattress you have now wasn't good for your back."

"It's not, but Ms. Evers from the church has an unused mattress that she was gonna give to me for a very good price."

Andrea gave Thelma a serious look. "Mama, do you really wanna take a mattress from out of somebody's house?" she asked.

"What's wrong with that?"

"I mean you don't know what people have in their house. For all, you know that mattress could be loaded with germs, bed bugs, or something."

"True. However, I was told that the mattress was still wrapped up and in storage."

"Well, if you think it's good, then go for it." Andrea said as she brought her cup to her lips, took a long sip, and then placing it near the edge of the coffee table.

"She's gonna let me have a look at it first before having it's brought over here. Meanwhile, you and the boys can go out and get lost today if you want."

Andrea let the idea run through her mind for a moment. "I don't see a reason why we couldn't," she replied. "The boys and I use some new clothes. So I guess we can go hang out at the mall for a while." Slowly standing up, Andrea headed towards the window and looked out across the street.

"Yeah," Thelma said cheerfully. "Go and have a mother and sons day."

From the second floor window, Andrea eyed the black Suburban truck parked right across the street from the building. "Yeah," she said in an unhappy way. "Let me try and make this a fun day for us."

After spending nearly an hour at the mall, Andrea ended up buying three outfits for herself, and then helped Miles and Ted find two nice outfits each. She was having a good time, although the outing could've been better if Andrea didn't have to see her two special friends somewhere in sight, every time she looked over her shoulders.

"Boys, let's sit and rest for a minute," Andrea said as they approached a bench.

"Come on, mama," said Miles. "This is the most fun we had in a long time. Let's keep going."

"Just give me a minute, and then we'll go to any other store y'all wanna go to, alright."

"Can we just go without you?" asked Ted.

"Yeah mom, it's not like we're *little* kids anymore." Miles agreed.

Andrea looked back and forward to the both of them. She didn't think it would be a good idea to let the two of them out of her sight. "Just give me a minute," she repeated. "Let me rest my feet for a moment and then we'll be on our way."

"Mama, it's won't be the first time Ted and I walked around the mall by ourselves," Miles told her. "We'll be fine."

Andrea kept eyeing them. "Alright," she finally agreed to let them go wander around the mall by themselves. "But remember, if anybody you don't know comes up to you…"

"… Mom," Miles cut her off. "This is not our first time, we'll gonna be okay."

There was total silence between the three of them for a few seconds.

"Yeah, you're right," Andrea replied, pulling some money from her purse and placed it in Miles's hand. "Here's a twenty. That's no more than ten dollars for the both of you."

"No more than ten dollars, Miles," Ted repeated.

"I heard her," Miles told him.

Andrea let out a chuckle listening to them. "Alright, you two," she said for their attention. "When I get up from here, I'm gonna head down to Starbucks. So, when y'all ready to go, come down and get me, alright."

"Okay," both Miles and Teds responded as they started walking away.

As Andrea watched her sons walk away, a thought came to her mind that just maybe Miles and Ted would be better off away from her than with her.

Andrea sat at a table outside Starbucks for almost ten minutes, slowly enjoying Java Chip Frappuccino, and could only wonder how her children were doing.

"May I sit down?" asked a familiar voice.

Without looking up, Andrea answers, "Why not, you already follow me everywhere I go. So go ahead."

The tall man with the hazel eyes took a seat across from Andrea.

"Where's the other guy that's always with you?" she asked.

"Watching Miles and Ted," he answered.

Andrea almost jumped out of her seat when she heard those words.

"He with my kids," she almost shouted out loud.

"Calm down," he told her. "He's just keeping an eye on them, because as you already know there are some crazy people out there."

Andrea gave a strange look as she tried calming her nervous.

"What do you want?" she asked.

"To talk for a minute or two," he answered.

"What is there to talk about?"

"Look Andrea…"

Andrea cut him off before he could finish what he was about to say. "Just how do you know my name?" she asked.

The man took a deep breath and exhaled very loudly before answering. "We have someone who's good with computer and other technology working with us. The boss had him to run the numbers on your license plate and that gave us your name and address."

"And how do you know so much about my family?"

"We had the computer whiz work his magic and learn almost everything there is to know about you, Andrea. You were born May 31, 1977, to Ben and Thelma Walker. Married Charles Harris on March 15, 1997, and then had your first born, Miles Harris, nine months later. Few years later had your second born, Ted Harris, shortly after your husband death in 9/11. We know your social security, past residence, banking information, and a whole lot more if you'll like me to go on."

Andrea could've almost passed out on how much they knew about her, as she beat her head against her right hand.

"Is there anything you don't know about me?" she asked.

"I think we have everything I need to know about you," he answered. "But look, if it makes you feel any better to know something about me, my name is Marcus. Not that it would do you any good to know."

"Why would I wanna know your name?"

"Well, that's you, if you wanna know it or not, I really don't give a damn. I didn't come over here to get to know one another. I came over here to talk about what's happening."

"Well, I guess that would be something we need to talk about, wouldn't it?"

"Yeah, like whom you were with last night."

"Those were just my friends that I've known for a very long time. I went to Columbia University with them." She sat still for a moment staring at him. "Or did you already know that?" She then said.

The man who is now known as Marcus stared back at her silently, before replying, "I'm talking about the man you were with at the bar."

Andrea's heart fell with fear when he asked about the detective who approached her last night.

"Oh… him," she replied, quickly trying to think of something to tell him. "That was just some guy that was trying to pick me up and pay me a drink."

"What was all that stuff he was showing you?"

"He was trying to impress me with what he did for a living."

"And you want me to believe that."

"You can believe what you want, I really don't give a damn, but it's the truth."

They briefly stared into each other's eyes.

"I really do hope you don't think I'm stupid," said Marcus. "I know that was a cop that came up to last night – and don't you dare tell me it wasn't because I know it was." He paused and watched as Andrea tried keeping a serious face. "I also know you don't wanna see anything bad happen to anyone else. So if I were you, I'll be careful on what I say the next time he comes back around, because he will."

"What makes you think that man's coming back?"

"He's a cop. They always keep coming around the person who they believe can help them." Marcus leaned forward and started whispering. "Now, when that cop comes back, you continue acting like you don't know anything. As long as you continue to do that, no more lives will be taken – capiche?"

Andrea didn't respond.

"You have no idea what you're facing right now, Andrea," Marcus said still whispering. "If you think what you saw in the garage was awful, then trust me, you haven't seen anything yet. Believe me on that. Now this will all be over for you the morning when you'll wake up and don't see Mark and me parked across the street from your building. Then after that, it will do you no good to go to the police or say anything, because we will be long gone."

"Who's Mark?" Andrea asked.

"The other man," he answered. "It's short for Marcus Jr."

"So… this is like a father and son project for you two."

"If that's how you wanna look at it," Marcus replied just when his cell phone started vibrating in his jacket pocket. He pulled it out and viewed the text that came. Looking back up to Andrea, he placed the phone back in his jacket pocket. "Remember everything we talk about here," he said, standing to his feet. "… and when that morning comes, everything will be the way you want it to be."

Then without another word, Marcus leaves Andrea sitting there quietly until she heard Miles and Ted coming up behind her.

"Mama, we're ready to go," said Ted, startling Andrea.

"Okay," Andrea replied, standing up. "I'm ready to go as well."

Andrea picked up her two shopping bags from the chair next to the one she was in when out of nowhere, somebody walks by bumps right into Andrea and dropped something inside one of shopping bags. Keeping very calm, she saw that it was the young man she now knew as Mark as he kept on walking like nothing happened. She glanced down inside the bag to see what he dropped in there. Andrea couldn't believe her eyes when she found a stack of money labeled five thousand dollars resting on top of the new clothes she had just bought.

Attached to the money was a note that she reached in and pulled out to read:

There's more where this came from.

Andrea balled up the note and threw it in the trash as she and the boys left the mall. She also pushed the money underneath her new clothes so no one – not even her, could see it until she found a place hide it.

CHAPTER TEN

On the ride home, Andrea made small talk with Ted and Miles. Mostly to see what happened after they departed back in the mall, she wanted to know if anybody came up and started talking to them for no reason at all, since knowing Mark was watching them. But to Andrea's relieve, there wasn't – so they told her. When arriving in front of the apartment building and parked, she let Miles and Ted grabbed all the shopping bags, all but the one that had the money down at the bottom. Unsure on what to do with the money, Andrea wasn't letting it out of her sight, not until she was able to hide it in an inconspicuous place.

Miles and Ted moved a bit quicker stepping out of the car and heading inside the building. After Andrea stepped out and followed behind them, she didn't have a foot on the first step when she heard somebody calling her name. She wished she could've ignored the person as she turned to see that it was Detective Ronking, from last night, walking very smoothly up the sidewalk towards her.

"What are you doing here?" she asked.

"I need to talk to you," Ronking replied.

"I don't have anything to say to you."

"Oh, but I believe you do."

"Mom is everything okay?" asked Miles who was standing side-by-side with Ted. They were both eyed the strange man that was standing only a foot away from their mother.

Andrea thought they were already in the building, heading upstairs when she looked up at them. "Everything's fine," she told them. "Go in the house and I'll be there in a second."

They didn't move. They stood their ground, continually staring at both their mother and strange man.

"Go ahead," Andrea ordered them.

They listened to her the second time and slowly enter the building.

"You have some handsome boys," said Ronking.

"Look," Andrea said sounding very serious with what she was about to say to him. "I don't know anything about what happen in that garage the other night. Secondly, I don't appreciate you coming to my home asking me about something I don't know anything about. So will you please go away and leave me alone?"

"You know, I have been doing this job long enough to know you're hiding something," Ronking replied as he removed his sunglass and took a step close to Andrea. "Now, I'll be more than happy to leave you alone, if you tell me what I need to know."

"There nothing I can tell you, what part of that aren't you hearing?"

"I'm hearing what you're telling me, but I know that's all a big lie. Now, if you tell me what I need to know, then you won't ever again see me as long as you live. However, that won't be until after we go to court."

"Well, we won't be going to court, because I have no reason to have to go to court. Now do I?"

"I'm not sure, 'cause I'm not sure of what all you know."

Andrea stood and stared him in the face, wishing this whole ordeal would go away.

"Come on," Ronking said, staring deep into Andrea's big brown eyes. "Like I told you last night if you're worrying about somebody coming after you then we can place you all into witness protection."

"And like I told you last night," Andrea said, staring back into Ronking's eyes, "That won't be necessary because I don't have any reason to go into witness protection." She then started marching up the steps, but before even touching the doorknob, she turned back to Ronking, and said, "Don't come around my home anymore."

With those final words spoken, Andrea entered the building and slammed the door close. She moved fast up the staircase, when reaching the second floor, Andrea slowly walked towards the apartment door. Getting more the half to the door, Bobbi comes stepping out into the hall with a trash bags.

"How was the mall?" she asked when Andrea passed by.

"It's was fine. I bought three new outfits," Andrea replied

"Anything I might wanna borrow?"

"If I do, you won't be getting it."

"Oh, we'll see about that."

They both laughed.

"Okay," Bobbi said, slowly heading towards the staircase. "I'm gonna have to talk to you later because I think I threw something away last night that has my whole apartment smelling awful."

Just when she said that, Andrea noticed the unique odor. "Yeah, I see what you mean because I'm starting to smell it from here." She told her. "I'll let you go throw that out and talk with you later."

By the time Andrea had her hand on the doorknob; Bobbi quickly calls out for her attention.

"Andrea some cute guy stopped by looking for you while you were out," Bobbi informed her.

"Do you know who it was?"

The name had slipped Bobbi's mind, but then it slowly came back to her. "I believe he said his name was... Justin... yeah, that's it, Justin Ronking."

Andrea became silent as thought rushed through her head on what all Detective Ronking might have said to Bobbi.

"He said that he was an old friend of yours," Bobbi continued as she sat down the trash bags in her right hand, then reached down inside her pant pocket and pulled a card. "He wrote down his number so you could give him a call sometime." She held the card out for Andrea to take.

Andrea very careful reached out and took the card from Bobbi, and took a quick glance at it before throwing it into her purse. "Thanks," she said very unhappy.

"You don't seem too happy about hearing from him," Bobbi replied, staring Andrea in the face.

"Yeah, we have a little misunderstanding going on right now."

"Wanna talk about?"

Andrea reached for the doorknob and started turning it. "No, I'll be fine, don't worry," she answered. "Everything will work itself out eventually – but anyway, I'll talk to you later." She then enters the apartment and closed the door, before Bobbi even had a chance to say anything else.

"Child, why are you storming in this house like somebody's after you?" inquired Thelma, sitting near the edge of the couch with Miles and Ted, as they showed her the two outfits Andrea had purchased for them at the mall.

Not paying attention to how fast she entered the apartment, Andrea didn't have to think too long on a lie she could give her mother. "'Cause I need to use the bathroom," she said, and then rushed down the hall and entered the bathroom with her purse and shopping bag still in hand.

She closed the bathroom door – almost slamming it. She sat the bags down on the floor while looking around the room for something to pour in the toilet to make it sound like she was actually in there peeing. Looking at the sink, Andrea eyed the bottle of Listerine mouthwash. Although it would be must of a waste, she grabbed the bottle, removed the top, and begin slowly poured it into the toilet. After flushing the toilet, Andrea lightly turned on the sink to replace the little she poured out with water. Then, she fully turned on the sink so it could be heard down the hall, and then grabbed the bar soap from its dish to wet – in case Miles or Ted came in after her.

She then dried her hands, picked up her purse and shopping bags, and eased across the hall to her bedroom.

"Andrea," shouted Thelma, before Andrea even had a foot in her room. She heard Andrea when coming out of the bathroom.

"Ma'am," Andrea answers.

"Aren't you gonna come down here and show me what you bought from the mall?"

"Later. I have something that I need to do real fast."

Andrea went into her room, closed the door and locked it.

She dumped the contents of the Sears's shopping bag in the center her bed. Picking up the money, Andrea had a seat on the edge of the bed and flipped through the stack of hundreds. She couldn't believe she was holding so much money. It would've taken her almost four months to earn this amount of money, and she had no idea what to do with it. She didn't want to spend it, because it was dirty money – or more of blood money, and most definitely couldn't spend. But now that it was in her possession, she had to make sure that nobody found it.

Viewing every area of the room, she looked hard for a place to stash this money, but she needed a place no one would come across it accidentally. There really wasn't a good place in the room Andrea saw or could think of to hide the money. Then, glancing back at the bed gave Andrea a great idea. For a moment, she thought to hide the money between the mattresses, but then thought it to be too obvious. A second and much better thought came to mind, and Andrea thought about hiding it inside the bottom mattress. She glanced over to her dresser, and saw the needle and threads, that she used to fix a button on a shirt of hers' a week ago, sitting next to a pair of scissor.

Standing up from the edge of the bed with the cash still in hand, Andrea grabbed both needle and thread and the pair of scissor. She got down on the floor and lay on her side. Using the scissors, Andrea cut a small hole in the bottom mattress, very close to the edge, that way she'll be able to sew it back easily to make it look natural.

By the time she was finished hiding the money in the mattress and sewed back up the hole, the mattress looked as if nothing had been down to it. And it took Andrea no more than five minutes to do so.

Just as Andrea was getting up off the floor, there came a knock at her door.

"Just a minute," Andrea shouted, standing back on her feet, and then placed the needle and thread and scissor back on her dresser.

"What are you doing in there?" Thelma shouted back through the door.

When Andrea finally opened the door, she was standing face to face with Thelma.

"I say I had some things to take care of." She answered, easing past Thelma and headed down the hall to the living room, and then had a seat on the loveseat.

"Why don't you two go and hang your clothes up in your closet," Thelma told Miles and Ted.

"Yes ma'am," Miles and Ted replied as they grabbed their bags and took them to their room.

Once they were out of sight, Thelma stared down to Andrea with a smile, as Andrea tried to relax her body and mind a little.

"What?" Andrea asked when noticing Thelma staring at her.

"They told me you were downstairs talking to some man," Thelma replied.

"No mama," Andrea said, knowing what her mother was thinking.

"I'm just wondering because they said he was a good looking man. They also said you asked him what he was doing here, so I figured you knew this man from somewhere."

"Yes, I know him, but not for the reason you're thinking of. And if I was seeing somebody, it wouldn't be that guy, because he is not my type."

"Well, you did say the same thing about Charles, and look what happen between the two of you."

Andrea thought back to when she met Charles back in college. She thought Charles was nothing more than a pretty boy who thought every woman wanted him – until he met Andrea. He approached Andrea several times; however, she wouldn't give him the time of day. Within his eyes, Charles saw Andrea to be a very special young lady and wasn't gonna let her get away. He ran into her at a college party and nearly made a fool out of himself for Andrea to go out with him. Finally, Andrea agreed to, and then later, once she really got to know him, Andrea found that Charles wasn't as bad of a man as she thought he was.

"Charles was different," Andrea said still in thought.

"Oh, is that right?" Thelma asked.

Coming out of thought, Andrea looked up to Thelma and changed the subject. "Is there anything else you have to do today?" she asked.

"Not that I know of," Thelma answered. "Why you ask?"

"I need to make a run."

"A run where?"

"I wanna go see Charles." she said, standing up, and headed back to her room for her purse.

"You wanna do what?" Thelma asked.

Andrea came back to the living room with her purse up on her shoulder. "I wanna go see Charles," she repeated. "I'll be back shortly." Not waiting for Thelma to reply, she quickly heading out the apartment.

Upon arriving at the cemetery, Andrea took a moment before heading towards her husband's grave. She hadn't been there since the day they placed the coffin in the ground, which was the worst day of her life. What made it even worse for her is that her husband wasn't even in the casket when it was placed it in the ground. His body was never found. So all that was buried in the plot was a few of his belongings, along with a cream colored suit that was his favorite and Andrea always loved seeing him in.

After sitting still in the car for a few second, Andrea finally got out and made her way towards the headstone that read:

CHARLES MALIK HARRIS
JANUARY 2, 1975 – SEPTEMBER 11, 2001

Loving Husband & Father

Just looking at the date of death brought a stream of tears to Andrea's eyes. It was a reminder that he wasn't here with her anymore.

"Hey baby," she cried, staring at his name. "I know it's been a long time... and I know you've probably wondering what brings me out here today." She wiped away the tears that were running down her face. "I just wanted to come tell you... that I may be coming to be with you soon..., because I don't know what more I can do. I'm in the middle of something that I don't know how to get out of. The boys will be fine... I know my mama will take care of them." She paused for a second to try and keep herself together. "God I wish you could see them now. Miles is so big... I think he might get as tall as you were. And Teddy... oh, I wish you could've seen him from the day he was born... he is so must like you. They both are."

She got down on her knees and placed her right hand on the headstone.

"I wonder what things would be like if you were still here," she said. "Would I be going through what I am right now? I wish you were here to hold me... make me feel safe like you used to, and let me know that nothing would ever happen to me... I really need you, Charles."

She continued eyeing the headstone, before leaning forward and placing a kiss right above the name. She then stood back on her feet, and before walking away, she said, "You told me we will always be together no matter what. I just never thought it would be in death."

The whole ride home from the cemetery, Andrea pondered on what would happen to her children if the two men following behind her decided to end her life. The thought caused her to move slowly after she arrived home and headed up to the apartment. After entering through the door, she found Thelma on the couch holding both Miles and Ted in her arms, asleep. She tried not to wake them as she closed the door, but Thelma woke up when the floor creaked on Andrea's way past the couch.

"You're alright?" Thelma asked, sensing something was wrong in the way Andrea was walking towards the hall.

Andrea gave little of her attention to Thelma. "I'm fine," she answered. "I just wanna go lay down for a while."

"Is everything alright? Andrea, come sit down and talk with me, please."

Andrea came around and sat on the loveseat. "I was just wondering…" she started, not giving Thelma a change to ask the same question again. "… What would you do if something happens to me?"

"Andrea, where is this coming from?"

"This been on my mind since the day Charles died. What if something unexpected happens and my babies lost me too?"

"You shouldn't think like that."

"Well, I can't help it, mama. Life is so scary sometimes and I don't know what to do?"

Thelma listened to her daughter's words. She just knew something serious was going on with Andrea, but just didn't know what. She wanted to ask but didn't want to wake Miles or Ted if things went back and forward between the two of them. So she thought of giving some encouraging words to speak into her heart.

"Remember what the Bible says: God does not give us the spirit of fear; but of power, and of love, and of a sound mind. As long as you have God in your heart… you shouldn't fear anything." Thelma told Andrea.

Andrea leaned back against the loveseat as she took her mother's encouraging words into her heart.

Meanwhile, Thelma thought of what could possibly be wrong with her daughter.

CHAPTER ELEVEN

Sunday morning, Andrea and her family went to church together like they always do. She thought being inside a holy place could take away some of the fear she built up inside, even if it was just for a moment. However, she was wrong, because what she dreaded, followed her right inside the church, and sat in the far back of the sanctuary on the opposite side of where Andrea and her family sat.

Andrea sat in between Miles and Ted holding them gently in her arms because she had no idea when will be the last time she would ever hold them. During the whole church service, while listening as the Pastor preaches, she thought about what Marcus said yesterday, '*She would wake up one morning and they will be long gone.*' She had only wished that moment would've come this morning when she awoke.

As the service went on, Andrea felt the need to be alone for a moment. She stood to her feet, eased around Miles and from in between the paws, and excused herself towards the door leading to the back of the church. There, after no long than five minutes, she sat on the toilet in the second stall of women's bathroom, breathing easy to keep her nerves calm. Not daring to spend too much time in there, and have Marcus and Mark searching the church with the idea that she was up to something, Andrea stood up from the toilet, opened the door, and stepped out the stall.

"You don't hear too good, do you?" asked Marcus.

Andrea quickly turned and found Marcus in the bathroom, leaning against the first stall. She never heard anyone come in or even the bathroom door open.

"What are you doing in here?" she replied. "This is the girl's bathroom. Men's is one over."

"You're tryin' to be funny?"

There was silent in the bathroom.

"How many times do I have to tell you to stop making eye contact with us?" Marcus said.

"I haven't looked at either of you all morning," Andrea answered.

"Lying in a church, you must wanna go to Hell. You looked at us when coming in here, twice during the service, and once more when you were excusing yourself to come back here. That's the total of four times your brown eyes slightly drew attention to us."

Andrea gave no responses.

"Do you wanna dead, Andrea?" he asked.

It fell silent in the room yet again.

"If you don't do as I tell you, Andrea, then you're gonna be a dead woman."

"Why are you doing this to me?" Andrea finally said. "If you're gonna kill me, go ahead and do it, and stop torturing me. I can't take it anymore."

Marcus stood up straight and took a few steps forward, as Andrea happen to take a step back and was against the sink.

"Is that really what you want?" He asked. "Uh…"

Andrea didn't answer as she looked up to Marcus.

Very quickly, Marcus grabbed a hand full of Andrea's hair, snatched her head back, as he reached back for his gun, and pointed it beneath her chin. There was hardly space between the two of them, as Marcus was slightly pressing his body against Andrea's.

"Uh – is that really what you want?" he repeated as he saw tears welling up in Andrea's eyes. "See… I knew… you weren't really to face death. Now if it comes to us having this convention again, I may not hold back."

He then moved the gun from Andrea's sight, put it back in his pants, behind his jacket, and left the bathroom, leaving Andrea with a clear understanding to Marcus's final warning.

Shortly the next morning, after taking Miles and Ted to school, and then arriving at the café, Andrea entered inside, but as she was closing the front door behind herself, someone that Andrea wanted to avoid, held the door with one hand to keep it from being closed.

It was Detective Ronking.

"What are you doing here?" Andrea asked, trying to close him out.

"I just wanna talk to you," he replied.

"How many times do I have to tell you, I don't know anything?"

"And how many times do I have to tell you that I know that's bullshit."

Andrea tried hard to close the door and lock it, but Ronking prevented her from doing so.

"Okay, if I talk to you will you please go away and leave me the hell alone?" she asked after giving up the fight.

As the door open, Ronking stepped inside, staring Andrea in the face. "That depends on what all you can tell me," he told her.

"Well, that won't be much," Andrea replied, walking around to the other side of the counter.

"The shooting happen around after ten o' clock. Can you tell me your whereabouts around that time?"

"I had just finished up some paperwork here and was on my way home."

Ronking pulled a pad and pen from his jacket pocket and started writing down the things Andrea said. He then asked, "May I ask how you got home that night?"

"I drove myself home... in my car."

He wrote down her response and then glanced out the window. "Is that your Ford, Mustang outside?" he asked.

"Yes, it is."

"Is that where you always park?"

"No – I mean yes," she quickly changed her answer.

"What is it yes or no? Or did you just start parking there?"

Andrea thought quick of what to tell him. But the only thing she could think to do was give him a little of the truth. "I started parking there," she answered. "Where I use to park at isn't available for me to park at the moment."

"Where did you used to park?"

"It was a walking distance from here."

"Was it anywhere near the parking garage where the murders took place?"

Even though it was a risk, Andrea looked Detective Ronking in the eyes, and replied, "Yes… I used to park near the garage… I… I heard gunshots and I ran because I was scared. I swear on my father's graves that's what happened."

"Is that all?" Ronking asked. "I have a feeling there's something you're not telling me."

"I swear to you… there is nothing else."

Ronking put away his pen and pad. Just when they were back in his jacket pocket, he had a text to come in on his phone. He quickly pulled it from his pants pocket and read the text. "Okay," he said, looking back up to Andrea, "If that's all you say you know, then I don't believe you'll be any useful for us in court. However, I will say that there are still have a lot of unanswered questions that has to do with you that needs answering."

"Then can you ask them so you can get out of my life?"

"I have an urgent matter that just came up. We'll talk later."

Andrea tried calling for him, but by the time she had a chance, Ronking was out the door.

Meanwhile, across the street where Marcus and Mark were parked, Marcus had received a call on his cell phone that sat on the dashboard. He had put it on speaker so Mark could hear the conversation he was having with another member in on the operations. His job was to listen to Andrea's conversation through the surveillance device that was installed in her cell phone.

"Do you think Dean would do anything with this?" asked the man on the other end.

"Not if I can get through to him," replied Marcus.

Mark blew his breath angrily out of his mouth as he sat back in his seat. "Come on, dad," he snapped, "Just let Dean take care of her. It will make our job a whole lot easier."

"Look!" Marcus shouted as he turned to look Mark in his face. "She has nothing to do with this. She didn't get into this like the other guy did. Now in just a few days this will all be over with, and she won't matter to us anymore." He turned and faced the phone. "Listen, Brian, tell Dean she didn't say anything worth killing her over. Maybe if he would've handled those three in private like I told him, none of this would be happening."

It went quite for a few seconds.

"I'll let him know those were your words," said the man they called Brian before ending the call.

"This will all be over soon," Marcus said out loud to himself.

When the clock struck nine o' clock, the café was almost cleaned, but fully closed for the day. The only two people still inside were Alex who was finishing up washing the dishes. And Andrea who had just turned out the lights in the manager's office, with her purse up on her left shoulder, ready to head out the door and to go home for the night.

"I'll see you in the morning," Andrea said stopping by the kitchen.

"Wait a minute," Alex said very smooth, placing a plate he just picked up back down in the sink then turn off the water. "You mean to tell me that you're out the door before me tonight."

"Yeah, I'll do that small amount of paperwork in the morning when I get in."

"Oh okay," Alex said as he turned to finish cleaning the dishes. "Well, I'll see you bright and early then."

"Okay," Andrea replied, heading towards the front.

Andrea was no more than about five steps away from the kitchen door when Alex comes running out calling for her.

"I need to talk to you for a minute," he said when standing in front of Andrea.

Andrea gave Alex her full attention. "About what?" she asked.

"Well, it won't be long until I'll be getting Jordan… and you know… bad unexpected things can come at us when we less expected it."

"You can say that again," Andrea replied with the thought of the hell she was living at this very moment going through her head.

Alex chuckled. "Yeah, anyway," he said, continuing with what he wanted to say while sounding a bit nervous about it. "I wanted to ask if you wouldn't mind being Jordan's godmother. So if anything should ever happen to me... you'll take him, raise him, and love him as if he was your own."

This request wasn't much of a surprise to Andrea. She would've been more than honored to have Jordan's godmother, but with the problem she had parked across the street and who know where else, she wasn't sure of the respond she could give to Alex at the moment.

"Oh, Alex, I... I don't know what to say right now." She told him. "I'm sure nothing is going to happen to you anytime soon. So I know you and Jordan are gonna have one long father and son relationship. I'm sure of it."

"Yeah, but you can't be too sure about some things. I just wanna make sure that's my son has a good life with somebody trustworthy, and not ended up in some orphanage. But while I am here, I would like for Jordan to have someone in his life to look up to like a real mother. Since you know Sabrina isn't much of a mother for him."

Andrea found Alex's last comment to be a good point.

"So will you be Jordan's godmother?" Alex asked once more, although he wasn't taking no for an answer.

She smiled, knowing she did not want to let Alex down. Andrea playful thought for a quick moment. "Sure, I would love to be Jordan's godmother," she answered. "I don't believe I would want anything else... other than to see my boys graduate from high school and then go to college."

"I want the same here."

They both laugh.

"By the way," Alex said, "I kind of already told my lawyer who's helping me with the custody hearing that you would be the one taking Jordan if anything was to ever happen to me. He's gonna make sure that will happen because I want him living with the best woman I know."

"Alright, is there something you're not telling me here?" Andrea asked with the feeling that she was missing something.

"Everything is fine," he answered with a chuckle "I'm just planning ahead for all possibilities."

"Are you sure about that? You're making a contingency plan."

"That's my story and I'm sticking with it."

"Okay. Well…, I'll see you in the morning." Andrea said once again and started heading towards the front door. "I'm ready to get out of these clothes. I think I may even take a nice long hot bubble bath when I get home."

Alex turned his body to head back to the kitchen. "Well enjoy it," he exclaimed, "I'll be out of here once I finish these dishes and take out the trash."

After exiting the café, Andrea locked the door back with her keys, and then she quickly found the car key as she was turning around. She took a few steps towards her car, with the keys ready to unlock the door. Little startled but not too surprised, Andrea saw a shadow that wouldn't stop pestering her.

"Good evening, Andrea," said Ronking, leaning against the café wall.

"Why I'm not surprised to see you again?" Andrea asked very calmly.

Ronking stood up straight and started walking towards Andrea until he was standing face to face with her. "I told you I would be back to finish those questions that were unanswered," he replied.

"You wanna ask them right now."

"Right now is the only little time I have to ask them."

"Is pestering me part of your job or is it because you're delusional in believing that I know something."

He took a second to think on Andrea's question. "I think it's both," he answered. "Mostly it's because I have a photo of you running out of the garage and not from, along with that photo being time-stamp that coincides with the murders. And also, no one that claimed to have been around the garage at the time of the murder – heard gun shots. Now, I want some real answers and no more of the bullshit you fed me with this morning."

From the corner of Andrea's eyes, she saw Marcus and Mark looking right in her direction. Her heart was beating faster and faster, and she was trying not to panic. She was trying to mask her feeling and not do anything that would show on her face to Ronking – giving him little of the truth.

"It has been a long day," she said, "I really just wanna go home, take a bath, and get in the bed. So, can we do this some other time, please?"

"If I can just get five minutes of your time, I'll let you be on your way."

"Come on, I–"

"If you can give me only five maybe ten minutes of your time, then I won't come anywhere near you again.

It almost seemed as if Ronking wasn't giving Andrea much of a choice.

"Just five minutes?" she asked, knowing what she was about to do would be very risky. She was quickly pondering what she could tell this detective to explain the photo and anything else he may ask so that it would sound plausible and make him leave her alone.

"That's all I'm asking for. We can go sit in that all night diner around the corner and talk if you want. Since you've locked up here…" He notices the lights on inside, "and I don't believe you'll want who's ever in there to know what we're talking about."

Taking Ronking's last advice, Andrea agreed. "Fine," she said.

Ronking held out his hand in the direction to go, and started walking side by side with Andrea towards the all night diner he told her about. Marcus watched with many wonders of what Andrea was doing.

"Shadow them," he ordered Mark.

Mark climbed out of the truck and hurried across the street, then quickly tried to catch up with Andrea and Detective Ronking without being noticed.

Only a moment after Mark disappeared around the corner of the building, someone came up and knocked on Marcus's window. When Marcus rolled down his window, Alex rested his arm against the roof of the truck and eyed Marcus.

"Can I help you with something?" Marcus asked.

"I was about to ask you the same thing," Alex answered.

"And who are you?"

"Don't worry about who I am. The question is who are you?"

"What do you want?"

"I want to know why you're following Andrea."

There was silence for a second between them.

"What are you talking about sir?" Marcus asked without taking his eyes off Alex.

Alex made strong eye contact with Marcus, before saying, "I have seen you and that other guy sit out here in this truck every day and all day and you don't leave until Andrea does. I have seen the two of you come into the café and speak to Andrea very suspiciously. Now, I just saw that other guy get out and follow behind Andrea and whoever that was she was with. Now I wanna know why you two are stalking her?"

"Son, are you sure you wanna get into this?"

"I'm sure I'll call the police if you and that other guy don't leave Andrea alone."

Marcus stared at Alex with a very calm face. "You have no idea what you have just stepped in," he replied.

"We'll see about that," Alex said, taking one last look at Marcus as he back away. He then turned and headed towards the alley to go back into the café, through the back entrance of which he came out front when coming to confront Marcus.

By the time Alex was about to step back inside the café, he felt something hit him in the back – worse than a bee sting, knocking him over onto the floor of the café. It didn't take him long to figure out what it was that hit him, but exactly where he was not sure. Not able to really move, Alex slowly turned slightly over to find Marcus standing over him.

"You know next time you shouldn't get into something you don't know anything about," Marcus told Alex.

They both stared into each other's eyes, Alex unsure of what would happen next.

"Oh wait…," Marcus continued as he pointed his gun with a silencer towards Alex's head. "There won't be a next time, now will there?"

Alex's eyes open wide as he shouted, "No don't –"

Before Alex could say any more, it was too late. Marcus had released another bullet that ended Alex's life.

Marcus stared down at the body, while placing his gun in the back of his pants, and then pulled Alex's body back out the door into the alley. He propped it up against the wall to be in the shadows, so nobody from the streets could see it. Stepping back inside the building, Marcus looked hard on the floors and walls for any visible blood that may have splatter. There were two small spots that he wiped it away with a nearby cloth. Then, having another look around, he noticed the camera hanging above the back door but quickly noticed that it wasn't even working. He found the light switches and turned off all the lights, and walk out the back down – which locked on its own, making it appear as if Alex had closed and left the building himself.

He quickly crossed back to the other side of the street and moved the truck into the alley to hide Alex's body in the trunk, until he was able to dispose of it. Marcus then moved back across the street and parked – just in time. Andrea and Ronking were just returning to the front of the café – both appearing a bit happy. And Mark passed right by them, making his way back towards the truck.

"She a good one," Mark said, closing the door. "What she told him was believable and filled in everything he had on her. There shouldn't be any reason for him to come back… unless he would wanna try using her in court, but if she sticks with the story she just gave, she still wouldn't be any use for telling what exactly happen on the third level."

Marcus ignored Mark as he watched Ronking open Andrea's car door for her. "Look," he said for Mark to listen to his every word. "When she gets home, I'm gonna need you to stand on the street and watch everything until I get back."

"Where you're going?"

Marcus glanced back to the trunk to give Mark an idea on what he was about to tell him. "Like Jay we had someone who wanted to get into something he had no business in," he said and then paused for a second. "So, I had to take care of him in a way Dean would have."

Mark gives Marcus a crazy look as he said, "But then –"

Marcus cut him off. "I'll handle it," he said.

"We're gonna be more on the edge then we were to begin with."

"Boy, I realized that the moment I did what I did."

Andrea started the car and headed home, and Marcus followed. As soon as Andrea parked and went inside, Mark did as Marcus instructed him. He stood in the shadows across the street from the apartment and kept a close eye on Andrea until his father return.

Marcus drove to a secluded area where he could dispose of Alex's body, and no one would come across it by accident, or link him to it. That place was in the East River near the Williamsburg Bridge, where he wrapped Alex's body in a black sheet and tied it to some heavy objects that were stacked nearby, so the body could sink straight to the bottom.

CHAPTER TWELVE

It was thirty minutes after the café opened, and there was no sign of Alex. Andrea asked all the employees if they had heard from him and they said that same thing: 'not since last night.' Her woman intuition was telling her that something was wrong. She tried calling Alex on his cell phone more than three times, but all calls went straight to voicemail, and that was really making Andrea worry.

"Still no word from Alex?" asked Hakeem, standing in the doorway of the manager's office, eyeing Andrea sitting behind the desk while trying to call Alex for the twentieth time.

"No," Andrea replied. "I mean this doesn't make any sense. If he wasn't coming in today he should've at least called or at by and said he wasn't. But for him to not do either isn't like him. Then, to make it worse I keep trying to call and can't get in touch with him. I called both cell and home phone." She paused. "Something isn't right. Something isn't right at all here."

"No Argument here. Alex and I may not have always seen things eye to eye, but I will say that I knew him well enough to say this is not like him at all."

She blew air heavily. "I am really worried right now," she said holding herself together.

"Are you sure he didn't say anything to you last night about not coming in today?"

In her mind, Andrea replayed the conversation she had with Alex before leaving last night. There was nothing said about him not coming into work. However, there was something else about their conversation that got Andrea to thinking there could really be something worse.

Andrea stood to her feet. "Hakeem, can you handle the café until I get back?" she asked.

"Yeah I can do that, but where are you going?"

"I need to go check on Alex, and make sure he's okay," she said, picking up her purse that was resting on the edge of the desk instead of being in her lockers. "I shouldn't be gone no longer than an hour, depending on the traffic out there. Just hold things down until I get back."

She passed by Hakeem and speeded walk towards the front, as she pulled her keys from her purse and quickly find the car key. Andrea walked out of the café, got in her car, and drove all the way to Brooklyn to Alex's apartment. There was no question in her mind that Marcus and Mark were behind whatever it was going on with Alex.

When she arrived at Alex's building, Andrea walked swiftly all the way up to his apartment, where she frantically started knocking and calling his name through the door. Nonetheless, there was no answer. She reached into her purse and pulled out the spare the key that Alex had given her for emergencies. Entering the apartment, she briefly noticed the apartment looked no different from the day she helped him move in a few months ago. She then heads towards the bedroom in hopes to find Alex lying in bed, asleep. Andrea rushed through the cracked opened door and saw no sign of Alex anywhere. She did, however, noticed he had moved the furniture around, and added a new – but used – cherry wood crib for Jordan.

"Alex, where are you?" she said aloud to herself while placing a hand on the edge of the crib.

The apartment phone then started ringing.

"Hello," Andrea answered.

"Oh, I'm sorry. I must have dialed the wrong number," replied a man on the other end. "I'm looking for Alex Anderson."

"You have the right number. May I ask who this calling?"

"My name is David Morgan. I'm a lawyer representing Mr. Anderson on getting custody of his son Jordan."

"Okay, well, I haven't seen Alex since last night, and I have no idea where he is at the moment."

"I've been calling Alex on his cell phone and it goes straight to voice mail. So I decided to call his home phone because I needed to set up another meeting with him to talk about the next custody hearing coming up soon."

"Alex, please be alright," she said, forgetting she had the phone up to her mouth.

David heard Andrea and started wondering what was going on. "May I ask who I'm speaking with?" he asked.

"I'm sorry, I'm Andrea Harris," Andrea answered, remembering she was still on the phone talking to someone. "I'm good friends with Alex.

"So you're the Andrea that Alex was telling me about."

"What are you talking about?"

"Alex made it clear that if anything should ever happen to him, you would become Jordan's legal guardian. That's if he gets custody. The mother has already been proven to be an unfit parent, and she's not even trying to fight for custody of Jordan."

"Does it look like Alex has a chance of getting custody?"

It was silent for a moment.

"To be honest with you Andrea," said David. "The custody hearing really appears to be in his favor... we're just waiting for the judge to say it."

"It does?"

"Yes, that's why I need to meet with Alex as soon as possible. So if you hear from him could you have him call me, please?"

"I will do that. It was nice talking with you."

"Nice talking to you as well, Andrea."

They both hung up at the same time.

The phone call started making Andrea worry even more. Bad feelings begin building inside Andrea that was accompanied with fear. She wasn't sure what was going on, so she prayed that Alex was okay. But until she was sure that he was, she had to talk to somebody who could help her. Far from being sure of who she could talk to, Andrea was about to take one big of a risk when she started looking for Detective Ronking's card that was given to her by Bobbi that passed Saturday. Once finding the card, Andrea called the number on Alex apartment phone.

"Hello," Ronking answered.

Andrea was lost of words. She couldn't believe that she had taken this big risk of making this phone call.

"Anybody there?" asked Ronking.

"Hey Detective," she finally said. "It's Andrea."

"Well, this is a very big surprise call I'm getting."

"I know. I don't believe I'm making this call myself."

"Is everything alright?"

The line fell silent for few seconds.

"Andrea, are you still there?" Ronking asked, breaking the silence.

"Yeah, I'm still here. Look, is there any way we could meet for a few minutes to talk?"

"About?"

"Not on the phone. I need to talk to someone face to face."

"Are you at work right now?"

"No. I'm over in Brooklyn. I'm trying to find a friend, and I have no idea where he is. So can we meet somewhere?"

"Yeah, I'm actually in Brooklyn as we speak. There's a diner near the Brooklyn Bridge call *Henry's End.* I can meet you there and we can talk. It shouldn't take me long to get there. I just have a few things I need to finish up here and then I'll be right there."

"Okay, I'll see you when you get there." She said just before hanging up the phone. Then, before leaving the apartment, Andrea took a quick glance back at the crib in the bedroom, praying hard for everything to be alright, and then walked out the door.

Andrea parked a block away from the *Henry's End Diner*. While trying not to seem so nervous, she heading inside and stood at the door, scanning the room to see if Ronking had happened to get there before she did – since he knew the area better than she did.   However, Ronking wasn't there, so she found an empty table to have a seat until he arrives.

"Can I get you something?" asked a waiter that approached the table.

"Yes, I'll have a glass of water, please," Andrea ordered.

"Will that be all?"

"Yes, that's all."

When the waiter walked away, Andrea looked back out the window to see Marcus and Mark parked right across the street like they would be at the café. It wasn't much longer when Ronking came walking through the doors and had a seat across from Andrea.

"So how's everything going?" he asked, leaning forward on the table with his hands locked together in front of him.

"I wished I knew," she answered. "Right now I have a problem… and I don't know what to do about it."

"Well, what's going on?"

The waiter returned and sat Andrea's water in front of her. And then saw Ronking sitting with her. "Can I get you anything, sir?" she asked.

"No, I'm good. Thanks." He replied.

The waiter headed back to the kitchen again.

"A co-worker... that is also a very close friend of mine... is missing... and I have no idea on where he could be." Andrea explained.

"Well, have you filed a missing person report?"

"I haven't because I'm not sure if he's just missing or if his missing, missing."

Ronking tried to make sense of Andrea's words. "Well, what's the different?" he asked.

"Come on you know what I mean."

"I know what you mean, but what's keeping you from filing a missing person report."

"Because I don't wanna believe something has happened to him. I've been calling him and calling him, but all my calls go straight to voicemail. I just really wanna believe that nothing has happened to him."

"I understand, but you won't know if anything has happened to him if you don't report it," Ronking told her, but then thought out a question he should ask the moment the conversation started. "Has he been missing more than twenty-four hours?"

"What's that got to do with anything?"

"Well, if an adult hasn't been missing more than twenty-four hours then there's nothing we can do. When was the last time you saw him?"

"Last night... I was leaving the café to go home. He was the last one in there." Andrea thought a little more. "Now that I think about it, Alex had to have left before you walked me back to my car because the lights were off."

"That was after nine o' clock?"

"Yeah, it was."

"Then there's nothing that can be done until nine o' clock tonight. I'm sorry, but that's how it works with any police department."

Andrea hoped Ronking saying was a sigh to be patient, as she rubbed her hand against the top of her forehead. "God, I seriously hope he's okay," she said.

"Look, if you don't hear from him by morning then give a call to me personally and I'll file the report for you myself."

Andrea didn't say a word, she just shook her head yes.

"I'm sure everything is alright," Ronking told her. "I'm sure there's a good reason for whatever it is going on with your friend."

"I hope you're right."

"Let me ask you something. Do you know of anyone who would want to hurt him?"

"... No," she replied, but really wasn't sure. So she told Ronking a little about Alex without saying him much. "I mean... he does have a little of a past, but I couldn't say that any of it has to do with his disappearance. That's if you don't count the problems that he has with the mother of his child. She always threatens to do something to him, but I don't know if she meant the things that she said or not."

"Do you have her name?"

"Sabrina Winter, if I remember correctly."

"Well, if I get that call from you in the morning, she'll be the first person I'll talk to."

"Thanks."

Ronking looked at his watch. "Look, I need to get going," he said, standing up. "I hope everything is alright with your friend. Still call and let me know if he shows up."

"Okay," she replied, taking a big sip of the water, and then followed behind Ronking out of the diner.

The drive from Brooklyn back to the cafe, Andrea thought what she would tell Marcus when he comes asking why she had met with Detective Ronking. The only thing she could think of was telling him the truth: Her best friend is missing and she was worried.

CHAPTER THIRTEEN

It was the end of the day. Andrea stood against the front counter, gazing out deep in thoughts as she waited for the last customer to finish their meal. She pondered long and hard on Alex's whereabouts. She tried keeping a positive thought, but it wasn't easy. Everyone she knew to known Alex hadn't seen or heard from him since last night. Also, the last conversation Andrea had with Alex was tearing at her mind as well. She wondered if he could've gone and gotten himself into some kind of trouble and couldn't walk away from it too easy.

"Long day," said the last customer as she came to pay her bill.

"Tell me about it," Andrea replied, taking the bill and money out of the woman's hand. "As you can see all of my co-workers have cleaned up and left for the night and soon as I close up, I'll be doing the same thing." She placed the money in the register and pulled the change that was owed back to the lady.

"I didn't mean to hold you up."

"Oh, you didn't. I like staying late some times. It gives me some time to myself, before going home."

"I guess you don't get a chance to do much thinking when you get home?"

"Not when you have two boys running around the house."

"Oh, I know what you mean. My husband and son always are running around making all kinds of noise."

"I wish I know what that sounded like. I lost my husband back on 9/11."

"Oh, I'm sorry to hear that."

"It's alright. I wasn't the only one who lost someone close that day."

"Yeah, I lost my husband too in 9/11."

Andrea gave the woman a strange look. "I thought you said you had a husband and son making a lot of noise at home?" she asked.

"I remarried," the woman answered. "I couldn't spend the rest of my life alone because I lost the one man I truly loved. I had to learn that life goes on, and I had to go on with it as well. I then found another man who was just as good as the first one I was with… and in a month, we'll be celebrating six years of a happy life together."

"Wow," Andrea said as she thought about the woman's story. "I don't think I could do that."

"I can understand that. I mean Joshua may not be Michael, but I do thank God for bringing him to me." The woman took a step back from the counter. "Okay, I'm not gonna hold you up any longer. I know you want to get home to your children. So, maybe I'll see and talk to you the next time I'm in here."

"Well, I'm here every day, except weekends," Andrea told her.

The woman then headed towards the door.

"Hey," Andrea stopped her.

"Yes?" The woman asked, turning back towards Andrea.

"May I ask how you and... Joshua met?"

"Oh, well, to make a long story short," The woman said, taking a step back towards the counter. "Joshua was my neighbor... and he was also a therapist. After the loss of Michael, I was trying to convince myself that I was alright when I know I wasn't. Joshua was there for me not only as a free therapist... but as a friend. That showed me how much he really cared about me. I can't say I fully got over Michael, but after hearing this so many times, I've learned that God doesn't close one door without opening another... or less a window. There I was thinking I was gonna be alone for the rest of my life, and then God sends me someone else to make me happy."

Andrea found the woman's words really moving and started wondering why she couldn't do the same thing for herself. Charles was a good man, but could there really be another man that was just right for her out there.

"Well, even though I don't know you, I will say that I'm happy for you," Andrea told her. "There are not many people out there who would've thought like that. I know because I'm one of them."

"Sometimes you just got to let things work itself into place."

"Yeah," Andrea said, grabbing hold to the wedding ring that Charles place on her hand years ago. "There could be someone else out there for me. I'm just still unsure on how to let go yet."

"Just give it time."

They stared at one another for a moment. Then, without another word to be said, the woman turned around again and walks out the door. Andrea came around the counter to lock it.

However, by the time she could even get a hand on the lock, the door was pushed open and in stepped Marcus and Mark, which scared Andrea only a little, since she knew they were coming sooner or later.

"Closing so soon," said Marcus.

"Yeah, what's your hurry?" asked Mark. "I'm sure you knew we were coming to speak with you."

"About?" Andrea asked with a straight face.

"Don't play with us," Mark advised her. "You going to Brooklyn and meeting with the Detective."

"Oh that," Andrea said as if she didn't know what they were talking about in the beginning. "I needed to talk to him about something – and it had nothing to do with what's going on with me or you two."

"Then you wouldn't mind telling us what it was," said Marcus.

Andrea stood quite for a second before coming out and saying, "A very good friend of mine and employee here went missing. No one has any idea where he is. I've been calling him all day long, but I can't seem to get in contact with him."

"Is that why you went to Brooklyn earlier today?" Marcus asked.

"Yes, to see if he was home and overslept or something. But he wasn't there, and I'm really worried."

"So then what?" said Mark, stepping closer towards Andrea, "You called the Detective to have him look into filing a missing person report?"

Andrea took a deep breath. "Yes," she exhaled. "But it can't be filed unless he's been missing for at least twenty-four hours."

"What makes you think he's even missing?" Marcus asked with a slight straight face. "For all you know he could've got arrested and now in jail waiting for somebody to get him out."

"They have phones in jail," Andrea replied, wishing Marcus comment to have been true. "I know Alex would've called and told me if something like that happened. I know Alex... he wouldn't just up and disappear like this." She then looked directly at Marcus. "Did you see anyone leave out of here last night after I left?" she asked him.

"Nope," he lied.

"All the lights were off in here before I got in my car and went home, and you were the only person still around during the time he could've left since Mark here followed behind me and Ronking when we went to talk."

"Maybe I did... maybe I didn't. There were a lot of people walking through the area. He could've walked right past me and I wouldn't have noticed it. Besides, I really don't care, because the only person I'm watching is you."

"Yeah... that's right," she said sadly, showing Marcus that she understood. "Well, if there's nothing else, could you two please leave? So I can finish closing up."

"No problem," replied Marcus.

With that said, they turned and headed back out the café without speaking another word.

Later that night, Andrea couldn't sleep. She lay in bed wondering about Alex. She had her cell phone lying on the pillow right next to her, plugged up to its changer, and the volume up as high as it could go. She was hoping that Alex would call at any minute, to tell her that he was alright. However, the call never came. Andrea was extremely worried. Even though Alex was nothing more than a friend, he was the only person who could really make her smile. However, she did have belief that Alex may have had stronger feelings towards her as she thought back to the day she was helping him move into his apartment:

"Which cabinet do you want these cups in?" Andrea asked from in the kitchen of Alex's apartment. She held two freshly bought cups in the air for Alex to see which ones she was referring to.

Alex was in the living room with his shirt off. He had just finished hanging a picture on the wall above the spot where his well-worn, dark red, crush velvet couch, which at the moment was sitting in the middle of the room. Glancing into the kitchen, Alex prepared himself to push the couch up against the wall, after first pointing to which cabinet he wanted the cups to go.

"You can put them in the cabinet on the right side of the stove," he instructed Andrea.

Doing as he wished, Andrea opened the cabinet to the right side of the stove and begins loading the cups inside on the bottom shelf.

Once the couch was against the wall, Alex back away to check and see if the couch was aligned correctly under the picture. "I have to thank you again for helping me move in," he said, then noticed that the couch was a little far off to the left, and moved it over to the right some.

"It was not a problem at all," Andrea replied. "I just hope you'll return the favor when I save up enough money to get a place for me and the boys."

"You know you don't even have to ask."

"I hope not," Andrea said as she looked at her watch and saw the time. "I'm gonna have to leave soon. I told Miles and Ted that today I'll take them to see some movie that came out two weeks ago, and Miles have been begging to go see it."

"Okay," he answered, once seeing that the couch was now perfect, and head into the kitchen. When coming up alongside Andrea, he saw that Andrea had placed the cups in the correct cabinet, but on the wrong shelf. "Actually, I wanted them on the second shelf," he told her.

Andrea looked inside the cabinet. "Okay, that won't be a problem. I can just move them around." She reached back into the cabinet and started moving the cups up to the second shelf.

"Here, let me help you," Alex offered, and started helping Andrea move the cups around before she could even say if she wanted his help or not.

With one cup left to move, they reached for it at the same time. Their hands met on it and Alex's blue eyes happened to gaze into Andrea's.

Alex reached out with his free hand and rubbed it against Andrea's cheek. Then, without a second thought, he moved in and placed a passionate kiss on her lips.

"Alex, stop," Andrea said, breaking Alex's kiss.

"What's wrong?" he asked.

Andrea looked away. "I can't do this," she told him.

"You can't do this," he repeated, leaning back against the counter as he pondered why. "Is it because I'm white?"

"No, it's nothing like that," Andrea answered quickly, but honestly.

"Is it because of my background history?"

"Alex, it has nothing to do with you," she said, placing a hand on Alex's shoulder. "I'm just not looking to have a relationship with anybody."

Alex gazed into Andrea's eyes again. "Andrea, you are a wonderful woman and I want…"

"Alex…" she said, cutting him off. "You are a good person… but I'm not looking to go down that road again."

There was silence in the room.

"I have to go," she said, grabbing her purse from off the table, and then headed towards the door. "I'll call you later… and maybe come by tomorrow and see how things coming with the apartment."

Alex shook his head to say *okay*.

Then, without another word said, Andrea opened the door and walked out.

While lying in bed, wondering where Alex could be, Andrea wondered if she had hidden deep down inside her heart the same strong feelings towards Alex as he did for her.

With no contact still yet to come from Alex, Andrea spent most of her free time in the manager's office. Worried out of her mind, she couldn't keep her mind focused on work. When Andrea first came in the café that morning, she didn't even take time out to put her purse and phone away in her locker like she would normally do. She just brought them in the manager's office and sat them on the desk. Andrea always kept her phone in the locker so she wouldn't pull it out while on the job and make it a distraction. She would check it every hour to make sure an emergency call that had to do with her family didn't come while she was working. But with Alex missing, she kept it close.

Even though it was another risk, she did as Ronking told her, and gave him a call.

"Hello," Ronking answered.

"Hey, it's Andrea," she replied.

"You know you keep surprising me with all these phone calls," he joked.

It was then silent on the line.

"Still no word from your friend?" Ronking asked.

"No... and I'm starting to get scared. I mean what if he's somewhere lying dead right now."

"Try not to think like that."

"Well, I don't know how to think right now. I just know something is wrong."

Ronking started thinking. "You think it could be possible that he could've gotten arrested or something?" he asked. "This is a big city and many things can happen to a person."

She remembered Marcus giving the same comment. Now, hearing it from Ronking had Andrea thinking that maybe it could've been possible that Alex had gotten arrested and thrown in jail. Then, remembering something else, Andrea had bought a new cell phone, after breaking her last one on the sidewalk three weeks ago, and had a number change. She knew Alex had the first number memorized, but maybe hadn't memorized the new one.

"You think you could check for me and see?" she asked. "I don't believe that's what happened, but I won't know if it's not looked into."

"I'll see what I can do. With everything going on around here with this triple homicide case, it could take me awhile to get to it. But as soon as I can, I'll see if there's been an arrest on your friend. Alex is his name, right?"

"That's right. Alex Anderson."

"Okay, well, I'll check and get back to you as soon as possible."

"Thank you…"

"No problem."

With enough said Andrea hung up the phone and ended the call.

By seven thirty Andrea had to get away. She shut down the manager's office, gathers all her belongings, and pulled a spare key to the café from the desk's center hand draw. She pulled Hakeem to the side and gave him the key and asked him to lock up tonight because she wasn't coming back until in the morning. Hakeem may not have cared much about the people he worked with, but however, he was aware of how close Andrea and Alex were. And with the way Andrea has been acting lately, he knew something serious had to have happened.

Tonight was Bible Study at the church, so Andrea thought she'd go sit in on the remainder if she made it on time. Except by the time walked through the front doors, the Pastor had just finished closing out. She then spotted Thelma, Miles and Ted standing in the pew near the front, and headed towards them.

"Oh my Lord," said Thelma when seeing Andrea coming towards them. "How did you find time to come out to bible study tonight?"

"Hey mama," Ted said happily.

Andrea reached her arms around Ted from behind and placed a kiss on his forehead. "Well, I didn't make time, I took time," Andrea told Thelma, resting her head on top of Ted's. "I wanted to talk to Pastor for a moment about something. You think he'll see me right now?"

"Oh yes, I'm sure he will. Just go and knock on his office's door." Thelma replied.

"Okay. Give me about five minutes and I'll drive us all home."

"Take your time. I have a few people here I need to talk to."

Andrea headed to the back of the church towards Pastor J.R. Mansell's office. She knocked on the door three times and then waited for an answer.

"Come in," said Pastor Mansell with his deep voice.

She slowly cracked open the door and stuck her head to see a tall and round, brown-skinned man, with a salt and pepper mustache, sitting at his desk.

"Well, Sis. Harris," Pastor Mansell said, standing up from his seat and then walking around his desk. "Come on in, it's good to see you." He welcomed Andrea warmly.

"It's good to see you too," Andrea replied. "How have you been?"

"Oh, I've been doing just fine, trying to take it easy and better care of myself with this heart conditions. You remember I had a heart attack a few months ago."

"Yes, I remember. I brought you flowers when you were still in the hospital, remember?"

"Oh yeah, I remember. You brought the purple tulips."

"That's right. I know you like the color purple and when I saw them in the store I knew you would have loved."

"You know me well, don't you?" He chuckled, and then changed the subject. "So what brings you by here tonight? I thought you worked late on Wednesdays."

"Well on Wednesdays I don't get off until little after Bible Study has ended. But tonight I just took the rest of the day off, because I needed somebody to talk to. Somebody I could trust and maybe help me, and I thought you might be the one."

"Well, what's going on?"

"It's about something that happened last week. I've been trying to keep it to myself, but after this evening, I don't think I can anymore. I really need to talk to somebody about this."

"Well, come have a seat and tell me what's on your mind." Pastor Mansell guided Andrea to one of the two chairs in front of his desk. "Now, what's going on?" he asked as she walked back behind the desk to his chair.

Andrea sat her purse down on the floor and took a moment before saying anything. "You heard about that triple homicide that happened last Wednesday?" she inquired. "About how those three men were gun downed in cold blood."

"Yes, but I don't know what that's got to do with anything."

"Well, you're not gonna believe this."

Pastor Mansell leaned forward in his seat. "What's going on, Andrea?" he asked very curiously.

"I saw it," she let out without a thought.

"What do you mean you saw it?"

"I saw it," she repeated as she started breaking down. "From the moment they had them tied down on the ground, to the moment he pulled the gun on them and shot them all dead. I saw it all. I witnessed it."

"Are you serious?"

"I wish I wasn't."

"Oh my God," he said, standing back up from his seat again and came over to the other seat next to Andrea. He pulled her close for a hug and held Andrea tightly. "Why didn't you go to the police?"

"I was scared. I tried to go to the next morning, but they found me. He pulled a gun on me and threatened me and my family if I went to the police."

"Was it the man who killed the three?"

"No, this was another guy. I didn't see the face of the man who killed those three men."

"I can't believe this is happening to you."

Andrea pulled away. "That's not the end of it," she told him. "One of my co-workers who I'm very close friends with have been missing since yesterday… I think they killed him."

"What makes you think that?"

"Before I thought about leaving work early today… something just told me to look in his locker. When I looked inside his locker; his jacket, his phone, everything else that he usually brings to work with him was still in there." After a moment pause, she wiped away the tears from her eyes and then continued. "I think he started seeing what was happening around me. I think he learned that I was being followed by those men and…"

"You're being followed?" Pastor Mansell asked cutting Andrea off.

"Yes," she answered. "I'm followed by the man who threatened me. He follows me wherever I go. He even followed me here. Alex was one that some time saw things I didn't. And he's not afraid of anything. So if he did catch on to them, I believe he would've confronted them, and then they killed him because they saw he wasn't afraid. If that happened, it had to have happened while I was with this Detective Monday night, because it was the only time it could have."

"What Detective?"

"There's this Detective who found me because he had a picture of me running out of the garage that night. When I wouldn't answer questions, he kept coming around. So I made up a story that was good enough for his questions, and hoped he wouldn't come back because I'm afraid they might go after him." More tears rolled from Andrea's eyes, but she didn't wipe them away this time. "I don't wanna die… and I don't one anyone else to die because of me either."

"And nobody else will," Pastor Mansell said, standing up once again. "I have a friend in the FBI that can help us." He then helped Andrea up as well. "Now you say this man follow you everywhere you go. Does he follow you home?"

"Yes, he parks right across the street from my building in a black truck – every night."

"I'll get my friend on the phone right away. I'll tell him everything you told me, and I'll have him pick up this man."

"But what if the others come after me?"

"That is why I'm gonna have him put you and your family somewhere safe until he catches this monster and this whole thing is over. I'm gonna pray for the Lord's protection and that everything works out."

They made eye contact, Andrea could see the assurance in Pastor Mansell's face, and it made her believe every word that he had said.

"Pull yourself together and go on home, leave this in the Lord's hands," Pastor Mansell told her. "Don't let your family know what's going on. When the police knock at your door just be ready to go. You hear me?"

"… Yes."

"Everything is gonna to be fine. Now go."

Andrea picked up her purse and slowly headed out the office, and joined back with her family to go home.

Pastor Mansell picked up the telephone, but before dialing any numbers, he felt a slit bit of pain come into his left arm. He placed the phone back down for a moment so he could go into his top right-hand desk drawer to retrieve the bottle of pills that he needed. He had eight bottles in the drawer, and it took him a few seconds to find the correct one.

Just when he found the right bottle, there came a knock on his office door.

"Come in," he shouted opening the bottle.

The door opened.

"Are you Pastor Jason Mansell?" ask a man wearing all black and a full-length coat.

"Yes, I am. How may I help you, Mr....?"

"Jackson... Dean Jackson," he answered, coming all the way inside the room and closed the door behind him. "I was wondering if I could have a moment of your time."

"Could you maybe can back?"

"This will only take a moment if you don't mind."

"Well okay, I guess I can give you a little of my time to talk, but make it quick, because I have a serious matter I have to attend to."

"Oh, I'm sure you do," Dean said with an evil grin. "So, I'll make this quick, I won't hold you long. You see, I have this new friend who by accident discovers a little secret of mines... she made it clear that she would tell anyone, but she just did. Now, it's kind of got this person she told into a little trouble."

"I'm not sure if I understand your problem, son." Pastor Mansell replied, eyeing Dean as he popped the pill in his mouth. He had been holding in his hand since the moment Dean knocked on the door.

Dean chuckled, slowly steps towards Pastor Mansell. "I guess what I'm trying to say is..." he stopped speaking, until he was standing side by side with Pastor Mansell, and placed a hand upon his shoulder. "It was I that Andrea witnessed killing those three men..."

Pastor Mansell quickly made eye contact with him.

Dean continued, "And now, I'm afraid you'll only gonna be able to tell Jesus Christ about it."

Before Pastor Mansell could react, Dean slammed his hand downward against the back of Mansell's neck. Once Mansell was almost lying flat on the floor, Dean came down hard with his elbow against Mansell's chest where his heart was – knocking the breath out of him. Dean stood over the lifeless body – just as Marcus did with Alex's. Then without another moment to waste, Dean slowly made his way out of the Pastor Mansell's office, as if nothing happened.

CHAPTER FOURTEEN

Time felt as if it was moving extremely slow as Andrea kept glancing at the time on her phone. She sat quietly in the living room, waiting for that knock to come at the apartment door. Thelma was right alongside her, watching a *Lifetime* movie, and making small talked about what was happening in it. Miles and Ted were to watching television in their room, although, it was passed time for them to be in the bed. However, Andrea didn't give them a reminder of that. She was allowing them to stay up, so she wouldn't have to wake them once the police arrived.

"So what did you talk with the Pastor about?" Thelma asked, still watching the movie.

"It was nothing really," Andrea answered. "I… just needed to share something with him. It was something that's been on my mind for a little too long."

"Wait a minute, you mean you couldn't come and talk with me... your mother about it."

"I don't think it was something I could've really talked to you about."

"That's the first. When you were younger you use to talk about almost everything to me."

Andrea turned to look Thelma in the face. "Well, I'm older now, mama, and I need other people to talk to sometimes." She replied.

"Yeah, I know." Thelma looked back at Andrea. "I used to be you once. Always talked and shared things with my mother all the time. But as soon as I got grown and moved out of her house, I started talking and sharing more with my friends about the thing I had going on in my life. Until they made me mad or upset, then I went running back to my mother to talk to her about it."

"Yeah, I have had those moments," Andrea replied, remembering the two or three times that she had to come and talk with Thelma because of something that happened with a friend.

"Well, I wish you had more moments like that."

"Why you say that?"

"Andrea, a mother knows," Thelma said, continuing strong eye contact. "You should know that. A mother knows her child, and therefore, I know there's something going on with you. I just wish you would come out with it to me."

"Mama, there's nothing to come out with."

"You came out with what was on your mind Saturday afternoon when you returned home."

For a moment, Andrea had to think back to Saturday afternoon to remember what Thelma was talking about. "Oh that," she said when the little talk they had played again in her head. "That was nothing. I just got caught up in a little moment after visiting Charles's grave, that's all."

"Okay," Thelma replied, not believing Andrea's responds. "Then tell me about yesterday when you got in from work… and this morning when you left to take the boys to school. You seem more outside yourself than you were this past week. Don't think for a second 'cause I'm getting older and my eyesight is fading that I don't see and feel something going on with you, Andrea. A mother's instinct is always strong even when we are on our last breath."

Andrea let out a chuckle. "I remember when grandma said that to you." She said.

"And she was right, because while laying on her death bed that woman let me know I needed to get myself together. Now can…"

Before Thelma could get another word out, the house phone started ringing.

"I'll get that," Thelma said, reaching for the phone on the coffee table. She looked at the caller ID before hitting the talk bottom and placing the phone to her ear. "Hey, there first lady… No, it's alright that's you're calling me because I was really just thinking about you. There was something I need to ask you." She paused for a moment. "Is… Is everything alright…?"

Andrea's eyes were focused on Thelma as she wondered what was being said on the other end of the phone.

"Oh my God," Thelma nearly shouted, while placing her hand over her heart. "What happened…? Are you gonna be okay…? I'll come by first thing in morning… Alright, I'll see you then." She ended the call and placed it back on the coffee table.

"Is everything alright?" Andrea asked.

"Pastor Mansell had another heart attack." she answered.

Andrea was very shocked when hearing the news and quickly asked, "Is he gonna be okay?"

Thelma turned and looked into Andrea's eyes. "He didn't make it this time. They found his body lying in his office at the church."

"I don't believe this."

"I do. His heart wasn't really good anymore. They've been looking for this to happen for a while now. It was just a matter of time."

Andrea felt bad that Pastor Mansell was gone, but that also meant he didn't have the time to help with her problem. "I'm going to bed." She said, getting up from the couch, and then headed her room. "Miles and Ted get ready to call it a night." She shouted just before closing her bedroom door.

No later than four forty-five in the morning, Andrea was lying asleep in her bed. Until out of nowhere, she woke right up out her peaceful sleep, crying. Tears rolling down her face onto her pillow. Her mouth covered with both hands so no one could hear her. She really believed this whole nightmare was going to be over. But now Andrea had to face the facts that this whole event happening was going to be her life for God knows how long.

For the remainder of the night, Andrea laid still, staring out her bedroom window, watching the sun as it began to rising over the same tall buildings the moon disappeared behind.

Half past nine o' clock the next night. Andrea kept herself busy in the manager's office, catching up on some paperwork she was falling behind on – even though she wasn't in the mood. She worked on them in hopes it would help keep her mind focused away from how dark her life have become.

"How are you holding up?" asked a voice standing in the office's doorway.

For a slight second, it sounds like Marcus until Andrea looked up and found Hakeem standing there.

"I'm fine," she answered, turning her attention back to the papers scatter all over the desk. "I thought you were gone."

"I was on my way out the door, but I thought I come see how you're doing."

"Well, I'm doing just fine. So I guess you can go on home now."

"You still haven't heard anything from Alex?"

Trying to keep from crying, Andrea calmly answered, "No, so a missing person report is being file."

"None of his family has seen him?"

"He doesn't really have any family. His mother and father are both dead. He's an only child. The only family he really has is his..." Andrea pauses as she thought about the last part of the sentence, and it hit Andrea almost like a ton of bricks. "Is his son... who he is fighting for," she muttered.

"Oh, I knew about that," Hakeem replied. "But have you tried checking hospitals? He could be lying in some hospital, unconscious, after having some kind of bad accident."

Andrea wished Hakeem's comment was possible. However, after finding Alex belongings still in his locker the other night, Andrea knew that it wasn't. Nevertheless, to know what happened is the real question Andrea continued asking herself.

She then lifted her head up again from the paperwork to Hakeem. "It could be possible," she said in a very stressful way. "I'll have to look and see if that's what happened." Andrea then gathers a few of the papers and put them in folders.

"I could do it for you if you want."

"What?" Andrea gives Hakeem a confused look.

"I could look and see if Alex has been admitted to any hospital."

"Why would you go out of your way to do that when you and Alex didn't even get along with one another?"

"'Cause maybe then you will go back to your old self and help out around here."

Andrea slowly shot Hakeem a look that was far from being a good one. "What did you say?" she asked.

"Look," Hakeem said getting straight to the point. "Every since Alex disappeared, you stopped helping out in the kitchen and out front. The other five and I have been working our asses off to keep this café going. Now it really doesn't surprise me at all that Alex is missing with his background: illegal gambling, petty and auto theft. There's no telling what else he has done or was trying to do, and got caught by either the police or by some street gang behind."

Slow anger was building inside of Andrea from Hakeem words. She stood up behind the desk and slowly replied, "Get the hell outta here."

169

"What? You're mad now 'cause I brought up the truth about your friend."

"Hakeem, I want you to get outta my face – like right now."

"Andrea, I…"

"You better not let another word come out of your mouth," Andrea ordered, cutting Hakeem off. Then quickly comes around the desk and eased towards him. "If another work come outta your mouth, I will make sure this will be your last day working here."

"And what are you going do? Tell Ms. Blakemore?"

"I guess I didn't tell you."

"Tell me what?"

"Ms. Blakemore is turning the café over to me when she comes back next week. That will mean I have the authority to fire your ass without having to go to somebody over me because I will be over everybody in here. Now, if you're ass is not outta here in the next five seconds, you are gone. Do I make myself absolutely clear?"

With that said, Hakeem took a step back into the hall. He then turns and quickly leaves through the back exit. With everything that just happened, Andrea felt like she had the strength she didn't even know she had. Andrea then glanced to the paperwork she was working on and decided to finish it all up in the morning. She stuck the papers in the desktop left-hand drawer and then grabbed her purse resting on the edge.

After shutting down the back of the café, Andrea made her way to the front where she was able to see through the window in the door. She saw a visitor standing out front, leaning against a silver Lexus LS430.

"What are you doing here?" she asked as she stepped outside, and then locked the door as it closed behind her.

"I came to see how you were doing," replied Ronking.

"You couldn't just call?"

"I rather had come in person to not only hear how you were doing but to see as well."

Andrea stared at him with a smirk. "Well, that's very kind of you," she told him. "I guess I can tell you I'm doing alright. I had a little verbal fight with one of my co-workers about how things been going on around here... and about Alex."

"Yeah, about your friend, I looked to see if there have been an arrest on him, but there wasn't. Even looked in hospitals and didn't find anything. The only thing I found on him was passed arrests from a few years back."

"I know about those."

"Oh."

"Yeah, Alex and I were close." She informed him.

Ronking leaned back farther against his car and folded his arms. "Well, why don't you tell me about this relationship between you two?" He said.

"Maybe some other time," Andrea replied, turning to head over to her car. "Right now I wanna get home and get something to eat because I haven't eaten anything all day. So, I'll see you... around." She started walking.

"How about I take you out to dinner?" Ronking asked. "I know a good place not too far from here that I'm sure you'll like. It'll be my treat."

"That's nice of you, but I don't think so."

"I won't bite."

"I'm sure you won't, but I still don't know you that well."

"There's not much to know about me," Ronking said, pointing to himself with four fingers. "My name is Justin Nelson Ronking, twenty-nine years old, and I'm a Libra."

Andrea laughed at him as she wondered how Marcus and Mark were looking at them. "Look, you're a nice guy and all, but I don't think going out with you would be a good time," she said.

"Why, because of your friend's whereabouts."

"That and more," she said, making it seem as she was randomly looking around, but was just trying to see what Marcus and Mark were doing.

"I know I don't know what's all going on in your life right now. Maybe it's nothing, maybe you're going through hell. But sometimes it's good to try and get away from it all, even if it's just for a few minutes."

Andrea stared down. "I don't know…"

"Come on, I'm not gonna take no for an answer," Ronking said, cutting off Andrea.

Andrea saw Ronking wasn't going to give up. So she finally took the risk and said, "Alright. I'm Andrea Olivia Harris, thirty-six years old, and I'm an Aries."

"Alright, now we're talking."

"So I'll just follow behind you to the place?"

"Or how about you come and get in my car, and I'll drive us there. I'll bring you right back afterward."

Andrea knew Ronking's idea was far from being a good one, but she didn't want to keep making up excuses, and allow the wrong saying to draw a line of more questions.

"I guess I can do that," she agreed, coming towards Ronking's car as Ronking opened the passenger door he was leaning against for her. As she entered the vehicle, her eyes were focused over on Marcus and Mark, until the second Ronking got into the driver seat and pulled out.

Marcus and Mark waited until they were a good distance ahead before following behind.

Ronking brought Andrea to a kind of place she hasn't been in since college. It was a small bar, with live entertainment playing on a small stage, and a few people on the dance floor dancing to the music. They headed to an empty table and waited for somebody to come and take their order.

"Why are you looking so nervous?" Ronking asked.

Andrea had seen Marcus and Mark entered the building and have a seat at a table on the other side of the room. "I just haven't been out with a male in a long time," she told him. It was the first thing she could think to say – and she felt it to be a little of the truth.

"What about Alex?"

"I didn't start hanging out with Alex until after I got to know him at work." She paused with a small smile as she had a moment. "I remember the day I met him. Alex came in the café less than two years ago to have breakfast. I happened to have been his waitress. When I brought his order to him, he noticed the 'Help Wanted' sign in the window..."

"And let me guess, he asked for a job."

"Yes, with these big, blue puppy-dog eyes." She smiled for a second before continuing telling the story. "However, seeing his appearance, I wasn't sure about helping him get a job there."

"What was wrong with his appearance?"

"He had this thick bread that needed trimming, needed a haircut, a shower, and clothes that fit. It took me a good minute, but I thought he could've been someone that could've been given a chance – after I talked with the manager, and he turned out to be a good worker. Got his life together, and saved up enough money to get his first apartment and move outta this rundown hotel he was living in… and became a very good friend to me."

"Oh, I see," Ronking said, and then changed the subject. "If you don't mind me asking, what happen to your children's father?"

"That's a personal question."

"Sorry to get all up into your business, but I'm just a little curious. You told me you're a single mother, but you're wearing two rings on your married finger."

She gazed down to her rings. "I lost my husband on 9/11." She answered.

"I'm sorry to hear that."

"It's okay. We were married for only a little while and then he was gone."

"How long were you two married?"

"Four years… four short years. I was pregnant with our second child when he died. My two boys are the only things I have left from him. Well, my boys and that old car I drive around. He worked his heart out to get that Mustang. It was his most valuable possession next to me,

174

and since he put all that work into getting it, I won't let anything happen to it."

"Wow, that's nice of you."

With all the questions Ronking was asking, Andrea decided to turn the table and start asking Ronking a few questions about him. "So, what about you?" she asked. "Is there anyone special in your life?"

"Not really," he answered. "I've had someone special in my life, but things never really got serious between us. Not sure of why, but my guess is that she didn't care for what I do."

"How long have you been a cop?"

"… Oh… long enough to know how to do the job right… and to get done what needs to be done."

A server soon came to the table. She asked them what they would like to drink. Ronking quickly ordered both drinks and dinner for them. Andrea didn't object to what he ordered because she thought he may know the food better served here than she would have.

While waiting for their food to come to the table, they continue to chit-chat about everyday things. After the food arrived, they continue to talk while they enjoy their meal. Even though Andrea didn't really know Ronking, she was having a much needed good time telling stories about what happen in their lives years ago and nowadays. During the whole dinner, Andrea paid no mind to the ones who were watching them from across the room, even though she was a little worry about what they would do after tonight.

"That was delicious," Andrea said, drinking the last of her ice tea.

"I said you would like it," Ronking replied. "I bet you're glad you came with me now."

"Yeah, I haven't had this much fun over dinner since… since my first date with Charles."

"Well, I'm glad I was able to show you a good time."

The song "The woman's work" by *Maxwell* started playing over the speakers. Andrea didn't even notice the live entertainment had stopped play on stage ten minutes ago.

"Oh my God," said Andrea.

"What is it?" Ronking asked.

"This is the first song Charles and I dance to on our first date."

"Are you serious?"

"Yes. I remember that day like it was just yesterday." Her mind thought back to that day. "God, I haven't heard this song in years."

"You wanna dance?" Ronking asked after seeing a few people out on the floor dance, dancing to the music.

Andrea quickly looked at Ronking and said, "No, I'm good. Matter of fact, I think we need to get going. I need to get home."

"Come on, let have one dance."

"I don't think that's a good idea, because…"

"Don't keep making up excuses," Ronking said cutting her off. "You keep making up excuses then your life is gonna be lived on excuses." He stood to his feet and held out his hand. "Now, come have one dance with me and then we'll be outta here."

Andrea looked into Ronking's eyes before taking his hand, and following him out onto the dance floor. She wraps one arm around his neck, and Ronking wraps an arm around Andrea's waist. Then together with the hands that were free, they held them together and moved slowly to the music.

"You need to let lose," Ronking told her.

"What do you mean?"

Ronking pulled back some to look in Andrea's eyes. "I can feel everything going on with you through your body," he answered. "You need to let it all go and let your body relax. Let your mind be at ease." He then pulls Andrea back closer towards him.

Andrea tried doing what Ronking said. She closed her eyes and held Ronking close, as he held her back with respect. After releasing everything that was on her mind and let her body relax from the stress that it was in, Andrea actually for that moment felt free.

CHAPTER FIFTEEN

Ronking pulled up behind Andrea's car in front of the café.

"Well, thanks for dinner again. I had a good time," Andrea told him.

"You're welcome," replied Ronking, placing the car in park.

"Well, have a good night." Andrea reached for the door handle.

"I'd like to go out with you again, Andrea," Ronking said, just before Andrea could pull the handle and push open the door.

She stared back at him. "I had a good time tonight," she said, leading back into the seat. "But I don't know if I'll be able to do this again."

"Why?"

Andrea exhaled as she wished she could have just told him everything. "… So many reasons," she replied, "but I don't see why we can't just be friends."

"I understand. Maybe one day we could hang out as friends then."

"Yeah, I would really enjoy that a lot."

A smile appeared across Ronking's face from Andrea's responds. "Well, you have my number," he said, "just give me call the next time you would like to hang out. I believe I've know of another good place that you'll enjoy."

"Will do," Andrea said, opening the door. "Have a good night." She repeated as stepped out of the vehicle and walked over to her own.

While driving home, Andrea continued experiencing feelings that she hasn't felt in years. Just one night and one dance with a man she hardly knew made her feel alive again and didn't have to worry about anything else. However, Andrea knew the feeling wouldn't last long because she knew the reality part of her life was soon coming to turn her life back upside down again.

After finding a park in front of the apartment building, Andrea exits out of the car, locked the door, and headed towards the steps.

"What got you getting in so late?" asked Bobbi while coming up the street.

"I should be asking you the same thing," Andrea replied.

"I worked a double tonight. I needed the extra money."

"Are you behind on a bill?"

"No, I'm good on my bills. My wallet is just empty… maybe those bills have something to do with that. So I have nothing to spend on myself."

"I know what that's like."

They then headed into the building together.

"So, what's got you getting in so late?" Bobbi asked again after they started climbing the staircase.

"I went out to clear my head."

"Well, you must've cleared, because you're smiling."

When they reached the top of the second floor, Andrea turned and gave Bobbi a look as she wondered what she was talking about.

"No, I'm not," she said with a chuckle, making the smile a bit larger.

"Oh, yes you are, and it's not one of those pretend smiles you use to walk around with."

Andrea never really paid attention to the smile she wore most of the time. She was trying too hard to make everyone believe she was alright, but it seems no one was really buying it. That's why so many were asking if she was alright.

"Are you serious right now?" she asked.

Bobbi dug around in her purse to find her hand mirror. When she found it, she held it up to Andrea. "Here, look for yourself?" she replied.

When Andrea viewed herself in that mirror, it was like seeing an old friend from years ago.

"I haven't seen this person in a long time," she replied. "He brought back the old me."

"He?" said Bobbi, giving Andrea a surprised look after hearing her say that word.

Andrea looked up from the mirror Bobbi was still holding out to her and headed to her apartment door.

"Wait a minute," Bobbi said, catching up with Andrea, and then stopped her in her tracks. "Andrea, are you seeing somebody?"

"No."

"Then who is *he*?"

"Just somebody who's a little concern about me, because of something I have going on at work. He took me out tonight to try and help me take my mind off of what's going on."

"Is that all?"

"Yes."

Bobbi stood her ground, arms folded across her chest as she continued staring Andrea in the face. She wasn't letting Andrea go anywhere until she shared with her a little more about this guy she was out with tonight, and Andrea knew it.

"Bobbi, this is a nice guy," Andrea told Bobbi. "But I don't think he's somebody I would ever go that route with in life. I don't see him as anything more than a friend."

"And why is that?" Bobbi asked.

"Well, for starters, his job. With the job that he has I couldn't take being deeply involved with someone, and then losing them like I did with Charles."

"Well, what does he do?"

"Does Law Enforcement say everything?"

Bobbi stood her ground as she stared into Andrea's eye. She knew exactly what Andrea meant since she was at this very moment in love with someone who worked a dangerous job – her fiancé Jeremy was in the Army. She gazed directly into Andrea's face and said, "I understand how it feels. There's not a day that goes by I don't hear a knock at my front door and hopes that it's Jeremy and not somebody from the Army to tell me that Jeremy is dead." She took a moment paused. "I pray and hope every day that he comes home and we can finally get married… like we're been talking about since high school."

"I couldn't be that kind of person," Andrea said. It was almost like she could feel the pain Bobbi had inside. "My heart couldn't take that kind of pain."

"Neither can mine... but you can't always help who you love."

"... That's true." Andrea agreed.

The moment had seemed to have gotten to Bobbi as she wiped away a tear that fell from her right eye. "Okay, well, I'm getting tired," she said. "I gonna go in and get ready for bed."

"Alright..." Andrea replied. And they both headed inside their apartment.

Andrea was waking up as the sun rise up in the sky. Her mind was still wrapped around last night event. It was as if she was becoming infatuated with Detective Ronking, but she didn't want their relationship to progress any further. Andrea didn't want to face the same fear Bobbi was facing with Jeremy. She pondered if the real reason why she didn't want to fall in love again was because it was so hard losing Charles. After all, Charles didn't work a dangerous job, somebody just wanted to put fear in a nation, and it cost thousands of lives, including Charles's.

It was almost as if the smile was glued to Andrea's face. To those observing Andrea, almost immediately noticed the change in her. Even Thelma noticed it the moment Andrea entered the room, but she didn't say anything. Thelma wasn't going to ask any questions, she was just happy to see her daughter smiling again. So did Miles and Ted as they enjoyed small talk with their mother the whole ride to school.

While at the café, a few people who knew Andrea well noticed her new behavior. Hakeem wondered what had gotten into Andrea that she was kind of back to her old self again, even with Alex still missing. Marcus and Mark just wondered what Ronking had done to have made her so happy.

"Andrea," shouted the employee running the register. "You have a phone call."

Andrea had just brought a customer his order and placed it in front of him. She then heads behind the counter and took the phone of the employee's hand as he held it out for Andrea to take.

"Andrea Harris speaking," she said after placing the phone to her ear.

"Hey girl," answered Shanequa.

"Why are you calling me on the café's phone?"

"'Cause I know you don't answer your cell while working. And I could stop by there this morning because I had to come straight into the office."

Andrea already figured what this call was about. "So, what's the itinerary today?" she inquired.

"Just out to lunch to the place we went last Wednesday."

"… I guess I can do that today."

"Oh really, you're not gonna try turning us down this time."

"Well, I haven't seen my friends since last Friday, now have I?"

"True. I guess we all been busy the last couple of days."

"You can say that again. Do you think you can come pick me up again?"

"Same time as before?"

"See you then," Andrea replied, and then they both hung up the phone. Before she was able to head back around the counter to go take the order of three elderly women that walked in, Andrea was cut off by Hakeem.

"Can I speak to you for a minute?" he asked.

Andrea never got over the words Hakeem said last night. "Not now," she told him. "I have customers I have to get to."

"This will only take a minute."

"What is it?"

"I want to apologize for what I said."

"Why, because you feel bad or you don't wanna lose your job?"

Hakeem stood and thought for a moment. "Both, I guess," he answered. "Look, trying to take care and provide for a family of five and holding down a full-time job isn't easy. I have been a little overworked for awhile. For the past few days, I have come to work, and it feels like I'm getting extra work put on me, and that's not cool. I'm not getting paid enough to do extra."

After listening to what Hakeem had to say, Andrea stared him in the eyes and said, "I guess I can understand that," she replied. "However, that doesn't give you the authority to judge people of their past history, because you're having issues."

"You're right, and like I said I apologize, I'm sorry and it won't happen again."

Andrea continued staring at him in the eyes. "I guess I can let this incident slide – but if it happens again... then you are out of here because I'm not gonna have that kind of behavior happening here when I take over."

Without giving Hakeem a chance to ask about her taking over the café, Andrea walked away to take care of three elderly customers that were waiting for service.

After being seated at a table close by a window and getting their drinks ordered, Andrea tried starting up a conversation with her friends.

"So, what have you all been up to?" she asked.

"Nothing much, just working like always," replied Felicia.

"I could've guessed that. I mean has anything new happening."

"We should be asking you that with the way you're smiley?" Shanequa replied. She had been noticing Andrea's mood since the moment she picked her up from the café. "What's new with you?"

"Oh me, nothing, I wake up and did the same thing I do every day."

"Something gotta be new with you because your mood wasn't like this last week."

"She's right, it isn't," Felicia agreed.

Andrea started playing with her hands a little. "Alright, I'm gonna tell you all something, but it has to stay between us." She told them.

"No problem." They all replied.

Andrea took a deep breath and exhaled. "Okay," she started, a little nervous about telling them what's going on, because she knew how they can get. "There this guy that's been coming around to help me with this issue that I'm having. And last night, he took me out and showed me a very nice time. Something I haven't had in a long, long time. But, I don't think he's somebody I'll want a serious relationship with."

"And why not?" asked Felicia smiling at Andrea's news. "I think you should at least give him a chance."

"Yeah, but I don't think he would be the one I would try giving a chance to."

Shanequa held up her hand for Andrea's attention. "Is it that guy you work with at the café you're talking about?" she asked.

"No, it's not Alex," Andrea answered. "I don't even know where he is right now."

"What do you mean you don't know where he is?"

"It's like he disappeared off the face of the earth. Alex is the only male friend I have, and I'm very concerned about him. But having that I have seen him since Monday night, I hope he's not in any serious trouble.

"Welcome to the club," said Montica.

"What do you mean 'welcome to the club?'" Andrea asked.

Montica made eye contact with all her friends before replying, "Remember last Wednesday when I told you I had a colleague trying to get in on a case that had come up. And how he was supposed to be sending me some information about it, but never did?"

"Yeah," everyone answered.

"Well, he was more than just a colleague to me. He was an extremely close friend I've known a bit longer than I've known Brice. He was like my big brother to me. Without him, I may not have gotten where I am now. However… when I didn't hear anything back from him about the case, I tried calling him and nothing. I'd tried calling his family and they don't even know where he is. Next thing I know, I turn on the TV and I see over the word 'missing,' his picture and name: Steven Paige."

Andrea's eyes widen a little when she heard Steven's name come out of Montica's mouth. She couldn't believe one of her friends was close friends with someone she knew had been murdered and couldn't say anything.

However, Andrea wasn't the only one who could believe it. With her purse sitting on the floor between her and Montica, Brian who was to listening to the conversation from a far distance, couldn't believe what he was hearing. He picked up his phone and made a call to Marcus and Mark.

Marcus, who was parked less than a half a block away from the restaurant, answered the phone. "What is it, Brian?"

"I thought you would wanna know I just found out something very unbelievable," Brian replied.

"Found out what?" asked Mark.

"There's someone else who may know about what we're doing?"

"What?" Marcus and Mark both shouted into the phone.

"Andrea is talking to someone who knew Paige. He was bringing her in on the case too."

"Are you sure about that?" Marcus asked as he was able to look through the window and see Andrea and her friends, and wondering which one it could be.

"Well, she didn't say that it was Dean's case, but that was indeed the only case Paige had coming up."

"Well, how much of the case does she know about?"

"I'm not sure. She hasn't said anything about the case. Just know that she and Paige were friends – oh, and I got that her name is Montica, but don't have her last name to go with it."

"She hasn't said anything else that could tell you who she is?" Mark asked. "'Cause New York is a big city with a bunch of law firms that I'm sure has a Monica in it."

"Mon-t-ica," Brian corrected. "She did say she knew Steven longer than she knew somebody name Brice. You think that could be a boyfriend… or maybe husband?"

"How the hell I'm supposed to know," Marcus snapped. "You're the one with all the damn computers. Look it up."

"Just a minute," he said as he started his research on one of the several computers in front of him. "I researched a Marriage License for Brice and Montica Summer."

"Do you have a picture of her?"

"Hold on," he replied, clicking a few keys and pulling up a profile on Montica. "She's an African-American in her late thirties, brown eyes, black hair that comes to her neck, and is five-eight."

"That does sound like two of those girls that went in with Andrea," said Mark.

"Give me a second and I'll send you a picture."

188

Within ten seconds, a text came in a Marcus's phone and he opened it.

"That is one of the girls that went in with Andrea," Mark replied.

"Well, if that's her then she's a lawyer... if you haven't figured that out yet."

Marcus and Mark both stared at each other.

"What are we gonna do about this?" Brian asked.

"I have no idea," Marcus answered, placing his head down in his hands.

"I know what I'm gonna do. Exactly what needs to be done," said an unfriendly voice on Brian end of the phone.

Marcus quickly held up his head as he glanced at the phone. He knew exactly who it was speaking on the other end and what thoughts he had. "Dean... she may not have anything to do with this. Leave her alone," he said.

"Marcus, you continue keeping your eyes on Andrea... and leave Mrs. Montica Summer to me."

The call ended.

CHAPTER SIXTEEN

Montica was leaving her office for the evening. She stayed a little later than usual, signing off on a few documents that were left in the in-basket on her desk earlier. What she hadn't finished, she put in her briefcase and would try finishing them when she'd got home.

"Montica," someone called as Montica was heading towards the elevator.

She turns around and gives a big smile. "Oh, Christopher," she said, "What can I assist you with?"

While the man known as Christopher was coming towards Montica in a fast professional way, he replied, "I was wondering if I could have about three minutes of your time."

"Sure, what can I do for you?"

He stood face to face with Montica before continuing. "You are aware of the meeting that was called for Monday at twelve o' clock?" He asked.

"Yes, I was wondering what that was all about."

"Well, I shouldn't be telling you this. However, after having you waiting for so long as you have, I think you have the right to know."

"Right to know what?" she inquired.

"The meeting that we're having is with all the other partners of the firm."

"Okay," Montica replied, with one part of her body wondering what he was fixing to tell her and the other having a very positive feeling about it.

"Well, this meeting is also for you… to welcome you in with us."

"Oh my God," she said with much excitement in her voice. "Are you serious?"

"We're very serious."

"Oh my God," she shouted, dropping her briefcase and reached her hands to the sky seeming to praise God. She had waited for this moment for so long, and it was finally here.

Christopher reached out to shake her hands before saying, "Alright, calm down. You're not supposed to know about this until Monday."

"Well, I'm glad you told me about this now," she said, reaching down to pick up her briefcase. "That way, the other partners won't be thinking they're letting a child in with them."

"Oh, believe me, you wouldn't be the first to make a fool out of them when becoming a partner."

"Is that so?"

"Well, it wouldn't be normal for us if one didn't."

Montica stood and thought about the news that she was given. "I don't believe it," she said. "You have given me a bedtime story to tell my daughter tonight. Oh, I just wish Steven was here to hear this news. He would be so proud of me. He always told me I would one day make partner with all my hard work."

"And Steven always knew what he was talking about," Christopher agreed. "I'm pretty sure you two will soon be standing face to face again as he congratulates you making partner."

"You think?"

"I hope so. I really hate to think something terrible happened to Steven. He is one of the best District Attorneys New York has."

"You're right about that," she replied as she thought of all the times she saw Steven in action. "Anyway, I'm gonna head on home. Thank you so much for the good news. It means a lot to me right now."

"Anytime Montica," Christopher said, taking a few steps backward to head back to his office. "So I'll see you first thing Monday morning and then again at twelve o' clock P.M. on the dot."

"See you then." Montica stepped to the elevator and pushed the down button. This was the happiest moment to come – since the day she got married and the born of her daughter.

Once stepping off the elevator in the parking garage, Montica headed straight for her car. As she arrived, she sat her briefcase on top of the hood as she looked through her purse for her keys.

"Excuse me…" said a male voice from behind, startling Montica.

Montica didn't recognize the man as he approached her wearing dark sunglasses, black shirt, black pants, and full-length black coat that came a few inches below his knees.

"Yes, can I help you, sir?" she asked, finally finding the keys.

"If you are Mrs. Montica Summer then yes you can."

"Well, that would be me. So what can I do for you Mr....?"

"Jackson," he told her.

"Well, what can I do for you Mr. Jackson?" she asked again.

"I have a few questions that I need you to answer for me."

"What kinds of questions?"

"Well, I was wondering if you were working any kind of cases with District Attorney Steven Paige."

"Why would you need to know that?"

Dean removed his sunglasses from his eyes and placed them in his inner coat pocket. "I was talking to Mr. Paige about this case a little before he went missing," he answered. "I just learned that you may hold information to it."

"Paige was trying to get me in on a case, but I really don't know much about it."

"Tell me what you do know."

Montica stood and stared Dean in the face for a moment. "I'm sorry, but who are you?" she asked.

"Don't worry about who I am. Just tell me what you know about that case."

"I'm sorry, sir," she said, unlocking the car and then opening it. "I couldn't tell you, even if I did know something about that..."

Dean cut her off. "Don't walk away from me when I'm talking to you," he ordered.

Montica quickly looked back when she heard the tone in his voice, but then froze when she saw the silver gun that he was pointing at her. The sight of it made her heart started beating hard and fast.

"Now, I want to know how much you know about that case," Dean ordered her again to tell.

"Please, don't hurt me," Montica cried. "I have a little girl at home waiting for me."

"Is that supposed to mean something to me?"

"What do you want?"

"I have been telling you what I want and you haven't told me yet."

"I told you I don't know anything about that case. He didn't really tell me anything about it. Before Steven could send me anything to the case, he went missing. So I don't know anything about it. I swear I don't."

"Is that the truth?"

"I swear on my life."

Dean smiled as he gazed into Montica's eyes. "Now that I believe," he replied, right before pulling the trigger and sending a bullet into Montica's chest.

The force of the bullet knocked Montica to the ground. Dean stood over her body as he watched Montica's blood run throughout the parking garage – like he did the night he killed the Judge, Lieutenant, and Mr. Scott.

With the café closing an hour early on Fridays, Andrea was able to come straight home and have a little of a movie night with Miles and Ted. Everyone in the apartment still wondered what had all of the sudden gotten Andrea in such the good mood she remained in.

By ten fifty-two, Andrea finished taking a shower and was just walking into her bedroom when her cell phone, resting on the edge of the nightstand, begins ringing. She closing the door, quickly walked over to the nightstand, and picked up the phone. Quickly checking the caller ID, Andrea wondering who would be calling her this time of night. It was Shanequa.

"Hey girl," Andrea answers with much excitement in her voice. "What you doing calling me so late?"

There wasn't a respond. All Andrea could hear was crying on the other end of the phone.

"Shanequa what's wrong?" she asked.

"It's Montica..." she finally answered.

"What about Montica?"

"She's been shot."

Andrea nearly dropped the phone on the floor, and almost lost the strength in her legs. For a full moment, everything had gone a blank as Andrea slowly took a seat on the edge of the bed, with her hand rested across her chest. "What did you just say?" she asked, feeling as if it was hard to breathe, as she didn't want to believe the news.

"Montica was brought in here after being shot in the chest." Shanequa paused. "Who would do something like this to her, Andrea?"

Andrea was so worried about the life of her friend she didn't know how to respond. After learning earlier today that Montica was associated with Steven Paige, Andrea didn't pass wonders if it was discovered by Marcus and the others, and it caused them to come after her.

"She is going to be alright?" she asked.

"I don't know," Shanequa answered. "Brice hasn't heard anything yet. So she may still be in O.R."

"Brice is there?"

"He came in about twenty minutes ago. If I didn't run into him, I wouldn't have known Montica was even in here."

"What about Felicia? Is she there? Does she know about this?"

"She left to go to Chicago, three hours ago. She said she'll be on the next flight coming back, but she didn't know how long that will be."

"I'm coming down there."

"Andrea, I think it would be best if you'll wait until in the morning to come out here."

"Why should I do that? Montica is my friend I need to be there... and be there for Brice."

"I'm here with Brice. You just stay home. We all don't need to be down here worrying our heads off."

Andrea thought about it. "Shanequa, I wouldn't feel right if I don't come down there."

"Andrea, if you did come down here you really won't get in to see her until in the morning. She's gonna want to rest – but you know the police are gonna be asking her a lot of question and that's gonna take awhile. So, just wait until tomorrow afternoon to come here. I'm sure everything is gonna be fine. I'm praying that it is."

It went quite on the line for a moment.

"I'll be praying too," Andrea replied.

"… I'll call you as soon as I know something."

"Please do. You know we're all like sisters."

Shanequa was doing the best she could to continue holding herself together and keeping positive thoughts. "I got to get back to work." She said. "I'll let you know when ever thing is okay."

"Okay…" Andrea replied.

They hung up together.

Andrea slowly rocked back and forwarded sat on the edge of the bed, replaying the conversation with Shanequa over and over again in her head. Until she picked back up the phone and made a call.

"Hello," answered Ronking.

"Hey, it's Andrea."

"I know. I have your number programmed in my phone."

"Why doesn't that surprise me?" she replied in a very unhappy way.

Ronking chuckled. "Well, what can I do for you?" he asked.

"I need you to do something for me."

"Is everything alright?"

"No… I just found out that one of my best friends has been shot. Now she's in the hospital fighting for her life."

"What do you want me to do?"

"I want you to get in on her case. I know you may have your hands full with that triple homicide case, but it would really mean a lot to me if you help find the guy who shot her."

After all, Andrea has done with Ronking, she knew Marcus had something to do with Montica being shot and wasn't feeling as if she was taking a risk from what she was asking of Ronking. Maybe then, this whole nightmare would come to an end. And without Marcus being able to see what she had done, Andrea felt she had nothing to worrying about at this moment – so she believed.

"… I'll see what I can do?"

"No… promise me that you will help find the guy who did…, please."

"… I promise… I'll do what I can."

"Thank you," Andrea said releasing the tears she was trying so hard to hold back.

"I'm sure everything is going to be fine. So don't worry."

"I'll try not to. But you don't know how I'm feeling right now. I'm already upset about Alex disappearance, and now this."

"I understand. I'm going to do everything I can to help you help your friends."

"Thank you," she told Ronking again.

Ronking exhaled. "Alright, look, I have something I need to get done. So… maybe I'll call you back later, alright."

"Okay, I'll talk to you later."

They ended the call.

Hours later at the hospital where Montica was admitted in, everything was going fine. Montica was alive and conscious. Her husband, Brice, was right by her side, as two policemen asked a few questions about what happen tonight.

"He just came up to me," Montica told them. "I didn't know who he was. He just came out of nowhere asking me questions."

"What kind of question?" The tallest officer asked.

"About a case that I didn't really know anything about," Montica said very breathily.

"Did he ask you about anything else?"

"He just asked if I knew anything about this case. I told him I didn't, and if I did I couldn't tell him. That's when I was tried to get in my car and he... he... pulled a gun on me."

Brice's very large hands held Montica's very softly, letting Montica know that she had nothing to worrying about and that he was there to protect her from any harm. Brice has always made his family feel safe and protected for years, and hoped, after tonight, as long as he had breath in his body, his family would continue feeling safe.

"Were more words shared between the two of you?" asked the shorter office.

"He just kept asking about that case. Then... that's when he... when he..." Montica closed her eyes and try to not think about the worse moment of her life.

"I can see that this is hard for you right now," the tallest officer replied. "So we can come back in the morning and ask you some more questions, and perhaps bring in some photos and have you take a look through them to see if you can find the man who did this to you. If that doesn't work we'll bring in a sketch artist and let you describe your assailant."

Montica was so lost of words that she couldn't respond.

"That will be fine, officer," answered Brice, "Just as long as you promise to find the son-of-a-bitch that tried to kill my wife tonight."

"We're gonna do everything we can, Mr. and Mrs. Summers. Believe me, when I tell you that," said the shorter officer.

"Thank you," Brice replied.

Without another word, both officers made their way out of the room.

"I can't believe somebody did this to you," Brice said, looking deeply into his wife's eyes.

"This all just feel like one bad dream," Montica replied and then changed the subject. "Where is Destiny?"

"She's next door with the Clarks."

"I think you need to go be with her tonight."

"No, I need to be here with you."

"Brice, you and I both know Destiny can't stay with them. They have a lot of things going on. So you need to go get her."

"But babe…"

Montica cuts him off. "I'll be fine," she said, "Nothing else is gonna happen to me here. If Destiny happens to wakes up in the middle of the night, it would be best if you are with her, so she'll know everything is alright, and that she doesn't have to be afraid. So I need you to go be with her tonight. And if it comes to you needed to come back here then take Destiny to Andrea. I know it's a bit out of the way, but I don't want Destiny to see me like this."

Brice could see that Montica was trying to be strong for herself.

"It will also let me know that you will be fine," Montica added. "… Please, Brice."

Not willing to leave, Brice stared into his wife's eyes and said, "Alright, I'll go home tonight. But I'll be back bright and early tomorrow morning, and I'll leave Destiny with my parents tomorrow and she can spend the night with them because I'm gonna be here with you."

"Okay," Montica muttered, as Brice leaned in and place a kiss on her lips.

Brice headed towards the door, but took a glance back at his wife, before opening the door and walking out.

Montica rests her head back on the pillow and made herself a bit more comfortable in the bed. She then closes her eyes to she could get some rest after tonight's event.

Moments later, the door to Montica's room opened. Montica heard the door when it closed, and slowly opens her eyes to see who had entered inside. Her eyes could have fallen right out of her head, as she found herself staring eye to eye with the man who shot and left her for died.

Montica took the chance to try screaming for help, but Dean had started smothering her with his bare hands. Montica tried reaching for the call button on her bed, but Dean grabbed Montica's hand by the time she could push the button and continued holding her hand until he finished the job.

Once Dean saw Montica was no longer breathing, he pushed against the gunshot wound for it to start bleeding out. Then, being very sure this time, since he watched the lights leave Montica's eyes, Dean left Montica's lifeless body lying there, waiting to be found.

CHAPTER SEVENTEEN

The following Wednesday was a very sad day, as many people stood around the brown wooden casket that held Montica's body, and held obituaries that read:

MONTICA JASMINE SUMMERS
JULY 12, 1976 – APRIL 19, 2013

Little more than forty family members, friends, and co-workers had come to say final goodbyes to Montica. It was very amazing on how many people had cared and loved Montica and was going to miss her deeply. But no one was going to miss her as much as Brice, who was trying to hold back a few tears as he held his six and half years old daughter. He was sitting in between Felicia, Andrea, and Shanequa, who were all grieving the loss of their friend.

The Pastor had finished saying a few words and looked to a young lady from the church to come forward and sing the song *Amazing Grace*. As the young lady's beautiful voice moved everybody around Montica's casket, Andrea found herself eyeing Ronking standing a distance away from the funeral under an oak tree. Just seeing him standing there during her time of saddens, helped Andrea to see what kind of man he was.

After placing Montica in her final resting place, less than half the people that attend the funeral came to the Summers's house in Manhattan, for the repast. Everybody was moving around, few came up Brice telling him how good of a person his wife was. It made Brice wish hard that none of this was really happening. That it was all a bad dream he was having the hardest time waking up from.

In the kitchen, Andrea, Felicia, and Shanequa were responsible for preparing the food and getting it out for the guest to enjoy. Thelma helped.

"I should have gone to her room sooner," said Shanequa, standing against the kitchen counter, arms folded across her chest, as she thought back to Friday night. She was the one who found Montica, after coming to the hospital room to see how she was doing. It hurt her very deeply to have found her best friend that way. "Maybe if I would've gone to her room sooner, Montica would still be alive."

"There was nothing that could've been done, sweetie," Thelma told her.

"Yeah," said Felicia, coming close to Shanequa and placed a hand on her shoulder. "The doctors had a hard time stopping her bleeding during surgery. When they did stop it, they thought everything was good, but it wasn't. All they did was bought her a little time to tell what happened."

Shanequa wiped away the tears that had fallen from her eyes. "It's just so amazing," she then said. "One minute you're having a good time with someone and the next time you see them... they're... gone. It makes no sense at all."

"It doesn't..., but that's the way life is," replied Andrea, walking over to stand face to face with Shanequa. "I remember Charles showing me the most wonderful time of my life. It was a night I would never forget, and the next day I woke up and he wasn't there. I then later see and hear my husband taken away, out of my life, and I will never see him again... and that hurts so much. You ask why, but it's a question you just won't ever get the answer to."

"She right," said Thelma, "There are some things we can't get an answer for. The only thing we can do is to keep moving forward with our lives until we get to the end."

"What about Destiny?" Shanequa asked when the thought of Montica's only child came to mind. "How is that little girl supposed to get through life after losing her mother at the age she is?" She looks to Andrea directly. "How did Miles and Ted handle losing their father the way they did?"

Andrea thought about it. "Well," she said, "Miles was too young to really understand what was going on, and then I haven't even given birth to Ted when it happened. But there isn't a week that goes by they don't ask questions about Charles."

"All three of us are gonna be there to tell Destiny about her mother," said Felicia. "And maybe one day she might fill her mother's shoes."

A brief smile came across Shanequa's face. "That would be something to see," she replied.

They all came together for a group hug. Thelma stood aside watching them.

Releasing one another, Andrea said, "I'll be back. I'm gonna see how's Brice is doing."

"Please do," Felicia agreed. "He was doing everything he could to stay strong at the cemetery while holding Destiny."

Andrea headed out the kitchen and into the living room. She spotted Brice gazing out the front window.

"How you holding up?" she asked, approaching Brice.

"I just talking to some of Montica's colleague," he responded, still gazing out the window. "On Monday, they were gonna… make Montica a partner at the firm."

Andrea was more than shocked to hear the news. She knew how bad Montica wanted that position.

"Do you know how much she wanted that?" Brice continued. "How hard she worked? I mean she worked hard. Early in the mornings, worked all afternoon, and then worked late at night. Going through files and reading cases – hell she sacrificed out time together with me for the past five months and three days to get herself where she was gonna be this past Monday." He turned so that he and Andrea were looking face to face. "Andrea, why in the hell would someone wanna kill my wife?"

It hurt Andrea deeply to have heard Brice ask that question, and to know that answer but couldn't give it without it leading to cost her own life. She wondered what this Steven Paige was involved that not alone got him killed, but Montica as well.

"Everything is gonna to be alright," Andrea said, as Brice released every tear he was trying so hard to hold back. She reached out, and Brice lean in and cried on Andrea's shoulder.

"Andrea," Brice said finding words. "I don't know how you're able to be strong after losing Charles…, but I don't think I can be this strong."

"Its strength that comes with time," she told him. "You can't lose someone you love and then be over them by tomorrow. Sometimes when you really love someone… you can't ever let them go."

"I want her back Andrea… I want her back."

"I know you do. We all do."

Eyes of many guests were on Andrea and Brice. Many were able to sense his pain but knew there was no way to take the pain away.

Moments later, Destiny came slowly walking up to them.

"Daddy…" she said, getting Brice's attention.

Pulling away from Andrea, Brice looked down to his daughter, eyes full of tears.

"Everything gonna be alright, Daddy," Destiny said with tears building in her little eyes.

Brice bent over and picked Destiny up. Destiny held her father tight as she started crying on his shoulder. Holding her tightly in his arms,

Brice cried alone with his daughter as he carried Destiny into another room and closed the door, so they both could have a moment alone.

Andrea watched the door, wondering what was happening on the other side. She was startled when felt a hand came out of nowhere and touched her on the elbow. After seeing him at the cemetery, Andrea wasn't much surprised that Ronking had stopped by the house for the repast.

"It's just me," Ronking replied, seeing that he caught Andrea off guard. "How're you doing?"

"… There's a lot going on right now." She answered. "It's unbelievable, all that's happening to good people I know."

Ronking stood feeling sorry for her. "I'm sorry for the loss of your friend," he replied.

"Yeah, so am I." Know it wasn't the time, she asked, "Were you able to get in on her case."

"I wasn't able to get in on it, but I will tell you they do have some of the best detectives working on it to find this man."

"Oh… well, I guess that's good to hear."

"Is there anything that I can do for you?"

"At this point… the only thing you can do is to find the monster that did this."

"I understand. But if there's ever anything else that you may need, remember, I'm only a call away."

There were no more words spoken. Ronking took one last look at Andrea before heading towards the front door.

"Justin…" Andrea called when Ronking was just two steps away.

Ronking turns his attention back to Andrea. "Yes," he answered.

"Will it be possible for us to meet later today? Somewhere I can just get away from life for a while."

"… Yeah, I don't see why not," he said, taking a step back to Andrea. "If you want to come by my apartment in Queens later after my friends help me finish painting my living room, you're more than welcome to."

"How long will that take?"

"Well, once I get back there and move the stuff out from and off the wall, it shouldn't take any longer than an hour. It's just one wall, really."

"And you need friends to help you do that."

"Well, they're the ones with the free paint."

"Oh… well, when I finish up here which may be in another two or three hours, I'll come over there." She glanced around the room. "I really just need to get away."

"I understand." He pulled a business card from his inner coat pocket, wrote his address on the back, and handed it to her. "Give me a call or text to let me know you're on the way."

Ronking turned once again, headed out of the front door, and down the street to his car.

The repast lasted for another two and half hours, just like Andrea thought it would. After cleaning up, seeing that Brice and Destiny were going to be alright, and getting her family home, she used the GPS on her phone to get to the address Ronking had given her. The whole drive to Queens, Andrea cried. Glancing in the rearview mirror to Marcus and Mark, she wondered why they haven't just killed her. Every time she turned around they were doing something to cause her more and more pain. She knew they had something to do with both Alex and Montica, and she really wanted to know the reason why.

The GPS informed Andrea the destination of Ronking's apartment building after turning on the street. She found a park and quickly headed inside the building. While walking up to Ronking's apartment door, she prayed that Marcus and Mark didn't figure out where she was, but if they did, she hoped they didn't get the wrong idea of her visit.

Andrea knocked three times and waited for an answer.

The door was opened, but not by Ronking. It was a man built the same as Ronking, but a little shorter.

"Hey," Andrea said, "I think I might have the wrong apartment."

"You Andrea?" the man asked.

"Yeah, that's me."

The man stepped aside to allow Andrea to enter. "Justin in the living room," he informed her.

Andrea entered the apartment far enough for the man to close the door. As she followed him to the living room, she noticed that he had paint spots on his t-shirt, pants, and both arms.

"See you made it," Ronking said when seeing Andrea enter the room behind his friend. "Andrea, this is my friend Eddie." He introduced the man she walked in with. "And this is my friend Ray." He then introduced the man kneeling on the floor, packing up the stuff they brought to painting with.

Andrea greeted both of them.

"Alright, I guess I'll see you guys later."

"Yeah," said Eddie, "We have better things to be doing than painting your walls."

"I know that's right." Ronking agreed.

"Yeah, so we'll see you in the morning," said Ray, patting Ronking on the back on his way out with Eddie.

"Yeah, I will see y'all first thing tomorrow morning," Ronking shouted just before they exited the apartment and closed the door.

Andrea and Ronking were now together and alone.

"Can I get you anything?" Ronking asked, breaking the silence that was building in the room.

"No, I'm good," Andrea answered while looking around the apartment.

Ronking points to the couch with his hand. "You can have a seat if you want."

"Thank you."

Andrea took a seat on the couch and sat her purse beside her on the floor. Ronking came and had a seat behind her.

"So how was everything before you left Summers's House?" Ronking asked.

"About as well as you could be expected. One of Montica's cousins is gonna stay over there tonight with the family."

"Well, it's good that somebody will be there with them and maybe help out."

It became silent in the room again.

Andrea covered her face with both hands for a moment, before sliding them back, over her hair, and then resting them on the side of her neck. "Have you ever been in a place in your life where everything just feels like a dream?" She asked but didn't let Ronking answer. "You wanna wake up like it's a nightmare, but you can't. The whole thing is eating at you and you feel yourself about to lose your mind."

"I've been there before." He answered, "Then once it's over you don't wanna look back on it."

"That's exactly what I mean. It seems like my life is in an endless monster roller coaster." She jumped up from the couch, took a few steps forwards, and stared out the window. "First, I lose my husband and now I'm losing my friends. I'm starting to get afraid that I'm soon gonna lose the ones that mean more to me than my own life."

Ronking stood up and stepped over to where Andrea was standing. "Everything is gonna be fine," he assured her. "Now, I don't know anything about your past or what you may be going through in your life right now, except what you have told me. Nevertheless, as a friend, if you let me, I promise you will never be afraid of anything else in this lifetime again."

Gazing in Ronking's eyes, Andrea saw the truth in every word he had said. Seeing she had someone who wanted and maybe could help with her particular problem, made Andrea cry because she knew it was going to be a great risk to him if he became involved.

"Justin…" she said, with a tear falling from her left eye. "This is so much… it's…"

Not knowing is Andrea was accepting what he was offering, Ronking cut Andrea off by reaching out and given her the biggest hug he could. "Everything is gonna be alright, Andrea," he said. "I'm not gonna let anything else hurt you."

"That would really mean a lot." Andrea cried, holding Ronking back very tightly.

Ronking had no idea on how good he was making Andrea feel just by holding her. Then, as the moment continued to build, he started kissing Andrea's neck. Andrea couldn't say anything; she just continued holding Ronking as he continued kissing her until he was gazing into her eyes. She closed her eyes when Ronking leaned in and placed a kiss on her lips. When Ronking broke the kiss, Andrea reopened her eyes and felt as if the whole world was at peace.

No words were spoken as Ronking went in for another kiss, and Andrea held him as he did it. Andrea didn't know what was happening, her body was starting to feel so relax and so far from the way she used to feel. She felt even more relaxed when she felt Ronking unzipping the back of her dress, and allowed it to fall to the floor. Realizing what was happening, Andrea didn't stop it as she reaches to remove Ronking's shirt.

Andrea was then lifted off her feet, and up into Ronking's strong arms, as he carried her through the open space of the hallway and into the bedroom, where Ronking relaxed her slowly down on his bed.

Nervous, for it has been a long time since a man has touched her in this way, Andrea's body became a bit tense as Ronking begin kissing almost every inch of her smooth skin. He started from her thigh, worked his way up to her stomach, breast, neck, and then finally to her lips. Ronking pulling back and came up to his knee with removing Andrea's panties, then lay back in between Andrea's legs and kissed her soft lips again.

She would have never in the past let a man come this close to being with her – so soon. Andrea didn't even let herself be alone with Charles until after their third date. But at this point, it really didn't matter to Andrea how long she has known Ronking, she just needed someone to be with during her stressful time.

Within a moment of time, Andrea exhaled hard the moment she felt Ronking enter her. From how long it's been since the last time she was intimate with her husband, this came to feel like Andrea's first time all over. As Ronking went on, Andrea held her arms tightly around him, eyes closed while breathing very pleasurable, and nearly forgetting all of the problems she was currently facing.

She had no regrets.

"Are you alright?" Ronking asked as Andrea rested across his chest.

"I fine," she replied, "I was just thinking."

"About?"

"… What happens next?"

"What do to mean what happens next?"

Andrea rises up, holding an arm across Ronking, as she gazed down into his eyes. "You're the first man I've been with in a long time," she told him. "This is all new to me. It's like a new start for me and I don't know what could happen between us." She paused. "I'm not even sure if this should've happened." She then moved from across Ronking and sat straight up in the bed, with the sheet covering her. "I mean we don't really know each other to have done this."

"Okay, maybe we did move a little fast," Ronking agreed as he too sat up. "But I think things could maybe work out between us if we take our time." He paused and stared at Andrea. "Andrea, I have never felt this way about any woman in a long, long time."

"What is it about me that you like so much?"

Ronking couldn't help but gaze into Andrea's eyes. "There is so much about you that I admire," he said. "You are so different than most women. You have an inner smile that you hide from the world – why – I don't know. You walk with the confidence. When you walk into a room... to me... everything stops as your radiant appearance glows throughout the room. And when I look into your eyes, I see the stars that God took from the night's constellation and placed in your instead. But there's still so much more to you that I would like to get to know."

"There's more to you I would like to get to know too," she replied.

"And perhaps you will soon." He said, lying back flat on the bed.

Andrea gazed out the window, wondering of what could possibly become of her life once this ordeal was finished. Then, she started thinking about the things Ronking said to her earlier when they were in the living room talking.

"Would you really be there for me if I needed you?" she asked.

"Of course," he answered.

"Would you try and protect me from any harm that comes my way?"

"… Yes."

She closed her eyes, took a deep breath and exhaled. Then, Andrea slowly said, "I witnessed the homicide." She was feeling very strong telling Ronking, much stronger than when she told Pastor Mansell.

"You did what?" Ronking asked, raising himself back up in the bed.

"I witnessed the homicide," she repeated. "I was there when those three men were killed. I didn't get a good look at the man that pulled the trigger, but I know a way you could find him and maybe the rest of the people that work with him."

"How can I do that?" he asked, listening to every word she said.

"I'm being followed by two of them. Anywhere I go, they go. They're parked right across the street of this building right now, in a black suburban. Hell, I'm lucky if they don't know it's you I'm with right now."

"Now it all makes sense to why you wanted me to leave you alone so bad?"

"Yes. I couldn't say anything. They threatened to kill me if I did. But by me staying quiet cost the lives of my friends – and I can't stay quiet any longer and let someone else die because of me."

"And no one else well. Thanks for finally telling me," he said, placing his arms around Andrea's shoulders and led in to give her a very passionate kiss.

"So, what happens now?" Andrea asked, staring deep into Ronking's eyes, believing she could really trust in him.

"I hate for you to continue this, but things are gonna have to remain the way there are until I can inform my partners about this," he answered. "We don't wanna make the wrong move and cost someone else their life. But don't worry, I got you. I'll let you know what will happen as soon as possible."

It wasn't until a little after one o' clock in the morning when Andrea returned home. Continue resting in Ronking's arms made Andrea feel so safe and protected, that she lost track of time. However, she felt so much better about herself after finally speaking – like she should've done a long time ago. And on the way home to the moment Andrea's head touched her pillow, all she could think about was freedom… and how life would be for her with Ronking in it.

CHAPTER EIGHTEEN

Remembering Ronking's instructions, Andrea did what she always did from the moment her eyes opened to the second she walked out the front door with Miles and Ted to take them to school.

"Mama, will it be alright if I went over to a friend's house after school?" Miles asked when Andrea was two blocks away from the schoolhouse.

"What friend?" she asked.

"Max… we have a class together."

"I don't know any of your friends name Max."

Miles was quite for a second. "Well, actually… it's short for Maxine," he replied.

Andrea made a surprise face when she learned it was a female Miles was trying to go with after school. She shared the look with Miles.

"No mama," he replied. "Maxine is just a friend."

"Sure she is," said Ted.

"Mind your business." Miles snapped as he glanced back to his brother.

"Make me."

"Enough you two," Andrea said to the both of them. She pulled up into the school's parking lot and parked so she could ask Miles a few questions. "Miles, exactly why do you wanna go over to this girl's house after school?"

"Ms. Green gave an assignment to the class Friday and we have to work with a partner on it, and I got teamed up with Maxine," he answered. "The assignment is due Monday, and Maxine wants to try and have it done before tomorrow. So she was wondering if I could come over to her place after school so we could try and get it done today. But I said I had to ask you first."

Ted chimed in and asked, "Why can't you finish it in school?"

Andrea looked back and pointed a finger to Ted," You stay out of this," she told him, and then turned back to Miles. "Do you know where this girl lives?"

"Not too far from us. She lives in the same area. Her mother was gonna pick us up after school. That's if you allow me to go with them."

Andrea took a moment to think about it. "I'm gonna allow you to go," she said, "But if it gets too late, you have her mother – or father to bring you home. I don't want you out by yourself at night."

"Okay," he answered with a smile. He then opens the door and got out, with Ted right behind him.

218

As Andrea watched them head inside the school, she smiled as she realized her children were really starting to grow up. She only wished their father was there to witness it.

While focusing on the road, Andrea couldn't help but ponder what she would tell Marcus when he comes asking questions on her little visit to Queens, and to why she was there until after twelve o' clock in the morning. She could answer the question on the visit honestly, but to why she was there so long was too personal to tell. However, they may not have cared if she got intimate with Ronking, but Andrea didn't want them having the wrong impress towards her.

This was Andrea's first day back to the café since Monday after. Andrea came in for half a day to inform her co-worker that she was taking some time away, due to a death. Many thought it to be Alex, but she continued to tell them that Alex was still just missing, and shared with them that it was Montica that passed. They gave Andrea hugs, including Hakeem, who she left in charge while she was out.

However, when Andrea entered the café, she thought Hakeem may not have been the best pick to leave in charge for a long period of time. Andrea found the chairs in the front weren't stacked on top of the tables, and there was a light left on in the back. Then, she happens to see that the light was coming from the manager's office, not along after, the sound of something being dropped.

"Hello?" she said but didn't get an answer. She slowly took small steps towards the back. "Is someone back there?" she then shouted.

Almost out of nowhere, an old woman, with middle cut brown and gray hair, comes walking out of the manager's office, wearing a big smile that made Andrea smile when she realizes who it was.

"Ms. Blakemore, what are you doing here?" Andrea asked, placing her purse down on the closest table, and then walked over to embrace Ms. Blakemore with a hug.

Ms. Blakemore held her arms wide open. "Well, I told you I'll be here on the 25th which is today." She then gave Andrea a big motherly hug. "And how have you been?"

Andrea exhaled. "I've been okay," she answered

"Well, that didn't sound too good."

"You have no idea. So much has happened in the past week alone."

"Well, tell me all about it." Ms. Blakemore said, pulling out a chair from underneath the table they were standing by and had a seat.

"You wouldn't believe half if I told you," Andrea replied, having a seat across from Ms. Blakemore at the same table. "I mean everything that's happened isn't something that happens every day in someone's life, and I've never thought it'll all would be happening to me."

"What exactly has been happening?"

Everything within the past two weeks flashed through Andrea's head, but she could only share the things everyone else saw. "… Alex went missing for one." She answered.

Ms. Blakemore gave a confused look when Andrea said what she did. "What do you mean Alex went missing? Missing how?"

"I don't know where he is – nobody knows what he is. I've been looking for him, repeatedly calling his phone and I only get his voice mail. So I had a missing person report filed with the police and still haven't heard anything back yet."

"Oh my goodness," Ms. Blakemore said, reaching across the table for Andrea's hand. "I know how close you two are. You were like brother and sister. I'll hate to imagine that something terrible has happened to him."

"Same here," Andrea agreed. "Not only have lost track of a brother, but I've lost a sister as well."

"What do mean?"

"You remember my friend Montica?"

"I believe so… she's the lawyer, right?"

"Yeah, that's her." Andrea paused for a moment. "Anyway… this past Friday, someone shot and killed her when she was leaving work."

Ms. Blakemore placed her other hand over her heart. "This is a world gone mad, dear," she said. "Who would've wanted to kill her? She was a very kind and sweet woman who I don't believe wouldn't say anything bad to anyone."

"No, she wouldn't… but like you said it's a world gone mad."

There was then a moment of silent between them as they thought of the loss of Montica.

"All of this must be very hard for you," said Ms. Blakemore.

"It is… and it all continues to go through my head every time I close and open my eyes."

Ms. Blakemore sat and thought for a moment. She was very concerned for Andrea and what she was currently dealing with. "… When was the last time you had a day off?" she asked.

"… Well, I'll be honest; I took the past two days off."

"Well, take this day off as well – no take today and tomorrow off. Then first thing, Monday morning, when you get in, we'll go over and sign those papers, turning the café over to you."

"Are you serious?"

"Have I not ever been more serious?"

"Are you sure? I mean I haven't been there the past two days, but I know the café can get a little crazy. You sure you don't want my here to help out?"

"Andrea, go home and get some rest… relax. I can handle things around here. I did it long before you came along."

Andrea chuckled while remembering Ms. Blakemore's comment was known to be the truth. "Okay," she replied, standing up from the table. Ms. Blakemore stood up with her, and they shared another hug before Andrea headed to the table where she laid her stuff down on. "Well, I'll see you first thing Monday morning."

"I'll see you Monday," Ms. Blakemore said, watching Andrea leave out the door.

Thelma hadn't too long returned home from the market. She was in the kitchen unpacking the few items she bought for dinner tonight when she heard the front door open. After placing the item she had on hand in the refrigerator, Thelma glanced in the living and saw Andrea putting down her purse on the couch, and then coming towards the kitchen.

"Why you home so early?" Thelma asked as Andrea entered in the kitchen. "I thought you said you were going to working today."

"I did," she answered, opening the refrigerator and pulling out the cranberry juice. "But my boss me I could have today and tomorrow off."

"I thought your boss was in England."

While getting a glass from the cabinet shelf, Andrea replied, "She was, but she came back, because she had some papers that she needed me to sign."

"What kind of papers?"

After pouring the juice into the glass, Andrea took a quick sip before answering, "Ms. Blakemore wants to turn the café over to me." She then turned and put the juice back into the refrigerator. When she glanced back, she finds a shocking look on Thelma's face.

"You mean you're going to own that café?" Thelma asked.

"That's right."

"Then what is Ms. Blakemore gonna be doing afterward?"

Andrea took another quick sip of her drink. "She wants to go back home and be with her family – for her own reasons. Since the café had a good thing going on, she didn't wanna just close it down and sell it. She knew how much I enjoy working there, so she's gonna pass it on to me."

"So does that mean you'll be making, even more, money now?" Thelma asked with a wondering look on her face.

"Maybe… maybe not… who knows?" Andrea answered as she headed into the living room and got comfortable on the loveseat.

"I hope you do? Maybe then with more money entering your hands will help you get that own place you've want so much for you, Miles and Ted. And then leave me here all by myself."

"Well know you will always be welcome over."

"I should hope so after all the time you spent here." Thelma then changed the subject as she finished putting away the last of the groceries. "So since you're off again today, you're gonna be able to get Miles and Ted from school."

"Yeah, I'm gonna pick up Ted. Miles is going over to a friend's house to work on an assignment that's due Monday, so he's won't be home until later."

"Speaking of getting home late…" Thelma said, closing the refrigerator, then came and stood behind the loveseat. "Why was it after one o' clock this morning when you got in?"

Andrea stared straight ahead when Thelma asked the questioned. "I just needed some time to myself, mama," she answered. "After Montica passing and so many other things going on just put me in a place where I had to be alone."

"So where did you go, because you had me a little worrying. I was starting to think I was gonna have to call the police."

"Mama, I'm a grown woman and I know how to handle myself."

"Yeah, that's what they all say until they get found in an alley… dead."

Andrea paused after her mother's comment. "Well…, you don't have to worry about anything like that happening to me," she replied.

"I'm always gonna worry about what might happen to you…" Thelma said, bending over and wrapping her arms tightly around Andrea's neck, giving a big motherly hug and a kiss on the forehead. "… Because you're still my little girl and I care about what happens to you."

Andrea held onto her mother's arms. She felt like a little girl having Thelma holding her the way she was.

The sun had set.

Andrea, Thelma, and Ted were all at the kitchen table, having a nice dinner – almost like one big family. The only problem was that Miles still hasn't come home yet. And Andrea has looked over at Miles's empty seat more than twice since they all sat down to eat.

"I hope Miles gets home soon because it's late," said Andrea, looking out the window to how dark it was.

Before speaking, Thelma finished chewing the food in her mouth and sending it down her throat. "He didn't say what time he'll be home?"

"No, and I forgot to ask."

"Did you at least find out where this child lives?"

"Four blocks from us," answered Ted.

Andrea and Thelma both eyed Ted.

"And how do you know, Teddy?" Andrea asked.

He chuckled. "I live in the same room with him, mama," he answered. "Miles may not always talk to me, but I could still hear him. That's how I know Maxine isn't just a partner for that assignment, but she's also his girlfriend."

"His girlfriend…" said Thelma. "When did he get a girlfriend?"

"Oh, if I heard right, I believe they've been together for two weeks ago."

Andrea stared at Ted for a moment. "Boy, are you making this up?" she asked.

"Nope," Ted answered, picking up his drink.

"Lord, I need to start spending more time with you two," Andrea replied, picking up her glass of red wine, and then lean back in her seat. "I'm coming to a point where I hardly know my own kids."

Suddenly, there came two slow knocks at the front door.

"I'll get it," Andrea said, standing up to go see who was knocking.

"Mama, even if you did spend more time with us, we're not gonna tell you everything," Ted replied.

Andrea unlocked the door. "Yeah, we'll see about that," she said.

When she opened the door, Andrea quickly reacted when Miles collapsed into her arms, causing them both fall and hit the floor. Both Thelma and Ted jumped up from the table and over to see what had happened.

"Oh my God," Andrea shouted after seeing Miles's face.

Miles's left eye was black and his upper lip was busted open. There was blood running from his mouth and nose, and his right jaw was swollen.

"Miles, what happen to you?" Andrea asked trying to help him.

"... I... I was attacked," Miles answered in pain.

CHAPTER NINETEEN

There was blood spattered all over the front of Andrea's shirt and hands from helping Miles downstairs to the car. Fear had built inside Andrea while rushing Miles to the hospital. When they arrived and checked in at the emergency room, the doctors took Miles to the back, while Andrea, Thelma, and Ted had to wait in the reception area. It felt like eternity had passed as Andrea paced back and forth on the waiting room floor, waiting for the doctor to come and tell them how Miles was doing.

"Andrea, I know you're worried, but please come sit down," said Thelma, while holding Ted's head in her lap as he slept. "You're gonna walk a hole in the floor."

"I can't sit down, mama," Andrea replied, pausing in her tracks, directly where Thelma was sitting, and stared Thelma right in the face.

"These – I mean somebody… put their hands on my child and could've almost killed him tonight." She then started pacing again.

"Sweetheart, I'm sure it's not as bad as it seems."

While continuing pacing the floor, she replied, "It wouldn't seem like anything if he did like I told him, and had that girl's parents bring him home."

"He said they were in a hurry to get somewhere and weren't heading in our direction."

"That's no excuse, mama…" Andrea snapped. "It wouldn't have taken them long to drive him four blocks. Those people knew that it was too late for Miles to be out walking the streets alone in the rough neighborhood we live in."

"Okay, I will agree with you there. Miles shouldn't be out alone this time of night. But you know how Miles is. He's always trying to do things on his own. He gets that from you." Thelma then thought back to when Andrea was a little girl. "Remember when you were little, and I always told you not to play in the streets, but you did it anyway because you thought you were big enough to do so."

"…Yes, mama, I remember." Andrea answered after finally taking a moment to sit down.

"And remember almost getting hit by that speeding car that was coming right at you. If it wasn't for that nice lady being there at the right time, you wouldn't be here today."

Andrea thought back to the same event Thelma was remembering her about. "But mama…" she said, "There was nobody to help my son when somebody was pushing their fist in his face." She then looked

Thelma in the eyes. "Mama, times have changed since I was a little girl."

"I know," Thelma replied. "But that doesn't mean we have to start thinking negative because things are changing in the world."

Only a second later, a doctor entered the waiting room and called out, "Andrea Harris."

Andre quickly jumped from her seat and headed towards the doctor. "How is he?" she asked. "Is he gonna be alright?"

"He's going to be fine," the doctor answered.

"Can I see him?"

"Yes, you can. If you would, please follow me and I'll explain everything to you."

Andrea looked back at Thelma. "Mama, I'll be right back." She told her.

"Go ahead. I will be right here with Ted," Thelma said, rubbing Ted's head.

The doctor started walking down the hall, with Andrea following alongside him.

"Mrs. Harris, I'll have to tell you, your son had a rough encounter tonight." The doctor told her. "I have had patients come in from off the streets beat up worse than what your son was tonight."

"Well, how bad is he?"

The doctor started going down the list – using various medical terms to describe Mile's injuries. Andrea had to stop him and asked to put it all in plain English.

"Busted lip, bruised face, and he bit down on his tongue a little," the doctor explained. "He has a few bruises around his stomach, so we did a couple of x-rays and found no broken bones. So I don't see any reason why he couldn't go home tonight."

"Thank you, God," Andrea whispered to herself.

"We also inquired if he could describe his assailants, but he said it happened so quickly, and that it was too dark to make out any facial features." The doctor added.

"I know, he told me the same thing when we were bringing him here."

They were soon standing right outside the treating room Miles was in.

"I'll give you two a moment alone." The doctor said. "I'm gonna run and get the release papers and a prescription for medication, and then after that, you and your family can go home."

"Okay, thank you so much, doctor," Andrea said, just before the doctor walked away.

When slowly stepping in the doorway, Andrea heart almost stopped when she saw Miles's face again. Not only did Miles look bad, but the look on his face told Andrea more than what she already knew. He was scared.

"Mama," Miles said when he saw his mother standing by his bed.

"Yeah, I'm right here, baby," said replied, making her way to his bedside and grabbing a hold of his head.

"Mama, I'm sorry. I shouldn't have tried walking home by myself. I'm…"

Andrea quickly cuts him off. "It's going be alright, Miles," she said, taking Miles into her arms. "There's nothing we can do about it now.

The important thing is that you're still alive… and I can hold you in my arms again."

It went silent in the room as they held each other very tightly.

"I wanna go home, mama," Miles cried.

"And I'm gonna take you home," Andrea told him, not ever wanting to let him go again.

When returning home, Andrea didn't say much of anything. She just stormed to her room and closed the door to have a moment alone. Thelma sent Miles and Ted to their room to get ready for bed. After they were changed into their nightclothes, Thelma came and stood in the doorway right after Ted had finished saying his prayers and was climbing in the bed.

"You boys okay?" she asked.

"I'm good," answered Ted.

Miles didn't respond as he lay facing the wall.

Thelma came all the way in the room and had a seat on the edge of Miles's bed. "You okay, Miles?" she asked.

"I'm fine," he replied.

"Then look at me."

Miles slowly rolls over. It was hard for Thelma to see how badly her grandson had been beaten. She closed her eyes and started praying deep down in her heart.

"Lord," she said before reopening her eyes and looked at Miles. "It's like I can't, but then I can believe that somebody would do something like this to you... and for no reason at all. I could only imagine what you went through tonight."

"Hell..." Miles told her. "I was just trying to get home... and somebody just comes out of nowhere... pulls me into an alley... and started beaten me in the face. They then throw me on the ground and starts stomping me into the ground." He paused. "I thought I was gonna die. I thought I was seeing that light everybody talks." Tears begin rolling from his eyes. "Stupid! I was so stupid."

"Don't you think like that," Thelma said, holding Miles's hand. "You were not stupid. If anything, the one that is stupid is the one who thought hurting you was smart... and they are far from it."

They then heard Andrea coming out her bedroom and slamming the door shut as she headed down the hall to the kitchen.

"Is mama gonna be okay?" Ted asked.

Thelma turned to look at Ted. "She should be," she answered. "You've gotta think, after losing a close friend, and then Miles getting attack tonight. There's a lot going on around your mama right now. And she gonna be a little down about it all for a while. So, we're gonna have to be there for your mama the best way we can."

"Mama was acting strange before what happened to auntie Montica and to me tonight," Miles replied.

"Yeah, mama isn't herself anymore." Ted agreed.

"Well, I know your mama..." Thelma was cut off by Miles.

"You think it could have something to do with the man she was talking to last Saturday?" he asked.

"The man you said she was talking to Saturday afternoon when you all got back from the mall."

"No. There was another guy she was talking to at the mall." Miles said, sitting himself up on his elbows. "And that wasn't the first time I saw him either. I saw him two Thursdays ago when mama overslept in here that morning and you had to take us school. He was coming in the building after we left out."

Thelma tilted her head to the side. "What does this man look like?" she asked.

Miles thought of an image in the back of his head. "He was very tall, hair braided, very muscular…" He paused for a moment. "And I think he had hazel eyes – I'm not sure, I couldn't really see them. But I do know that he was always wearing a black suit every time I saw him… and sometimes he wore dark sunglasses."

"Why didn't you tell me about this before?"

"'Cause mama doesn't want us to tell you everything we do."

"Yeah," Ted said, "like the morning she snapped at Miles because he was asking too many questions. She told us not to say anything about it."

Thelma had heard enough. "You two go on to bed," she said, standing up. "I need to go have a little talk with your mother." She cut out the light, closed the door behind her, and headed down the hall. She was trying to put together the pieces of information Miles and Ted had given, with the pieces that's been going through her head about her daughter's behavior for the past few days.

Andrea was in the middle of scrubbing the roasting pan that was used this afternoon to prepare dinner when Thelma entered the kitchen.

"We need to talk," Thelma told her.

"Mama, I'm not in the mood for talking at the moment," Andrea replied.

"I don't care if you are in the mood or not. We need to talk and I mean right now."

Andrea was trying to block her mother out. She continued to scrub the roasting pan as hard as she could to release out her anger.

Thelma took a few steps closer to her daughter. "Andrea Olivia Harris, do you hear me talking –"

Before Thelma could finish asking her question, Andrea slammed the roasting pan and the scrubbing pad down into the sink, causing the water splash out the sink and onto the floor.

"Mama I said I don't feel like talking!" She shouted. "I have a lot on my mind at the moment, mama. So I wish you would please stay the fuck out of my business."

Thelma raised her hand and slapped Andrea so hard that half Andrea's body turned.

"Now you may be a grown," Thelma said when Andrea was looking back at her. "But I am still you mother – and don't you dare ever again… in your natural born life… talk to me that way."

Silence had started building around them.

"Now… I said we needed to talk," Thelma said, breaking the silent. "I need to know what is going on with you. Why are Miles and Ted telling me that you are snapping at them for no reason? Why is Miles seeing you with some strange man, always wearing a black suit, coming around?"

Andrea tried hiding her facial emotions when not only to find out that Miles and Ted had told Thelma what she told them not to, but to learn that Miles have seen her with Marcus. "Mama, those boys don't know what they are talking about," she lied, walking around Thelma and headed into the living room, where she then stood silently in the middle of the room.

"Well at this moment, I seem to believe them more than I believe you," Thelma said, following behind her. "Andrea... I have to say it... I really don't know who you are anymore. You are not the child that I raised. You've been acting peculiar for almost the past two weeks." She then paused and stared at her daughter. "Andrea, what is going on? Are you into something illegal?"

With the pressure brought on, Andrea's eyes filled with tears. She finally turns and looks face to face with her mother. "I've been asking myself the same questions," she answered.

"What do you mean by that?"

"... I don't know how you would take the news if I told you."

"Will it really matter how I take the news, Andrea?" Thelma said, slow coming forward to where Andrea was standing. "Andrea..., I'm your mother... I worry about you... and I'm here to help you with wherever it is you have going on. Now, what is going on?"

The words were stuck in Andrea's throat as she stared into Thelma's eyes. But then, they finally came out. "I witness the murder," she said.

"You did what?"

"I witness the murders that happened in the garage. The one where they found the three men shot to death. I saw it."

"Andrea, this is nothing to be joking about."

"I'm not trying to be funny, mama," Andrea replied, releasing a tear from her right eye. "I really saw it. It happened right in front of me and it was unreal."

Thelma could look into Andrea's eyes and see the truth. "You're serious about this, aren't you?" Thelma asked.

"Does it all make sense to you now?"

There were no words spoken for the next few seconds.

"If what you are telling me is true…," said Thelma, "Then you need to go to the police."

"I can't."

"Andrea, you have to go to the police and tell them what you saw. Before more innocent lives share the same fate as those three that were killed."

"I think it's too late for that. Many lives have already shared that fate."

Thelma had a feeling towards what Andrea meant, although, she wish she didn't. "Andrea… you need to go to the police," she said for the second time.

"Mama, I can't," Andrea cried as she turned and faced the window. "I wish I could, but I can't."

"And why can't you?"

"Because…!" Andrea shouted, but then calming herself back down. "They're watching and everything."

"Who's watching what?"

When grabbed Thelma by the arm, Andrea didn't notice how hard she was pulling, as she led Thelma over to the window, cracked open the curtain, and pointed to what she was talking about. "They're watching me," she said.

Thelma's eyes followed to where Andrea was pointed and saw the black GMC truck parked across the street. With the truck's front window halfway down, Thelma was able to see the man Miles had described to her. When everything had come together, she placed her hand over her heart, as the truth was too hard to bear.

"They found me the next day after they killed the three," Andrea informed Thelma.

"They told me if I even thought of going to the police they'll kill you, Miles, Ted, and me. So I had to act like I didn't see anything – until the morning I wake up and they're long gone."

"I don't believe this," Thelma said, turning and walking to the spot Andrea was standing only moments ago.

"Neither can I mama, but it's happening, and there's nothing we can do about it."

Thelma stood and thought for a moment. "Do they have anything to do with what happen to Miles," she asked.

"… That's my belief. Why? I don't know. There are a lot of things that happen I believe they had something to do with." At that moment, a suicidal thought had come to Andrea's head. "I can't let them hurt another anyone else," Andrea said before heading towards the hallway.

"And just where do you think you're going?"

Andrea paused at the edge of the hall, and then quickly glanced back to Thelma. "Just have you and the boys ready to go when I get back," she replied. "We're gonna get out of here."

"How are we gonna do that with that man down there? When he sees us trying to leave town he's gonna kill us then."

"Don't worry," Andrea said, heading to her bedroom. "I'm gonna take care of him."

CHAPTER TWENTY

Andrea was leaning back against the closed and locked door of her bedroom, with hands held together against the lower part of her face, as she thought through the plan formulating in her mind. It wasn't something Andrea would have ever in her life thought of doing, but at this point, she felt like she had no other choice. She had to protect her family.

Quickly moving toward the bed, she got down on the floor and lay flat on her side to see underneath the bottom mattress. She searched for the area she sewed back together after cutting a hole to hide the five thousand dollars in. Andrea reopened the hole with her hand and retrieved the money. She remembers saying that she would never spend this money, but she had to go back on her oath.

She got up and reached for her purse that was lying in the middle of the bed, where she through it when storming into the room after returning home from the hospital. Andrea stuck the money deep down inside and then placed the purse up on her shoulder. She headed back down to the living room, where Thelma was still standing in the same spot Andrea left her in.

"What are you about to do?" Thelma asked.

"Mama... just be downstairs with the boys, when I get back." She replied.

Then without another word, Andrea headed out of the apartment. Thelma wondered what her daughter was up to, and it caused her to worry half to death. But at the same time, Thelma did as she was told and made sure she, Miles, and Ted were downstairs, waiting for Andrea to return.

Meanwhile, Andrea was standing outside Bobbi's apartment door. She knocked three times and then waited for an answer. However, there wasn't one, which was a good thing for Andrea as she placed Bobbi's spare key she was already holding in hand into the knob. Bobbi had given the key to Andrea in the case of an emergency. For Andrea, this situation was such an emergency.

The apartment was dark. There wasn't one light on inside. Using the light out in the hall, Andrea located a light switch and turned on the living room lights. Closing the door, she searched the apartment. Andrea glanced at the time on her watch and saw that it was passed time for Bobbi to be coming home. Andrea knew she had to search quickly for the object she came in for. She sat her purse down on the couch before first looking all through the living room, and then headed into the bedroom.

"I know Jeremy has one somewhere around here," she said out loud. "But where it is?"

She looked through all shoe boxes in the bedroom's closet and underneath the bed. Then, using only her hand, Andrea searched in between the mattresses, and still couldn't find what she was looking for. She had almost given up, until glancing towards the nightstand table. That's when she slowly opened the top drawer to find exactly what she was looking for: a Smith and Wesson three hundred fifty-seven revolver. She was extremely nervous, and slowly retrieved the weapon. She shook the whole time, as she was also extremely afraid of guns. She never thought she would ever have the need to use one.

There was soon the sound of keys jingling on the outside the front door. Andrea quickly closed the nightstand drawer and got up off the floor. She swiftly headed back in the living room, retrieved her purse off the couch, and very careful placed the gun in.

The door soon opened, and Bobbi walked in confuse to why the lights were still on. She was then surprised to find Andrea standing in her living room.

"What are you doing in here?" she asked.

Andrea didn't know what to say. "Well, I..." she paused for a very quick moment to seriously thinking. "I was trying to see if you had any... tampons."

Bobbi didn't respond until after giving Andrea a funny look. "It's that time of the month for you already."

"Yeah, already," Andrea answered with a fake chuckle. "Do you have any around?"

"To be honest… I used my last one this morning."

"Oh," Andrea replied as she started heading towards the door. "So it looks like I'm gonna have to make a store run. Thanks anyway."

"Oh, anytime. Sorry, I didn't have any, though."

"That's alright," Andrea replied, stepping out the door and closing it.

Wasting only a moment of time, Andrea glanced back, as if she could see Bobbi through the close door, before finally heading downstairs and out to her car. She sat still for a moment, thinking of a place to go – a place where no one would see them. An area within Central Park had come to mind. She thought hard on if that location was a good choice, but it was the only private place she could think of. So Andrea started the car and drove to where she thought was a good spot for privacy.

When entering Central Park, she parked in a spot where she figured to be a secluded area, as she picked up her purse from in the passenger, and placed it on her lap. When slowly pulling out the gun, Andrea figured out how to open the weapon so she could see how many bullets were in it. At first, Andrea was worried there weren't any bullets but was relieved to ding that it contained five bullets. Andrea closed the gun back, took a deep breath, and careful placed it in the back of her pants and pulled her blouse jacket over it. Her heart was about to beat right out of her chest, as exited the vehicle. She slowly walked over to Marcus and Mark that was parked right behind and given her a strange look – perhaps wondering why she was out here.

"You mind telling me why you're out here?" asked Marcus.

242

Taking another deep breath and slowly easing her hand underneath the back of her blouse jacket, Andrea replies, "I'm here to convince whoever to leave me, my family and friends, alone. I gonna take my family out of the city tonight... and there nothing you two will do about it."

Mark started laughing. "And just how the hell you plan to do that?" he asked.

Andrea didn't respond as she started sweating.

Staring at Andrea gave Marcus the idea that she was up to something. But before Marcus had a chance to do or say anything, Andrea pulled the gun and fired one round into his chest. When Mark realized what had just happened, he quickly reached for his gun in his holster on the side of his pants. He didn't even have a finger on it when Andrea fired three more rounds – two in Mark's chest and one in his head, and her eyes were closed the whole time.

All shaken up, Andrea slowly reopened her eyes, and not even on her own life did she believe what she had just accomplished. While staring at the two dead bodies, Andrea's hands shook, legs felt weak, and heart beating hard then ever against her cheat, as her breathing was labored. Never in her life did she believe she could be able to kill anybody, but it's was like she once heard: '*You do what you have to do to protect your family.*'

Without waiting around any longer, she rushed back over to her car, but by the time she opened the door, Andrea heard her name being called.

"Andrea...," said Marcus still alive. "Whatever... you're trying to do... don't do it. You don't know... what you're dealing with."

From the spot she stood in, Andrea stared at Marcus and said, "You should've thought like that before you put your hands on my son." She took a few steps back toward the truck, raising the gun again, and pointing it at her target. Andrea fired the last bullet in the chamber into Marcus's head, ending his life with her eyes opened.

As she drove back into Harlem, Andrea made a quick stopped by a nearby drug store, three blocks away from the apartment building, to pick up something she knew she was going to need. Then trying not to waste any more time, she finally made it back to the apartment, where she found Thelma, Miles and Ted waiting outside on the steps with their luggage in their hands. Andrea jumped out of the car and moved quickly to help Ted and Miles in the back seat, without time loading their bags into the trunk.

"Mama, what's going on?" Ted asked.

"I can't talk about it right now, baby," she answered, helping him in with his one bag on his back.

Thelma walked around to the passenger side, carrying one large bag, and one small that carried some of Andrea's clothes. "How did you lose them?" she asked.

"Don't worry about that right now, mama."

"So what – we're going to the police now, right?"

"Mama, I said don't worry about it." Andrea snapped, now helping miles who had two bags with him.

"Okay, well can you tell me where are we going?"

"Well we'll see about that when we get to Grand Central Station," she answered as she put the driver seat back into place. "Where ever the next train is going is where we are heading for now."

Thelma stared across the top of the car to Andrea. "Little girl, this isn't right and you know it." She then started whispering so Miles and Ted wouldn't hear what she said next, "You need to go talk with the police."

"Stop worrying about going to the police and get in the damn car," Andrea replied through her teeth.

Not trying to start a debate on the situation, Andrea got in the car and so did Thelma.

When arriving at Grand Central Station, they all quickly got out of the car, holding on tight to their bags, and rushed on inside. Andrea found a spot for her family to wait while she ran to get four tickets that will take them anywhere out of New York.

Less than ten minutes when Andrea returned to the area she left her family.

"Did you find anything?" asked Thelma, standing up come to Andrea, so that Miles and Ted wouldn't hear what they were discussing.

"I was able to get four tickets to Boston," Andrea answered. "I know that's not a far distance, but at least we'll be far enough while leaving my car behind if they come looking for us. While we're on the train, we can think what we're gonna do next."

Thelma looked at Andrea a disappointment in her eyes "What time does the train leave?" he asked.

"In eight minutes."

"Then we need to hurry... before we miss it," Thelma replied as she turned to her grandsons. "Come on, pick up your things and let's go so we won't miss the train."

"What is going on?" asked Miles, picking up his two bags. "Where are we going?"

"Stop asking questions and let's go," Andrea snapped while helping them.

They moved as fast as they could while trying to stay together all the way down to the platform. But before heading down the stairs to the platform, Andrea pulled Thelma aside to a water fountain and handed her two pills to take. She told Thelma they would keep her from getting nauseated on the train rides – as she often would. When they descended the stairs down to the loading platform, Andrea purposely turned her purse upside down and allowed the contents to spill on the ground.

"Damn!" she shouted.

Everybody turned to see what happen.

When Andrea saw she had their attention, she said, "Mama, take Ted and go ahead on the train. Miles come help me pick up my things."

"Okay, try and move fast picking that stuff. There's not much time," Thelma replied. "The train will be leaving at any moment." Without waiting for Andrea to respond, she took Ted by the hand, and they both made their way on the train.

"Mama, where are we going?" Miles asked, picking up few items.

"Boston," she answered.

"Why are we going to Boston?"

"… For the reason, I need to get you three out of town."

Miles stopped picking up his mother's belongings, gazed into Andrea's eyes and asked, "What do you mean you three?"

"… I'm not going with you," Andrea answered, gazing back into Miles's eyes.

"… Mama, what's going on?"

Andrea reached for her son's hand. "Miles, there are a lot of things going on that I can't explain to you right now." She told him. "A lot of people have gotten hurt and worse because of me… and I'm the only one who can put an end to it, but I can't if you all are still around. So I have to get the three of you as far away as possible before I can feel that I'm able to do anything."

Tears begin building up in Miles's eyes. "Mama, what are you talking about?"

"Miles, it's too much to explain right now. Right now, I need you to go get on that train and take care of your brother and grandma, do you understand?"

"Not without you."

"Miles, I will be fine. I know someone that can keep me safe until this whole thing is over. So you don't have to worry about me. I need you to be the big man of the family, be brave, and protect your brother and grandma."

"I can't do that, mama."

"Yes, you can. You are your father's son, and I know you can be just as strong and brave as he was."

"Was my dad really brave?"

"… He was the bravest man that I knew, and when I look into your eyes… all I can see is him in you."

Miles leaned forward and gave his mother a big hug. "I love you, mama," he said.

Andrea held Miles like she did back at the hospital. "I love you too, baby," she said, just before unwilling pulling away. "Look, I have something I need to trust to you." She unzipped one of the pockets inside her purse, pulled a little dark bag she placed the five thousand dollars it after leaving the drug store, and stuck it deep into Miles's backpack. "This is a little under five thousand dollars. I had to use some of it to get the train tickets. When y'all get to Boston, find a way to get to Concord, New Hampshire. So you all will be farther away from New York and nobody will know where you are, but me. Once I finish here, I'll be able to come get you and bring you home when it's time."

"Okay..." Miles answered, wiping away his eyes.

"And look, I gave your grandma two sleeping pills. So by the time you get on that train, those pills should be putting her to sleep. But if she happens to ask where I am, tell her I'm in the bathroom on the train."

"What I'm supposed to say when we get to Boston and she wakes up?"

"The truth is all you can tell."

They stared at one another for a moment.

"Go, Miles," Andrea ordered him.

Without another word, Miles got up from the ground and made his way onto the train. After locating his Thelma and Ted, he took his seat across from them.

"Where's your mother?" Thelma asked. She was already half asleep just like Andrea said she would be.

"... She's in the bathroom," he replied, just like Andrea told him to. "She'll be out in a minute."

"Oh, okay," Thelma said, laying her head back against the headrest.

Ted was right beside her, falling asleep himself.

Miles moved over to the window seat and looked out to see his mother, as she held up a hand and waved bye to him, and the train slowly started pulling away.

CHAPTER TWENTY-ONE

After seeing her family leave town, Andrea headed straight to Queens. For the meantime, she believes Ronking's apartment to be the safest place for her unless Ronking was to find somewhere else. Andrea knew she would have to tell him what she had done in Central Park, and had all hopes that it would be considered as self-defense. As Andrea was driving over, she tried giving Ronking a call but didn't get an answer, only the voicemail. So she left a message, informing him that she was on the way over.

Once arriving at the building and finding a parking space, she hurried upstairs to Ronking's apartment. Then, as she approached the door, she knocked once and the door cracked open.

Andrea looked inside. "Justin," she called out but didn't get an answer.

Slowly stepping inside, Andrea found a light switch and turned it on, and what she saw scared her out of her mind. The apartment was in shambles – like a fight had just happened. The coffee table was smashed, lamps turned over, a few holes in the wall, and papers and photos all over the floor."

"No…" she silently screamed with both hands upon her head.

Just then, Andrea's phone began to ring. She pulled it from her purse and looked at the caller ID. It displayed a block call, but it didn't stop her from answering it.

"Hello," she answered.

"I assume by now you realize we have your boyfriend," replied a cheerful male voice.

"Who is this?"

"That's not the question. The question is do you want to save Detective Ronking or not?"

"What have you done to him?"

"That's for me to know and you to find out."

Andrea was becoming more scared by the second. After all her careful planning and schemes, it looked like they would do her no good since Ronking was now in the hands of the enemy.

"Why are you doing this?" she asked.

"You seem to have gotten a little too close with this detective, and that doesn't sit well with us – and sure the hell doesn't sit with Dean. With how close you two have gotten, we figured you'll reached the point when you would risk telling him everything of our little activities, but guess what? That's not gonna happen, Andrea, because we have big plans and nothing is gonna interfere with them… not when we're so close to our objective."

"What do you want from me?"

"Well, again that's not the question, now is it? The question is if someone else will die tonight, because of you."

"What is that supposed to mean?"

"It means you have a choice to make. If you make the *right* choice… no one else will die. If you make the *wrong* choice… then there will be traumatic consequences."

Andrea closed her eyes and took a deep breath. "What are my choices?" she asked.

"Your first choice is to come to the location I give to you; alone, no police or funny business, and then we'll negotiate on what will happen next. This option will allow you *and* Ronking to walk away and live out the rest of your lives in peace"

"What's my second choice?"

"Well, you could not show at all, and perhaps others like an assistant manager, a head nurse, and a sweet old broad from the Blakemore café will die. Oh, and let's not forget both Detective Ronking… and you. Since I know you're at Detective Ronking's apartment at this very moment we speak."

Andrea almost stopped breathing from the caller last comment.

"Yeah, that's right," he continued, "Just because you killed two of our men don't mean we still don't have eyes on you. Now, I will be calling you back in exactly one hour to get your answer…, and I hope you make the right decision."

The call ended.

So scared, Andrea dropped the phone on the floor. She couldn't move nor breathe at that moment. Her mind was a complete blank. She thought that killing Marcus and Mark had freed her from being watched, but discovers that her enemies still knew her every move. And not only did she fear for her own life, but for her family as well, because it was possible they could've known where she sent them to hide.

Glancing down at her phone, she slowly bent over and picked her phone up, and then slowly headed out the apartment. While slowly walking down the stairs, Andrea thought about the conversation with the caller. Even if she goes to them without the police, she had the feeling that both she and Ronking wouldn't be walking away alive. If this Dean person was capable of killing three men without a second thought, who's to say he wouldn't be capable of killing two more just as easy.

There wasn't really a place Andrea could go at the moment. So she just sat still, behind the wheel of her car, with all kinds of thoughts flowing through her head. Would tonight be her last night alive or would she live to see another day? Whatever she decision she would have made, she felt that she would be facing death.

With her head against the steering wheel, Andrea said, "Looks like you were right, baby." She then slowly looked up at the moon. Her mind had gone back to the worse day of her life and the last words her husband had ever said to her. "You said we were always gonna be together…, no matter what. It looks like I'm coming to be with you… and we're gonna be together always… no matter what."

Andrea slowly closed her eyes like she was falling asleep, and thought back to that terrifying Tuesday morning, forty-five minutes after the second tower of The World Trade Center was hit. She was sitting in front of the counter at the Blakemore café, rubbing her unborn second child through her belly. She watched the event of The World Trade Center burning with Ms. Blakemore and a few customs that were refusing on going outside anytime soon.

"Mrs. Blakemore, am I dreaming?" Andrea asked.

"No you're not dreaming, dear," Ms. Blakemore answered. "This is reality."

"Do you think he's out of there? You believe Charles made it out of there alright?"

"He could have, who's to say," replied Ms. Blakemore with her hand over her heart. "Have you tried calling him on his cell?"

"I can't get through to him. All lines are busy." Andrea couldn't take her eyes off the TV. "God, I hope he's alright."

"This is just so unreal. I seriously can't believe someone would do this."

"Well, I for one can believe it," said an elder man coming over to the counter. "With all the money this country spends on intelligence, no one saw this coming." He said pointing to the TV. The emotion of the events he was seeing started tears build in his eyes. "I have a son on the other side of the world trying to fight for this not to happen. Now… now I have a daughter that may die in the war that was brought here."

"Your daughter works in there?" Andrea asked.

"… She started today in the north tower." The man answered. "God knows I don't want to lose my little girl. She has much to live for at home."

Slowly standing up, hand still rubbing her big round belly, Andrea came closer to the elderly man. "Well, my husband works in the south tower near the top." She replied to let him know she understood the pain he was in. "He too has a lot to live for."

For the first time, the elderly man noticed Andrea's belly.

Andrea rubbed the man on his back to let him that everything was going to be alright. Then at the same time, she tried and convincing herself of the same thing. "I'm praying that your daughter comes home to you just as hard as I'm praying my husband comes home to me, 'cause I need him home with me more than anything."

They both looked back up at the TV.

"This world has gone mad," said the elderly man. "May God help us? May God help us all?" He then made his way back to the table he was sitting, with an elderly woman who was crying her eyes out.

A moment later, Andrea felt her phone vibrate in her pocket. She quickly answered it without even looking to see who was calling her.

"Hello," she answered.

"Hey baby," replied Charles while sounding out of breath.

"Charles, where are you? Are you okay?"

"Baby, I'm fine. What about you?"

"I'm good. I'm at the café watching what's going on."

Charles was breathing very hard and loud into the phone.

"Baby, are you alright?" asked Andrea again.

Mrs. Blakemore came over to where Andrea was standing. "Is he alright?" she asked.

Andrea didn't answer because she was waiting for Charles to respond back.

"I'll be alright," Charles finally answered. "I'll be out of here in a moment."

"You're still in there?" she shouted.

"Yeah, but I'm gonna be outta here any second, and be there with you soon."

"Where in the building are you?"

"… I'm on the twenty-third floor." He lied. He was really on the sixty-sixth floor still trying to make his way down to the ground floor, but didn't want Andrea to know that, and really didn't want her to know that he had stopped to rest on the steps for a moment.

"You're almost home to me," Andrea replied while trying to smile, and a tear coming from her left eye.

Andrea then headed outside to look towards The World Trade Center that was visible from the cafe. Ms. Blakemore was right behind Andrea to make sure that everything was going to be fine with her and nothing happens.

"Yeah, I'll be there holding you, Miles, and little Teddy again in my arms."

"Who's Teddy?"

"Oh, that's my little nickname for the baby." He paused to catch his breath. "Every time I rest my head against your belly and the baby kicks, it feels almost like a teddy bear kicking me in there. So I've been calling the baby Ted and Teddy."

Andrea chuckled, "That's cute." She told him.

Charles begins breathing harder.

"Do you have your inhaler?" Andrea asked.

"Yeah, I got it," he answered, pulling his inhaler from inside his coat pocket.

"That's good because I know your asthma has to be bad under those conditions."

"I'll be fine, baby. Don't worry." He held the inhaler up to his mouth and squeezed. "Damn…!"

"What's wrong?"

"Nothing…" He lied again. His inhaler was empty.

"Charles, please hurry up and get out of there."

Charles was focused on trying to breathe. It felt like he was losing more and more air in his lungs. "I'm coming baby," he said lying back on the steps. "I promise… I'm gonna come home to you… and we all are gonna be one big happy family."

"That's what I want to hear you say. I want our family together tonight."

"… *We will always be together… no matter what.*"

Then at that moment, Charles spoke no more.

Andrea and Ms. Blakemore begin hearing a loud sound coming from the location of The World Trade Center, and it seemed to continue for a long time.

"What was that?" Andrea asked for anyone to answer.

"I don't…" Ms. Blakemore paused the moment she realized the south tower was collapsing. "We need to get inside," she said.

When Andrea's eyes were looking in the same direction as Ms. Blakemore, she raised the phone back to her ear. "Charles what's going on?" she said.

"Andrea, we gotta get inside," Ms. Blakemore repeated, grabbing Andrea by the arm and tried pulling her back inside the café.

"Charles!" Andrea shouted into the phone.

"Andrea, let's get inside," Ms. Blakemore struggle getting Andrea back indoors while a storm of ash was heading towards them.

"CHARLES!!!"

That was a day Andrea would never forget, and not because of the planes flying into the buildings, but because she lost her husband and best friend. Andrea had no idea that Charles died long before the south tower collapsed.

While thinking back eleven years ago, Andrea's cell phone began to vibrate from in the cup holder.

"Hello," she answered.

"Have you come to a decision?" asked the same caller from earlier.

Andrea glanced at her watch, and it was exactly one hour later.

Then, knowing there was no decision to make, she asked, "Where am I going?"

CHAPTER TWENTY-TWO

Remembering seeing keys on Ronking's apartment floor, Andrea quickly ran back up to the apartment and retrieved them. She then switched out her vehicle with Ronking's that was parked across the street from the building, before following the directions she was given. Unsure what all Ronking had inside, Andrea through having his car could've come in some uses if something unexpected were to happen.

The direction to head towards the East river near the Roosevelt Island Bridge had brought Andrea to some old abandoned warehouse off Vernon Blvd. She parked a few feet away and left all her personal belongings in the car. Andrea slowly got out the car, closing the door, and walked toward the man standing outside.

He was a light-skinned black man that appeared to be in his early thirties and was waiting for Andrea with a very serious look on his face.

"It took you long enough," the man told her.

She realized the man's voice from the phone call earlier. "Well, there's an accident on the highway holding up traffic. So it took me longer to get here, 'cause of the rubberneckers."

The man chuckled. "Thanks for that information," he said, looking towards the car Andrea came in. "I don't believe that's your car you're driving."

"Mines started having problems," she lied.

"Put your hands up, Dean wants to make sure you were clean."

Andrea complied.

The man searched every single inch of Andrea's body for any weapons or wires before proceeding. Andrea didn't like his touching and groping her, seemingly to get a cheap thrill.

He then stepped from in front the entrance. "Shall we…" he held out his hand for Andrea to enter through the door first.

Andrea took slow steps inside the big dark room with the smell of oil, scared because she was heading toward a cold blooded killer. "You don't have any lights?" she asked.

"Wait here while I get them," he ordered.

She stood in the middle of the dark room, with the feeling of being watch from within the dark. She really felt like somebody was watching her from the other side of the room.

"Hello?" she said after hearing something nearby fall. "Where are you?"

There was no answer.

"Is anybody there?" she shouted next.

Out of nowhere spoke a voice, "I'm right here," it said from behind Andrea.

The voice sounded very familiar. However, Andrea didn't have the chance to even turn around to see his face. A handkerchief containing chloroform was placed over her nose and mouth. After a moment of struggling, Andrea soon lost consciousness.

"Wake up my little eye witness," whispered the same voice from earlier.

Andrea slowly opened her eyes. Everything was a blur at first. But when her vision began to clear, she found herself looking into the eyes of the man who cared for her in the same manner of her husband.

"Justin," she said, happy to see that he was still alive.

"You surprise me by coming here," he replied. "I thought you would've tried running."

Andrea's vision began to clear even more. She tried reaching up to rub her eyes, but couldn't. She then realizes that she was tied down to a chair.

"Everything is going to be fine." He told her.

Andrea was scared. She thought she knew what was going on, but became more confused when she saw Detective Ronking stand straight up and walked freely to the other side of the room. She then found herself staring at four other men sitting at the same long table she was. They were all dressed in black suits and so was Ronking, except he was wearing a full-length black coat.

"Justin, what's going on?" she asked, very confused.

"I'm sorry," he replied, standing behind the chair at the other end of the table. "But I think you have me confused with the man in that photo in front of you."

She glances down and stared at the picture that was placed in front of her. In the picture was a dark skinned man covered in blood after being shot in the head.

"What is this?" she asked.

"She seriously doesn't get it, brother," said one of the four men who resembled Ronking.

"I can see that Jay," Ronking replied without taking his eyes off Andrea. "In that picture in front of you is the real Detective Justin Ronking. The man I pretended to be for the past few weeks."

Andrea couldn't believe what she was hearing.

"Andrea, you really don't recognize me?" he asked. "Did you really not see my face that night?"

"What are you talking about, Justin?"

"It's not clicking yet! I'm not Justin Ronking. Never have nor ever will be. My name is Dean... Dean Jackson. You only saw a badge, never asked to see ID. I'm the man you saw kill Judge Thomas Williams, Lieutenant James Arthur, and Martin Scott in the garage in lower Manhattan that night."

It was becoming hard for Andrea to breathe when the man she had developed feeling for revealed his true identity.

"No," she cried.

"... Yes Andrea," replied the man she now knows as being Dean. "Why do you think I stayed alive for so long? If it had been any other Detective or cop, they would've been dead the very night you were found. And the truth is... no cop knows about you or what you know. No cop even knows you were there. That photo I had of you running outta the garage was printed just before we erased the footage from every last camera in the area."

Andrea didn't want to accept the truth Dean was revealing to her. Yet, she had to admit that it all made a lot of sense. He was able to come around so much without Mark and Marcus confronting him.

"I needed to know if you had seen my face that night. So, I went to the man in that picture, made him tell his friends here in New York that he had a family emergency and he would be leaving town for a few days. Then afterward... well... you can see what happen next in the picture." Dean walked over to the left side of the table and stood behind two men that Andrea had seen just yesterday. "That's why I had my men Eddie and Ray who you have already met at Ronking's apartment yesterday, after painting the walls. I needed to hide his blood that was all over them."

"I can't believe you," she said as the truth was making it hard and hard for her to breathe. "Why did all this have to happen?"

Dean slowly walked back towards Andrea. "For my own reasons," he answered. "I had to be better than my father – stepfather really. Marcus raised my older brother, Jay and I like we were his own sons after our own father walked out on us with the girl next door."

"Marcus is your stepfather?"

"Was... you killed him and his son Mark not too long ago... remember." Dean then looked up seemingly thinking. "You know, I never thought you had it in you to kill anybody. Even after I heard it, it's still unbelievable."

"How did you hear about it?"

"Well, you see, even though you were being followed by Marcus, I wanted to keep my own eyes on you. So, I had a tracking device install underneath your car. That way if something happened and Marcus lost track of you, I would still know your location. Tonight when you were going to Central Park, Brian got curious and called Marcus to see where you were heading. Marcus then tells Brian that you stopped in the middle of nowhere, got out your car, and then the rest you already know."

They stared at one another in that moment.

"Anyway," he said, walking back to the head of the other end of the table and took a seat. "Marcus was the head of our organization before I took over. He sat in this very spot I'm now sitting in. He ran almost all of Queens and Brooklyn – until he was arrested a few years back. I looked up to Marcus... followed his every moved to the very moment the police took and had him incarcerated. So you could almost imagine his surprise when he returned and I had taken over everything. He wanted to resume his role here, but by then it was too late. We had all moved on from his old school operations. Marcus was a good leader up until the moment he was arrested. And it was time for someone new, had a vision, and focus to taking charge."

"You mean someone as big as Marcus didn't even try to get his position back from you," Andrea replied curiously. She still couldn't believe that the man who she thought cared for her was really the man who wanted her dead.

"Not with a gun to his head, he didn't," Dean answered. "However, between you and me… I could never have Marcus killed. Not with the way I once looked up to Marcus, I just couldn't. I just thought somebody with a bit more power and strength needed to be the head of the organization. The only person I thought was good enough for the job was… me."

"Why did it have to be you?"

Dean leaned forward in his high back chair and answered, "Unlike Marcus… I have no soft spots. If something went down, Marcus didn't have it in him to do what needed to be done. However, I am resolute to handle situations properly." He looked back and forth to the four men sitting at the table who were all agreeing with him. "You wanna know something else… there used to be more of us than you see to sit around this table. What happened to them – I'm sure you are wondering. I dealt with each and every one of them that wasn't fit. As they say, a chain is only as strong as its weakest link. If someone was judged to be weak, messed up, or wanted out of the organization, I made sure they were dealt with. This way we stayed pure to our operation."

"So, you're telling me you were able kill to all of these people and do God knows what other illegal stuff without the police coming on to you?

"I mean we had a few leaks to come our way, but like I said... I always dealt with them. I would have immediately dealt you if I didn't owe Marcus a favor."

Andrea gave Dean a confused look. "You mean... Marcus was protecting me?" she asked.

"Yes... he was." Dean replied.

It all became a bit clearer to Andrea on Marcus's strange; however, nice doing and his saying '*Do as you're told.*' Even the moment they had in the church's bathroom became a clear message when Marcus pointed his gun in Andrea's face for the second. Marcus wasn't threatening Andrea to be afraid of him, but more of Dean.

Dean then stood back on his feet and walked back towards her. "Marcus weak ass probably would've done more for you – if Mark wasn't always with him. Mark was one who saw things the way I did. Marcus, on the other hand, saw you as a woman that happened to be in the right place at the very wrong time. He didn't think anything should happen to you for that very reason. And for the first time ever, Marcus put a gun to my head to convince me to leave you alone. I told him I would – as long as he kept an eye on you and let Brian keep his ears on you until we left the country. With all that going, I thought why I couldn't have a little fun in this."

"What do you mean keep ears on me?" she asked, looking up at him even more confused.

Dean went into his pants pocket and pulled out Andrea's cell. "You recognize this?" he asked.

"That's my phone," Andrea replied.

He opens the back and pulls out the battery. "This was our ears," he said, holding it to her face. "This is a micro miniature microphone design by Brian to keep tabs on you. This is how we knew your plans for tonight. You told little Miles you had a friend who was gonna protect you, just before he boarded the train. I had Eddie and Ray to mess up Ronking's apartment and make it look like he's was kidnapped to give you a reason to come here. I also believe you have the rights to know that this is how we found out you told your pastor about what you saw that night… and so I dealt with him."

"How could you!"

"I had too. You told him something that he didn't need to know." He answered, throwing the phone nearly across the table. "Besides, he didn't look too healthy anyway."

"You're the devil."

Dean gave a devilish grin as he walked behind Andrea and started rubbing her shoulders. "Well, if I remember correctly, you seemed to enjoy this devil last night," he said, moving his hand across Andrea's breast. "You were so soft and sweet, enjoying every bite of what I was doing to you, and you held me tight like you didn't wanna let me go."

Andrea felt disgusted as the thought of being intimate with this monster entered her mind. She tried the best she could to get Dean's hand from off her. She tightened up as her body felt very dirty. It was almost like she could still feel him inside of her. It was very unbelievable that it happened.

"You and Marcus have something in common," Dean told Andrea. "You both see me as something other than human. You see me as the devil and Marcus… well, he felt like Dr. Frankenstein and I was the creature that he created. He was the one who taught me the business and almost everything I know – I just exceed him. And like I said I had to prove to everyone I could be better than he was." He bent down to Andrea's level. "And I did become better when you helped me prove my point to Marcus. He actually believed you would've been able to keep your mouth shut with him scaring you, watching over you, and had a little paper threw your way. But I never believed you could. I knew sooner or later you'll crack from the stress and say something to the right person and guess what… you did… twice. You were too much of a risk to me just like your friend Montica."

At that instant, Andrea lost control of herself, "You son-of-a-bitch!" she shouted as she tried jumping up from her seat. "I swear I'm gonna fuckin' kill you!"

Dean laughed hard and loud at Andrea's outburst. "And you wanna know what's really funny, though?" he said. "You were the one that called me and told me yourself that Montica was still alive. Brian didn't even have to say a word to me. But don't stay mad at me sweetheart, I mean after all, it was Marcus – and not me who dealt with your friend, Alex. However, that's still a bit of a shock to me, because I've known Marcus to be strong and hard, to beat some ass with a pair of brass knuckles, but I've never known him to be able to pull the trigger. So I know him handling Alex couldn't have been an easy thing for him to do. Nor to have dumped his body someplace near the Williamsburg Bridge in the east river."

"Why?" Andrea cried.

"He got nosy. Started sticking his nose in our business," he answered. "It was like dealing with agent Martin Scott all over again when he went through my brother's things in his office and found information that would've blown this whole operation. Apparently, the bank hired him to pose as a janitor and part of his duties was to report unusual activates from things employees left around or put in the trash. It's amazing what people will tell you when you start burning them with a lighter."

"What operation?" she asked, hoping to get the answered to what she was in the middle of.

"Since you won't be able to tell anyone, I tell you. The big job I have been planning for years." Dean walked behind the two men who sat on the right side of the table. "This is my brother Jay," he introduced the man to his right. "He's been working at The First National Bank for little over a year. There, he access locates various accounts from different organizations, charities, and banks near Boston, New York, Philadelphia, Baltimore, and Charlotte and provide that information to Brian here," he introduces the man to his left. "Brian, being the computer whiz that he is, helped Jay get secretly to access selected accounts and work some technology magic that will divert funds, and then covered it up. He also developed the technology to prevent anyone including the Feds or anyone else from detecting what was being done."

"What are you trying to accomplish?"

"Not trying... doing..." Dean corrected Andrea. "Tonight we tend to gain a little over ten billion dollars from targeted accounts. Then, we're gonna disappear, with the funds. By morning, there's gonna be a lot of head scratching by those financial institutions, and their customers."

"You can't do that."

"Sure we can. When Brian gives the command on his computer, all the targeted funds will go into six different untraceable offshore accounts that no one, but we will know about. I thought it would be somewhat poetic to name the accounts using the last six poor bastards that gave their lives in the course of this operation. I only wish Marcus could've been here to witness the result of my plan which once active will only take about… say five minutes." He said, facing Brian.

"That's about right," Brian answered.

"Yeah, that's how long it's going to take for us to become multi-billionaires. No more operating like small time gangsters, which is what we were when Marcus was running things for the past ten years by selling drugs, getting protection money, and other assorted operations."

"So you killed all those people over money."

Dean chuckled. "I killed all those people because they got in the way. When Martin Scott found out what was going down in Jay's office, he went running to Lieutenant James Arthur who has been trying to get dirt on me for the past two years. Scott took it to Arthur who took it to Judge Thomas Williams. That man has been trying to lock me up for a long time as well."

"What about that District Attorney?"

"Steven Paige was building a case to take us all out, and would have made him a hero to the city. Judge Williams just added more fuel to Paige's fire. So I dealt with Paige first and then… well, you know the rest. I had to make sure nothing interfered with what we had going down. So when I found out that your friend Montica may have held some of Paige's information, I had to kill her too."

"But she didn't know anything about you or what was going on. She told me herself that she never got the information."

"That's what she said. Well, I couldn't take any chances... I was close to the end!"

There was silence in the room.

"We need to get moving. Our private jet is waiting for us at LaGuardia airport." Dean told everybody while still staring down to Andrea. "It was nice knowing you, Andrea. But I'm afraid this is where I leave you."

"I swear to God you won't get away with this," she cried. "I will get out of here and when I do you will be stopped."

"You keep thinking that," said Eddie, standing up from his seat. "Because right beneath the floor at this very moment is enough C-4 that is set to blow in..." he looked at his watch, "... eleven minutes."

"Yeah, we need to get outta here, because C-4 is no joke," Ray replied, eyeing Andrea with a creepy smile. "And plus... we have all those gas lines up under this warehouse, and it could leave quite a mess in this area."

"You see Andrea," said Dean, "You were never gonna live even with Marcus protecting you. And if the phone would've been in the room with us last night after you told me what you witnessed, Marcus probably would've come to his senses and killed you himself." He paused as he and Andrea stared at one another. "You always had death mark on you, Andrea, and now death is about to take you. No one will even know you were in here because there will be so little of you left. However, I do have to thank you for bring Ronking's car here. Don't know what your plan was or the reason for driving it here... but I'm glad you did. Give the police a little of a belief to who remains they may find."

"We need to get outta here now," Jay reminded.

"Then let's go," said Dean, giving Andrea strong eye contact for the last time. "Die well my love." He grabs a hold of Andrea's face and places a wet kiss on her lip, but then Andrea shook loose and spitted.

Without another word, they all made their way out the room and up the stairs, leaving Andrea to die.

CHAPTER TWENTY-THREE

"We're gonna have to drive through Astoria," shouted Jay when exiting the warehouse.

"Why is that?" asked Dean, opening the passenger side door of his black BMW 7 Series and eased in.

Once everybody was in and their doors were closed, Brian answered, "When Andrea first got here she shared with me that there was an accident on the highway. I looked it up and there's traffic backup for five miles."

"Well then, get us to LaGuardia airport the best way you know how," Dean told Jay. He then glanced back to the back seat to Brian who was sitting in between Eddie and Ray. "I want that money in those accounts before we get to the airport."

Brian clicked a few keys on his laptop. After keying in the last command and executed it, he looked up to Dean and said, "The money is transferring as we speak."

"Good," Dean replied as he turned to his brother. "Park over by 9th street," he ordered.

"We have to get to the airport."

"But we really don't wanna miss the fireworks before leaving, now do we?"

Jay started the engine, drove over to 9th street, and parked in the Precision Auto Works parking lot to where they had a good view of the warehouse when it blows.

Meanwhile, Andrea was fighting to free herself from the tape holding her to the chair. The tape was wrapped around her arms and ankles extremely tight. Andrea knew she wasn't going to be able to pull herself free in time. So she leaned forward as far as she could and started using her teeth to try ripping the tape apart. There was so much taped holding her down, but that didn't prevent Andrea from trying to come free before the explosives went off at any moment. Suddenly, the tape began coming lose. Andrea's teeth were starting to hurt, but she didn't stop. Finally, when the tape started to rip, she continued using her teeth while lifted her arm up hard to help the tape finally pull apart.

With one arm free, she used it to quickly start unwrapped the tape from around the other arm. Andrea was scared to death that she wasn't going to make it. She finally freed the other arm, quickly stood up, and tried heading out the same way Dean and the others did. However, before Andrea was able to take a stand forward, she nearly fell to the ground but grab a hold of the table before doing so. Relieved of getting her arms freed in time, she nearly forgot that her legs were also tied to the chair as well. This had Andrea becoming more frantic that she wouldn't beat the timer on the bomb.

Andrea planted both feet firmly on the ground, grabbed a hold of both ends of the chair, and used every last strength in her body to pull up harder. The chair slowly moved from in between her legs and the tape. When the chair finally came free, it flew a few feet away from Andrea, as she fell to the floor. As she reached for the table for support, Andrea saw a Walther TPH pistol lying under the table in something wet. It had fallen from its holder underneath the table when she caught her balance with the chair. Andrea quickly picked it up for in case she would need it if she made it out in time.

While holding the gun in hand, she pulled herself up off the floor, ran for the door and up the stairs. She was out of breath when she entered the big room she entered in when she first arrived there. Almost tripping on something, Andrea quickly caught her balance, made it out of the warehouse, and ran as far as she could just as the explosives went off. The force of the explosions lifted her off the ground and sent her flying across the lot along with lots of debris.

"Beautiful," said Dean with a smile. "We shouldn't have any problems now if we wanted to return in a few years, now should we?"

"No, we shouldn't," replied Jay, shifting the car into gear and pulling off down the 9th and turning over onto 21st.

The explosion blew debris all over the place and several buildings were now burning. One of the big doors from the building fell at an angle on Ronking's car and shielded Andrea from the rest of the debris.

When Andrea woke she was able to get from under the debris and enter the car from the other side. She remembered Dean saying he had a private plane wait for them at LaGuardia airport. With traffic backed up on the highway, she knew the next best way of getting there was down 21st street towards Hoyt Ave.

Throwing the gun in the passenger seat, Andrea pulled the car keys from the glove compartment and started the engine. After shifting the car into gear, she slammed her foot on the gas, quickly moving the car from under the debris, and tried catching up with Dean before they got too far – or made it to the airport.

"Is that money in the accounts yet?" inquired Dean.

"It's almost there," Brian answered. "It's taking a bit longer than I thought it would."

"As long as it gets there, I'm good."

Brian eyed the loading bar on his laptop nearly finished transferring the money. Then, only moments later, the laptop was reading:

TRANSFER COMPLETED

"Dean," Brian called.

"What?"

"The money has been –"

Brian was cut off when Andrea slams Ronking's car into the back of their vehicle. Andrea wasn't sure what she was doing, but with the anger, she had built up inside, made her want to try and do something to stop them from going any farther.

"What the…," Dean said, looking out the back window.

He got a good glance at Andrea right before she slammed the car into them again. Dean couldn't believe what he was seeing.

"Eddie and Ray… kill that bitch now!" Dean ordered.

"You got it…" they replied, rolling down their window, stuck out their guns, and shot straight at Andrea.

Four shot went through the windshield and missed hitting Andrea. She screamed as she ducked behind the steering wheel, taking her eyes off the road. When she looked back up, she was driving against several cars parked on the side of the Hoyt Avenue, and quickly got back on the road and continued to follow behind them.

"She's not giving up," shouted Ray.

"Put a bullet between her eyes or I'll put one between yours," Dean responded back with burning fire in his eyes.

With that being said, both Ray and Eddie stuck their guns back out the windows and fired more shots at Andrea.

Two more bullets shot through the windshield, she ducked in time again behind the steering wheel. When Andrea raised her head again to look, she had steered the car to the opposite side of the street, with another car coming directly towards her. She quickly swerved back over to the right lane and pushed her foot flat down on the gas. They were only a few feet away from an intersection. Andrea once more slammed Ronking's car into the back right of Dean's, causing it to hit the corner of the sidewalk, flips upside down, and slide through into the intersection.

Andrea loses control of Ronking's vehicle before it finally stops a few feet away from where Dean and his men were.

After coming to a stop in the middle of the street, Dean used his elbow to break out the remainder of what was left of his window. Climbing out, he found himself looking eye to eye with Eddie who was hanging out of his window dead. He was crushed by the car when it flipped, and Dean knew if Eddie was killed while hanging out the window, then Ray would probably be the same. He looked around for a moment and didn't see a sight of Andrea, although, he did see the wrecked smoking car that she was driving. However, that wasn't Dean's primary concern; his mind was on his brother.

He slowly came around to the other side of the car, got down on one knee, and broke open Jay's window with the same elbow he used to break his. "Jay, are you alright?" he asked.

"Yeah… I'll live," Jay answered, trying to get out through the broken glass with the help of his younger brother.

Dean placed Jay's arm around his neck and helped him out of the car.

"Sweet Jesus," Jay said when his eyes saw Ray's crushed dead body.

"Yeah, Eddie's the same way," Dean replied.

"What are we gonna do now?"

"… We need to get to the airport before Carl and Archie decide not to wait on us any longer."

"And how the hell are we gonna get there?"

"Let's just find another car, hot wire it, and get the hell outta here, before the police get around here. And I'm not gonna rot in jail."

"Then let's get a move on it."

They weren't even one step away from the upside down the car when Jay heard coughing from the backseat.

"Brian…" Jay shouted. "We have to get him out."

"No, just leave him," Dean told him.

"Dean we have to help him. Without him, the money is lost."

"No, it's not," he replied with a big smile. "Brian gave me a copy of the account information and I have it right now." He patted to his inner coat pocket. "It's in a code only I understand – and if you're lucky, I'll teach it to you. So, I know where the money is and how to get it." Dean stared his brother in the eyes before saying, "Now, let's you and I go to the islands, sit by the beach with a cool drink, and some of the finest women we will ever see in this world. It'll be just you, me and a whole lot of bread."

"That sounds like a plan, brother," Jay replied with a smile.

"Then let's go."

Continuing their way around the car, Dean heard a gun fired just before hearing Jay fall. When Dean turned he found his brother on the ground with a bullet wound in his back. Before Dean could find where the shot came from, Andrea fired another shot at him but missed by an inch. Dean pulls the same silver gun he always used and fired three shots at Andrea who quickly ducked behind Ronking's car.

Not sure if he got Andrea or not, Dean got down on one knee to see if his brother still alive. "Jay," he whispered with his voice sounding like he was about to cry. Jay was his only brother – the only living blood relative he had, and now he was gone. "No." He grieved over his brother's dead body.

Andrea came out from hiding and fired another bullet at Dean, who quickly ducked and rolled behind his upside down car. She missed, and fired another round that too again missed. It became a gun fight between the two of them, Dean fired five straight shots at Andrea and then again ducked when Andrea shot back but missed yet again.

Dean's anger and grief had prevented him for aiming correctly. Trying to get a good shot, he took aim and shot his last two bullets. Without another clip to reload, Dean had no more use for the gun, threw it to the ground, and decided to make a run for it. Andrea fired a shot and missed Dean's left foot as he ran up the steps to a nearby house with a 'For Sale' sign in the yard. Dean smashed opened the window, unlocked the door, and enter inside.

Andrea carefully came from behind the car, pointing the gun directly at the open door of the house Dean run into. She saw a few spectators hiding from gunshots, and several were using their cell phones to take videos and snap pictures from a distance. Andrea slowly headed towards the house. She was slightly more than terrified about following Dean inside but knew she had to stop him before he got away and continued hurting good people, including all whose money he was stealing. Andrea was hoping one of the spectators had least called the police and they would arrive before she went any further.

Standing to the side of the house's front door, Andrea still wasn't hearing any sirens coming. So, without a second thought, she took a deep breath and entered the dark house which was under a bit of construction. There was a sound of a door closing from upstairs, and Andrea quickly pointed the gun up there. She tried easing up the staircase without making any noise. If Dean didn't hear her coming up, then she thought she could detain him until the police arrived.

Once reaching the top of the stairs, Andrea tried to use the lights coming in from the windows to make out where Dean was trying to hide. As she quietly scans for any clues of Dean's position, she caught the sight of a black coat hanging out of the closet nearly touching the floor in the first bedroom she came across. Andrea pointed the gun directly at the closet while taking small steps into the room, seemly unaware that she was breathing heavy from being scared. When she was about half to the closet, she opened her mouth to tell Dean that she had him covered and not to move.

However, Andrea wasn't able to say anything before Dean came out of nowhere, grabbed the gun straight out of Andrea's hand, and slamming her down to the ground.

"You shouldn't have tried to play hero," he said, pointing the gun at Andrea's head.

Andrea eyes filled with fear for she knew she was about to die.

Dean pulled the trigger, and all that was heard was a click. The gun was empty.

And like that, Andrea fear turned to rage when she pulled back and kicked Dean as hard as she could in his knees, causing him to fall onto the floor alongside her. Quickly Andrea stood to her feet and headed for the room.

"Where do you think you're going?" Dean shouted, grabbing Andrea by her left ankle and pulled her back down to the floor. He let Andrea go when she kick him again in the face, causing his mouth to bleed.

Andrea struggled to get up again but succeeded. So did Dean. He grabs Andrea by the hair and through her into the mirror that was attached to the wall. The mirror shattered into several pieces and falls on top of Andrea as she lay still, slightly dazed from hitting her head.

Turning Andrea around, Dean climbed on top and had her looking into his eyes. "I should've killed you the moment I found you," he swore in Andrea's face just before throwing a punch. "But no... I had to go and listen to Marcus's dumb ass and look at what all you've done!" He threw another punch across Andrea's face just before grabbing a hold of her neck and started choking her. "You're gonna die tonight, Andrea Harris. You're gonna die."

Unable to breathe, Andrea felt around the floor for a sharp piece of the mirror. When her right hand felt a piece that might have been good to use, she picked it up and shoved it into Dean's thigh, causing him to yell and fall over from on top of her. Andrea quickly got up, stormed out the room and downstairs to get out of there.

Dean yanked the piece of mirror out of his thigh and kept it in hand to use himself as he slowly stood up. He ignored the pain from his leg as he tried catching up with Andrea. When coming up to the front door, Dean suddenly stopped. It came to him that Andrea may not have run out of the house as he closed the door and started walking through the dark lower part of the house.

"I know you're still in here, Andrea," he said, taunting her. "Now where are you hiding?" Dean opens the first closet door he came across and then slammed it back when he saw that it was empty. "You know... just a moment ago you showed me where your punk ass son gets his lack of fighting skills from. You should have seen him tonight trying to fight back and get away from me, but he wasn't good enough to do so."

Andrea stood in the dark, listening to Dean, with rage building.

"I sure you're wondering why I did it. I had to send you a clear message that we were coming for you." He stood still in the middle of the room, trying to listen for Andrea over his own heavy breathing. He continued trying to bait her, "I think you got my message loud and clear because you made the move of getting your family out of town and thought you were gonna testify against us. You thought good old Detective Ronking could help you. But now… you gotta realize your pitiful plan has failed and that you're gonna die. Then guess what I'm gonna do afterward. I'm going to Concord, New Hampshire and take out your mother… and children. See, I know you told your mother everything, and I just can't leave any loose strings hanging. Then, all four of you will be one big happy family in the other world with your beloved Charles."

"You stay away from my family!" shouted Andrea, busting out another closet, swinging a metal bar. She hit Dean across his skull, knocking him to the floor, against a few paint cans stacked nearby.

"You stupid bitch," Dean shouted, moving quickly to get up.

Andrea hit Dean across the face, keeping him down. She repeatedly hit him over and over again across the skull. Suddenly, thoughts begin flashing through Andrea's mind, and every thought caused her rage to get bigger as she swung the metal bar against Dean's face. The first thought was the night she witnessed Dean killing those three men. Second, the morning Marcus found her and held her against the wall by her neck. Third, the nights Marcus killed Alex and the night Dean killed Montica. Then, the last thought that went through Andrea's head was an image of Dean beating Miles.

After realizing Dean wasn't going to be able to hurt anyone anymore, Andrea dropped the bloody pole and slowly backs away from Dean's seemingly dead body that was covered in blood. Then, at last, she heard the sound of sirens coming from up the street.

Scared for what would happen next, Andrea slowly headed towards the front door. That was until she was turned around and forced against the door. Andrea was looking Dean in his deform face as he tried using the last bit of strength he had left in his body to choke her. But with Andrea being a bit stronger than him, she kicks Dean between the legs, which got his hand from around her neck. Then, she smashed her hand into his face, causing Dean to fall back and puncher his neck against something sharp on the floor.

Stepping forward, Andrea stood over Dean's lifeless body the same way he used to stand over his victims. "Are we done?" she asked and receive no answer.

CHAPTER TWENTY-FOUR

Several dead bodies, shoot-outs, murders, and fires were nothing new to many of the cops in the city, but this was something else. Many Detectives, officers and CSI teams from all over the city were involved with the investigation and were working around the clock on all the crime scenes from the previous night. There was a team working on the Central park murders, the abandoned warehouse explosions, and on the area where three dead bodies were found by two wrecked and another on the inside of a nearby house. The answer to a question many wanted to know was, 'Who was responsible for the mayhem?' There were different stories coming from some of the conflicting eyewitnesses. Some of them said it was a man. A few told that it was a woman. Some ever said that there were two to three people. Many came out and said they didn't see or hear anything.

"First a triple homicide, now this," said Detective Sheppard from the Queens Police Department. "Life in New York is never boring."

"I've been saying the same thing for years," replied Detective Brown as he viewing some of the evidence that was collected at the scene. "Who could have done something like this?"

"I don't know. The witnesses are certainly no help, but whoever did it must have been really deranged to kill seven people.

"Maybe... who knows?"

"Hello boys," said Lieutenant Clint Troy upon entering the Crime Management Center investigation room with a much older man. "How are things coming along in here?"

"Everything is going fine," both Sheppard and Brown answered.

"That's good," Troy replied, turning to the man next to him. "Fellows, I would like you all to meet Detective Robert Smith from the Manhattan Special Investigations Division. Robert, this is Detective Phillip Sheppard and Detective Terence Brown."

"Nice to meet both of you," Smith said, shaking both Detective's hands.

"I asked Robert to come join us," said Troy, "because I wanted him to look through some of the evidence that we collected to see if last night's event had anything to do with the triple homicide case he's working on."

"Oh okay," said Brown. "From what was collected from the scene I wouldn't say that it was, but you never know."

"Well, what kind of evidence do you have?" Smith asked.

Sheppard held up a clipboard read the from the printed list, "Two crashed cars: one 2013 black BMW 7 Series and one 2006 silver Lexus

LS430, a laptop, a blood covered metal bar, a nickel plated Sig Sauer p220 elite handgun, a Walther TPH pistol, and a few shell casings. There were four dead bodies and one poor bastard in custody. Unfortunately, he's not conscious to answer any questions we have at the moment."

"Were there any identification found on them?" asked Smith.

"Yes, when we ran their data, we manage to find an identity on all seven of them."

"Seven? I thought you said there were five men found at the scene."

"Lieutenant Hawkins's Evidence Collection Team is investigating the two dead bodies that were found in Central Park, and they appeared to be tied with the five we have."

"Well is there anything you can tell us about them?" asked Troy.

Brown picked up seven folders and handed them over to Troy and Smith. "Three of them were in the system," He told them, before they started looking through the folders. "They were flagged in the DA's office as a person of interest as part of a special investigation. The two that was found in Central Park is still being looked at to ascertain their identities. And as for the last two, we did manage to get their identity and find out that they were siblings. Their names were Jay and Dean Jackson."

"Did you say Dean Jackson?" asked Smith, looking up from the file he was holding.

"Yes sir, I did. Does the name mean anything to you?"

"Yeah, Lieutenant Arthur told me about him just before he was killed. He didn't tell me much, though. Other than he was a person of interest. What happen to him?"

"According to the preliminary autopsy," Sheppard started explaining, "he was beaten with the metal bar and then fell on the edge of a toolbox with a handsaw hanging out on the side. The saw was weighted down by other tools, and was able to puncher his neck and cut his artery, causing him to bleed out." He paused and stared at Smith. "If you were to ask me, I'll say he must've really pissed someone off for this to have happened to him."

"Yeah, but there's something else you should know," said Brown, "His fingerprints were found on two of the guns we recovered. The Sig Sauer p220 we found on the street ten feet from the BMW that was upside down, and on a Walther TPH pistol found upstairs of the house where Dean's body was found. There were another set of prints found on the Walther TPH pistol, but unfortunately, the CSI team said they couldn't get clean readings of them. Also, whoever used the metal rod must've tried cleaning it, because the lab couldn't get any readable prints off it either."

"Hmmm, that's odd," Troy exclaimed.

"What about the two cars?" Smith asked, moving to the next piece of evidence. "Was there anything out of the ordinary in them?"

"The BMW was registered to Dean Jackson. That's where the laptop was located. But unfortunately, we can't tell you much about that laptop, because it has some type of weird security lock on it, and I mean tight too. Firewalls, passwords, and a whole lot more. CSU is working on it to see if they can break the security or get data off the hard drive."

"So," said Troy, "Whatever is on that laptop may have to do with what happen last night and why."

288

"It's possible... who knows," Brown said as he picked up a folder and open it. "As for the Lexus... it belongs to Detective Justin Ronking who's from your department, Smith."

"Are you sure about that?" asked Smith looking very shock.

"Yes sir."

Smith went into deep thought.

"Do you think he could've had anything to do with this?" Troy asked.

"I hope not," Smith said, facing to Troy. "But I haven't heard anything from him in a week since he –" Smith's phone started vibrating. He pulled it from his inner jacket pocket and answered it without looking at the ID. "Excuse me for a moment," he said, placing the phone to his ear then while heading towards an empty area. "Robert Smith..."

 There was no answer.

"Hello..." he said then waited for a response.

"Is there any way we can meet?" someone finally answers.

Smith removed the phone from his ear to have a look at the caller ID but found that it was a blocked call. "Who is this?" he asked, placing the phone back to his ear.

"I can't tell you that just yet," the caller replied. "I have some information that can help you with that triple homicide and what happen in Astoria last night."

"You know something about these two events?"

"I know more then what I wanna know... and I will tell you everything if you meet me alone."

"If you're trying to waste my time –"

"– Believe me, if I wanted to waste somebody's time it wouldn't be yours. I have information that won't be found at those crime scenes. I'm the only person who knows what you need to know to close at least the triple homicide case. If you meet me somewhere alone I will tell you everything."

Smith thought for a moment. Not sure if he was making the right move, he looked around the room before replying, "Where and when?"

"There a place call *Stella's coffee shop* in Harlem. Come as soon as you can get away."

Without waiting for a response, the caller hung up.

Smith placed his phone back in his jacket pocket and walked back over towards Troy. "I have to leave for a while," he told him. "I'll be back shortly."

"Is everything alright?" Troy asked.

"Everything is fine," he answered, taking a few steps backward. "I just have to make a quick run, but I'll be right back. I want to go over some more of the evidence that was collected." He turned around and walked out of the department.

Detective Smith surveyed the site and carefully entered through the doors of Stella's coffee shop in Harlem, without any backup or anybody standing by. He stood still for a moment as he quickly looked around the coffee shop, before taking a seat in a nearby booth. Smith looked around once more and saw that there were only seven customers in the place. None of them looked like they would've matched the voice from the phone call he received earlier.

"Can I get anything for you, sir?" asked a waitress who came out of nowhere. She had her pen and pad ready to write down his order.

"I'll have a cup of coffee," Smith answered. "Make that two... I'm expecting someone."

"Can I interest you in a slice of hot apple pie?" the waitress inquired.

"No thanks," he answered.

"Okay, two cups of coffee, coming right up," she said, walking away from the table.

Waiting patiently, Smith kept wondering who he was meeting and why. He would have never come if the person he spoke with hadn't mentioned something about the triple homicide and what happened last night.

"You're Detective Robert Smith?" asked someone standing slightly behind Smith.

Smith looked back to whoever it was standing behind him. "I am," he answered. He wasn't sure of what to think when he saw a woman standing there in dark sunglasses, a swollen cheek, and a busted lip.

"You came alone?"

"I did... Won't you have a seat?" Robert said with holding his hand out the booth across from him.

Very nervous, she slid into the booth without taking her eyes off Smith.

"So, what can I do for you Miss.?"

"… Harris… Andrea Harris." She answered, removing her sunglasses and revealed her swollen left eye. "I thought you should be the person I finally talk to about this whole thing."

"May I ask how you know me?"

"I saw you on the news about the triple homicide… and that's why I wanted to talk only to you about this."

"Well, Ms. Harris… you told me over the phone that you knew something about the triple homicide and what happen over in Astoria last night."

Andrea shook her head. "That's right," she answered. "I wish I could've come to you a long time ago with this and maybe… just maybe what happen last night wouldn't have happened the way it did. Maybe everything that happened after that night in the garage wouldn't have happened if I would've just gone to the police after I saw what I saw."

The waitress returns to the table with the two cups of coffee placed right in front of Smith and Andrea before walking away again.

"What exactly are you talking about Ms. Harris?"

Taking a deep breath, Andrea looked Smith in his blue eyes and very seriously answered, "I witnessed those three men being murdered that night."

Letting out a chuckle as if a joke was said, Smith replies, "You did what?"

"The triple homicide – in the garage – I saw it – I witnessed it."

"If this is some kind of joke, it isn't funny. We've had over twenty people confess to the crime, and have God know how many useless

292

tips. So, if you're looking to get something out of this, it's not going to work."

"I'm not joking or making this up," Andrea snapped while trying to keep her voice down. "I saw it… from the moment they were tied down on the ground to the moment the bullets were shot into their bodies. I've been trying to wipe it from my mind ever since it happened, but I can't. I can barely sleep at night because of it. I'm tired of being afraid."

Smith looked deep into Andrea's eyes and saw she was serious about what she was saying. He then asked, "If you saw all of this then why didn't you go straight to the police after it occurred?"

"I was scared and wasn't thinking straight. I was trying to pretend that it never happened, but it wasn't working. The very next morning I was gonna tell the police, but they found me. I didn't believe they would've, but they did. They threaten to kill me and my family if I went to the police."

"Who are they?" Smith asked as he took a sip out of his coffee, unsure if he should try believing in anything Andrea was telling him.

"The five men you found in Astoria and the two you've probably already found in Central park. They're the ones that killed the Lieutenant, Lawyer, and the other guy that was undercover at the bank or something like that. They even killed that District Attorney that went missing."

Unable to believe what she was now saying, Smith gave Andrea a look before replying, "Ms. Harris, the men we found in Astoria and Central park are all dead. So I'm sure those couldn't be the men you are referring to, are you?"

"Yes, those are the ones that I'm referring to. Two of them – the two that were in Central park, followed me around every day and night, from work to home and wherever else I went to make sure I didn't go to the police. I even found out that they bugged my cell phone to listen in on every conversation I had with anyone I was with."

Smith continued giving Andrea more confused looks as she told her story. "Ms. Harris," he said in deep thought. "Your story is really not making any sense at all. You're saying that these men are dangerous criminal that you witness do a crime, and now they're dead and you're still alive. How did that come to happen?"

Making eye contact, Andrea answered, "… because I killed them."

"You… killed them… all by yourself?" Smith asked with his head turn to the side.

"I'm not making this up. Do you think I would do this to myself?" She pointed to her face. "I know you don't believe me, I don't believe it myself." She paused as tears built up in her eyes. "But you gotta believe me. This whole thing has been a nightmare I really wanna wake up from. Many people started dying around me… people close to me… they even hurt my child, and that's what drew the line for me and declared that this had to end, one way or another. I don't know how I managed to do it, but I did."

"So you're telling me that scene in Astoria was done by you… and you alone"

Andrea took a deep breath. "… Yes…" she replied. "If I hadn't done anything, they would've gotten away and continued hurting and killing innocent people – including my family."

"Ms. Harris if what you are telling me is true… you're telling me that no one around you was able to see what was going on."

"I had a close friend named Alex Anderson who was seeing those two men following me around and got too close to them. They killed him and threw him in the East River."

"And how do you know this?"

Wiping away a few tears, Andrea answered, "They told me… they told me everything. I guess they wanted to impress me about their deeds and to let me know just how big and bad they were before killing me in that warehouse explosion off the river last night." Andrea took a few second to remember everything she was told. "God knows he really fooled me into thinking I was safe and was gonna be alright. He had me feeling like he cared."

"Who are you talking about?"

"Their leader… he killed a police detective and pretended to be him to prove a point about me to one of his men." She sat silent again in thought. "I mistakenly trusted him and risked my life for something that I thought was real and turned out to be a great big lie."

"Risk your life how?" asked Smith.

"I risked my life when I thought the leader was actually a police detective that they kidnapped on account of me. They told me if I met them alone at that warehouse and didn't notify the police both the detective and me would've walked away. If not, we both would've died. They said they were watching me and would've known if I did anything funny. They even knew I killed those men in Central Park. I know it was foolish, but I risked it because I thought I was risking my life to save and walk away from all this with who I thought was my friend."

"So you risked your life to save a police detective you hardly knew?"

"Well…" she paused as she leads back in the booth. "There's more to that story I don't wanna talk about." She looked away from Detective Smith.

It didn't take long for Smith to understand why Andrea wished not to say any more about why she risked her life to save someone she hardly knew. What Smith didn't understand is how things had gotten that far if what he was hearing was indeed true.

"May I ask what the detective's name was the leader was posting as?" Smith asked of curiosity.

"Ronking… Detective Justin Ronking…"

Smith gave Andrea a look of shock. "I don't believe it," he replied. "This can't be true."

"You still don't believe?" she asked.

Taking a deep breath, Smith stared Andrea in the eyes. "I'm starting to," he answered. "You see I'm close with the Ronking family. Joey Ronking was a dear friend of mine and was one of the best detectives in New York killed on a case nearly thirteen years ago. His son Justin Ronking wanted to follow in his father footsteps and become a detective in the big. So he moved back to New York five years after he and his family moved to North Carolina. Now, last Thursday, I received word that Justin went on leave, because of a family emergency. When I tried to call Justin to see what was going on, his phone kept going straight to voicemail. So I call his mother in Raleigh and asked how everything was going. She told me everything was fine and that she hadn't heard from Justin in over a week."

The conversation stalled again.

"Which one of the men was it posting as Justin?" Smith asked, putting together all the piece of Andrea's story. "Do you even know any of these men names?"

Andrea looked straight into Smith's eyes, very serious, and without a struggle, she answered, "It was Dean Jackson."

"Oh dear God," he replied, becoming more convince Andrea was telling the truth after hearing her say Dean's name. "What more can you tell me?"

Andrea began telling more details to what Dean shared with her. She told Detective Smith about the strange relationship with Marcus, and how Dean took over the organization to prove that he was a much better leader with more ambitions ideas.

"You said something about them doing an operation," Smith asked as he couldn't get over the news of Justin was dead. "Can you tell me what that operation was and maybe it could answer a lot of questions for us?"

"They were working on some elaborate operation to steal a bunch of money from organizations and charities from banks located in..." She struggles as she thought of each cities names Dean said. "New York..., Boston, Baltimore..., Philadelphia, and... Charlotte. One of them was like some kinds of computer genius helping Dean's brother access numerous accounts and other information while working at the First National Bank. I'm not sure if they succeeded or not, but if they did then the money is in six untraceable offshore accounts."

Smith thought about what was said to him back at the police department. "Now that might explain why that laptop is locked down so tight."

Andrea looked at Smith for a moment before saying, "I know the names the accounts are under. I'll give them to you if you don't take me in."

"They told you the names?"

"Yes. And I will give you all of them if you don't take me in."

Smith didn't say a word. He sat and looked at Andrea knowing he couldn't let her go if what she was saying was the truth; by her accounts, she killed seven people.

"Please," she cried. "I know how it works. But after everything I've gone through, I just really wanna go home and be with my family and act as if none of this ever happened."

Still sitting quiet, Smith thought long and hard before saying, "If you are sure the money is in those accounts and you give them to me... then I'm sure I can help you."

Breathing easy, Andrea replied, "Really?"

"But you're gonna have to come with me to the station."

"No," she cried with tears building up in her eyes. "I can't go to..."

Reaching across the table, Smith placed his hand upon Andrea's. "Ms. Harris, listen to me," he said softly, "If you do as I say... then I promise you... you will walk away from all this and won't ever have to look back on it again."

"How?" she asked, trying to calm herself down, seeing that Smith wanted to help her.

"Trust me," he replied. "I know the right people. Just let me take you into the station and get your statement about what happened at Central Park and the events that happened in Astoria last night, and then we can take it from there."

"Are you sure about this?" Andrea asked.

"Stop worrying and just come with me," Smith ordered Andrea as he placed money on the table for the coffee, alone with a five dollar tip. He then led Andrea out to his car and helped her in the back seat without putting any cuffs on.

CHAPTER TWENTY-FIVE

Smith had Andrea processed the moment they arrived at the station. Andrea had fingerprinted and had DNA samples taken for the investigation – even collected the tape from around Andrea's pant leg. While she was being processed, Smith made a few phone calls to the DA's Office, and to his friend, Agent Mike Harper of the FBI.

While Andrea was in unofficial police custody in the interrogation room, Detective Smith made sure the injuries on Andrea's face and right arm were properly treated. Afterwards she sat still with a cup of coffee and passed the time away by staring at herself in the two-way mirror in front of her.

Smith eyed Andrea from the other side of the two-way mirror, wondering how she had involved herself in the shooting in Central Park and Astoria. As Smith stood quietly in the room, the door opened, and in walked his long time friend, Agent Mike Harper.

Mike closed the door and then stood next to Smith.

"Is that her?" he asked.

Still eyeing Andrea, Smith answered, "Yeah, that's her. For the past three hours, we've been looking into everything she told us and it all turns out to be true."

Harper couldn't help but eye Andrea the way Smith was. "She doesn't look like someone who could've done all this," he replied.

"I know," Smith agreed. "We've looked into her background and found that she's just an everyday hard working single mother. I guess the saying is true... Hell has no fury like a woman scorned." "He then changed the subject from Andrea. "By the way, did you send a team to check out the East River?"

"Yeah, about that..." Harper paused. "We sent a team to search the East River like you asked, and so far five bodies were found at the bottom of a cinder block attached to them. We're gonna have them all identified, however, there won't be any need for one."

"And why is that?"

"'Cause there's no doubt that it's Steven Paige."

Smith continued eyeing Andrea, very pleased that she came to him.

Andrea was then taken to the fourth floor personal by Smith to a conference room. Two other people were already waiting very patiently in there.

After sitting Andrea down in the chair at the end of the table, Smith started introducing everyone in the room. "Andrea, this is Lieutenant Clint Troy and District Attorney Amelia P. Evans. You've already met

301

Agent Mike Harper. They're all here to verify a few things with you. So take your time answering any questions that they ask." He then looked to everyone in the room. "This interview is confidential. So nothing said here should go to the press."

DA Evans who was sitting on the other end of the table spoke first. "Ms. Harris, I'm gonna be reading the statement you've given to Detective Smith. If anything here is not correct, please let us know." She began, "You stated that you witnessed the triple homicide committed on Wednesday, April 10th, 2013. The homicide happened at the hands of (Dean Jackson). He was the leader of the seven men involved in the crime. Is that correct?"

Very slowly, Andrea answered, "Yes."

"You stated that after you witnessed the homicide you were too afraid to report it to the police. Then, because you were still out on your own, you were found by (Marcus Van Adams) who threaten the lives of you and your family if you went to the police. He also followed you around with his son (Marcus Van Adams Jr.) to insure that you didn't go to the police. In addition, they bugged your phone to listen to all of your conversations when and wasn't on the phone."

"That's correct."

"Within time, Mr. Jackson killed (Detective Justin Ronking) and posed as him to confirm with Mr. Van Adams that you were too much of a risk to have to walk around with information of that night. Also, during that time (Mr. Alex Anderson), (Pastor J.R. Mansell), and (Mrs. Montica Summer) were all murdered, because they became involved in what was happening. Mr. Jackson was making it seem as if he was looking into it while posing as Detective Ronking."

Andrea exhaled, "Yeah."

Lieutenant Troy then started talking, "Ms. Harris, we verified part of your story from videos and images that were uploaded online last night. Now, due to it being after dark when the crime occurred, we couldn't find a clear image of you. So, can you please clarify for us if that was you shooting (Jay Jackson) in the back, and then followed Dean Jackson into the house where his body was found?"

Andrea just shook her head yes.

"Did you kill Dean Jackson in that house after he did this to you?" He pointed to Andrea's face with a pen.

Andrea slowly shook her head again. "I felt like I had no choice," she said. "They killed my friends…, and they hurt my son. I'm sorry. All of this wouldn't have happened if I would have come to you that night the moment I got away. But I was too scared. I just didn't want to get involved. But I knew if I hadn't done something, they would be still out there killing innocent people, and I didn't want that. I didn't want anybody else out there feeling the way I do or witnessing what I did." Tears began to form in her eyes.

The room fell silent for a brief moment before Agent Harper began speaking.

"Now, before you killed Dean," he said, "you stated that he informed you that he had organized a plan to steal money from various organizations such as charities and banks out of New York, Boston, Philadelphia, Baltimore, and Charlotte. The money was put into six different untraceable offshore accounts. To help him pull this off, he brought in his brother, Jay Jackson, who provided accounts information from The First National Bank. They also worked with (Brian Carlo), who assisted in the transfer of the funds." Harper then looked to Andrea and said, "We looked into it and found that between all of the organizations, they stole a little over ten billion dollars. Now within your statement, you said that you know the names of the offshore accounts of which the money is in. Correct?"

"I do," Andrea answered.

"Write them down for us," Smith said, placing a pen and pad down in front of Andrea. "Andrea," Smith said softly as it looked to him that she wasn't gonna write the names. "If you help us then we can help you. We need the information to access those accounts."

Feeling that there was no way out, Andrea grabbed the pen and wrote down as much information as she could about the accounts. She wasn't able to provide any account numbers, but she was able to give a name for each.

When she was finished, Smith picked up the pad and looked at the list and became a bit confused about the names that were listed. "Are you sure these are the names the accounts are under?" he asked.

"I'm sure. Dean told me himself those were the names the accounts were gonna be under," she altered the truth a little. Dean didn't give her each name the accounts were under but had given her an idea.

"So," Smith said, still looking at the names, "he transferred the money into untraceable offshore accounts under the names of his last six victims he killed."

"What is gonna happen to me now?" Andrea asked.

With everything said and done, DA Evans leaned forward in her seat, eyed Andrea and replied, "Ms. Harris, the city of New York doesn't want any of our citizens to take matters of the law into their own hands, and we certainly don't approve of vigilantes." She paused as she and Andrea looked at one another in silence for a few seconds. "However, Steven Paige was a dear friend of mines. I also knew Montica Summers. I think you have done this city of great service by ridding us of this vile scum, and I personally feel you have endured enough crap. So, my office isn't going to charge you with any crimes. However…, we're gonna ask that you don't leave the city for the next few weeks. That is, until the police have wrapped up everything. I'm going to write this as… self-defense."

All heads nodded in agreement.

DA Evans continued, "Okay, well, let's just remember that the information we got here is confidential. Label this informant: eight hundred and seven, and put it in the investigation file." She viewed the time on the clock hanging over the conference room door and noted the time. "I believe we're all done here, gentlemen."

Everyone begin leaving the room and started making phone calls.

Andrea looked to Smith, very confused. "With everything that I've done," she said, "how can they just let me go?"

Smith looked back to Andrea and replied, "I told you… I know the right people."

It became quite in the room.

"Now, can I give you a ride anywhere?" Smith asked, breaking the silence.

The case wasn't yet closed, but Andrea was able to walk away, alive.

EPILOGUE

Three and a half months later

It appeared the nightmare Andrea was living in was over. Using the information given, the DA and Detectives persuaded Brian to give full testimony on Dean and his crew's action. They caught the remaining members of Dean's crew and were all sent to prison for a very long time. Andrea received a nice reward for helping recover all the stolen money from the bank heist. She put the money aside until she felt ready to use on a nice place for Miles, Ted, and herself.

After Andrea brought her family back home, you would've thought things had gone back to normal. But after everything Andrea has gone through, things didn't really seem the same to her anymore. She lost two best friends, she killed, and she came close to losing her own life. Those are things nobody would really get over, but she tries to act as if they never happened. And every day Andrea's family tries to help keep her mind from it as well.

Not long after that night, Andrea did what she said she would do. She went to Alex's lawyer and got custody his son Jordan. And like she promised Alex, she loved and was going to raise Jordan as if he was her own. Every time Andrea looked into Jordan's blue eyes it was like looking right into his father's. Miles and Ted were learning to love Jordan like a brother, and Thelma came to love him because Andrea loved him.

Ms. Blakemore signed the café over to Andrea and moved back to England. She still called to see how everything was going go the café and made sure Andrea wasn't having any problems now that she was not only the manager but the owner as well. And since Alex was gone, Andrea made Hakeem the assistant manager since he was the next best person working there, and then hired a new waitress. Even as the manager and owner, Andrea still enjoys working up front serving the customers like a waitress.

Every week or so, Andrea and her friend's Shanequa and Felicia would still go out to lunch and hang out every other Friday nights. It wasn't the same now that Montica was gone, but they made the best of it. Andrea never told them the truth about Montica or that she was a little responsible for her death. But it was reported on the news that Dean was the one who killed her.

A few times a month they all would drop by to see how Brice and Destiny were doing. Brice would often go through moments of depression and his daughter was his only source of joy. Destiny missed her mother, and would become sad from time to time. Andrea, Felicia, and Shanequa did all they could to help them through the situation. Brice was considering moving because the house held too many memories.

On a Friday afternoon, Andrea waited patiently on the edge of the examination table for her doctor to return with her results of her visit. With the way she's been feeling for the past few weeks, she had hopes that nothing too serious was happening with her body.

"Okay, Mrs. Harris," said a female doctor, entering the room with a folder in hand. "I have your results of your physical."

"So you can tell me why I've been feeling sick and always seem tired?" Andrea asked.

"I sure can."

"It's nothing serious is it? That accident I was in a few months ago was bad, and I hope I didn't wait too long to get looked at."

"Well, believe me that accident has nothing to do with what's going on with you at all."

"That's good to know," Andrea said, very relieved.

Detective Smith had made sure all Andrea's visible injuries from Dean's beaten were properly treated, however, her full body wasn't examined after she repeatedly crashed the front of Ronking's car into the back of Dean's.

"Yeah, I can assure that the symptoms you're having are all completely natural."

"In what way are they natural?"

"Well, according to your blood work, Andrea… you're pregnant."

Andrea stared at the doctor in sheer disbelief to the news she was given. "What?" she asked.

"You're pregnant," the doctor repeated.

"No," Andrea said, trying to breathe normally. "That can't be. I haven't…" She paused as her mind flashed back to the night she and Dean got together and did things she's been regretting since the moment she learned the truth. "Oh God, no… please no," she cried.

The doctor could tell that this was not good news for Andrea. "I'm taking this wasn't a planned pregnancy," she replied.

"This is something that shouldn't have happened at all."

It wasn't the first time the doctor heard those word from a patient. "Well, let's do an ultrasound, and I could tell you how far along you are," she responded.

"Okay," Andrea agreed.

"If you will, lie back on the table and I'll get everything setup."

Andrea did as she was told and laid back on the table while the doctor set up for the ultrasound to be done. Once everything was ready, the doctor lifted Andrea's shirt and placed the probe to Andrea's abdomen. They both looked at the monitor, and seconds later, they were seeing at a forming fetus.

"From what it can determine," said the Doctor, "I'll say you're about three months." She then reaches over and pushes a bottom on the machine, starting close together thumping sound. "And there goes your baby's heartbeat."

Unable to believe it, Andrea was beyond shock that at this very moment she was carrying life – the child of a man who killed others in cool blood and at the same time was trying to kill her. She lay still, eyeing the monitor, unsure on the move she should make next.

About The Author

Eric S. Swindell was born August 17, 1994, in Laurinburg, NC located in Scotland County. He and his family relocated to Raleigh, NC in 2004. He graduated from Southeast Raleigh Magnet High School: Class of 2013.

He began writing short stories at the age of twelve, and with much encouragement and enthusiasm, he continued. Eric found himself gaining an interest to extend his writing ability, and began writing Plays, Books, and Film Scripts. *The Soul of a Young Man* is the first book Eric published.

When Eric is not writing, he enjoys acting, cooking, designing houses and clothes, and reading books by his favor authors Carl Weber and J.K. Rowling.

Made in the USA
Columbia, SC
22 August 2022

65445489R00188